Red Clark, Range Boss

GORDON YOUNG

CENTER POINT LARGE PRINT
THORNDIKE, MAINE

This Center Point Large Print edition
is published in the year 2019 by arrangement with
Golden West Literary Agency.

Originally published in the US by Doubleday.
Originally published in the UK by Methuen.

The text of this Large Print edition is unabridged.
In other aspects, this book may vary
from the original edition.

Set in 16-point Times New Roman type.

ISBN: 978-1-64358-203-0 (hardcover)
ISBN: 978-1-64358-207-8 (paperback)

Library of Congress Cataloging-in-Publication Data

Names: Young, Gordon, 1886-1948 author.
Title: Red Clark, Range Boss / Gordon Young.
Description: Center Point Large Print edition. | Thorndike, Maine :
   Center Point Large Print, 2019.
Identifiers: LCCN 2019008513| ISBN 9781643582030 (hardcover :
   alk. paper) | IS͟‗‗‗‗‗‗‗‗‗‗‗‗‗‗‗‗‗‗‗‗‗‗‗per)
Subjects: LCSH: ‗‗‗‗
Classification: LC‗‗‗‗‗‗‗‗‗‗‗‗‗‗‗‗‗‗‗‗‗‗‗‗‗‗‗‗‗‗‗‗‗.52—dc23
LC record availab‗‗‗

Printed and b‗
by TJ Interna‗

CHAPTER ONE

The cowboy that rode into Nelplaid a little before sundown was lean and sun-scorched. He wore a blue hickory shirt, darkly damp with sweat splotches, an old gray vest and blue denim trousers, but the boots were of fine leather, with dollar-sized spurs strapped to them.

His hair was the color of brick dust, his face as brown as wind, with some swirling sand in it, and the hot sun could make a man's face, and he had eyes that were as blue as the lupine flower; but it would have made him mad if you had said so. He didn't like lupines. They were bad for cows; bad enough to be called locoweed. Besides, a proper man wasn't supposed to have eyes that anybody could call "purty."

Nelplaid was a measly little town, forty miles from nowhere, but much like other scattered lumps of 'dobe and rough boards that Red was used to. There was so much flour-fine dust in the midsummer street that anybody from a distance might have thought the town was on fire when a bunch of cowboys galloped through.

Not many people were astir when Red rode in; and such as happened to have their noses against dusty windows or loitered in doorways eyed him with suspicion. The big, barrel-chested black, with a claw hammer for a head, the sapling-thin legs and lean flanks of a greyhound, looked much too fine a horse for a mere puncher; and Red had not only an eight-square rifle under his leg but two long Colts on his thighs.

The Nelplaid was troubled country. There were a lot of little ranches back up in the hogbacks that flanked the big ranches of the foothills and valleys—which made it nice for rustlers. Big ranchers always, or nearly always, accuse little ranchers of being rustlers.

On top of that, outlaws rode the back trails, stealing horses, dashing off a hundred miles or so to hold up a train now and then, a bank here and there. The Kilcos, they were called, and folks were dead sure that the outlaws and rustlers had a way of giving one another a helping hand. So any heavily armed stranger that came jogging into Nelplaid was pretty sure to be put down by the townspeople as a killer on the dodge who was riding in on somebody's borrowed horse to throw in with the bad bunch.

Red came at a slow *chop-clop, chop-clop* through the ankle-deep dust, wiped his sweaty nose on the blue handkerchief about his neck, and was glad that the ride was over.

He passed four horses that were hitched to the ground before the long hitch rack under a scraggly cottonwood beside the narrow broken sidewalk that humped itself into two steps to get to the platform before the general store.

He turned in beside the other horses, dropping his reins as he came out of the saddle. Red shook himself, pushed back his hat, took a long, tired breath and hitched up the heavy belts. Their loops glittered with the bright brass heads of cartridges. Red, for all of his youth, had so many times had to scrouge down where there wasn't much of a place to scrouge, and stand off people who didn't like him, that he made a point of carrying a lot of bullets.

The long .45s were in slick black holsters that sagged low on his thighs, and the holsters were tied down by buckskin thongs just below the knees. He had all the earmarks of a bad man, or a man that wanted to be thought bad, except for the straight blue eyes that usually glinted with amusement if he didn't dislike somebody he happened to be looking at.

There was about a five-foot space between the general store and the building next door, which was "Dave's Silver Dollar"—so a weather-worn sign said.

Four men, lounging against the front of Dave's Silver Dollar, with thumbs in belts and backs to the 'dobe wall, sullenly sized him up.

He glanced their way, saw how they looked at him, and so he took a longer look on his own account. Red, with his quick-smiling mouth and good humor, made people who didn't know him well think that he wasn't much more than a fool kid; and he was a good deal like one until he was shouldered with some responsibility or got mad; then he might act pretty foolish, but he was dangerous.

He guessed that these fellows were not much good, sensed that something was wrong and wondered what. In cow camps and ranch houses where he had paused in heading for Nelplaid, he had heard that it was pretty wild country.

It made Red mad a little if even his best friends said that he nosed about, looking for trouble, or that he carried a chip on his shoulder; but he did have a stubborn way of not backing up from people that seemed to want to be disagreeable. He had worked for some big outfits and had been hired because of his unflinching readiness to shoot it out with cow thieves rather than for his ability as a mere cowpuncher. So when people stared at him, he stared back. For one thing, there was no way for him to tell, offhand, just who, of the men here and there that he had had arguments with—"argyments," Red called them— might have friends that knew him by sight and might want to do some revenging.

The four men were dusty, unshaven, rough fellows, with a wary tenseness behind attitudes of careless slouching.

A fifth man stood just inside the doorway with

an apron about his belly. He had a large black mustache, a fat red face, and a half-smoked dead cigar in his mouth. Made Red think of a big spider that had turned saloonkeeper. He didn't much dislike spiders, but any man that made him think of a fat spider was regarded unfavorably.

The four rough fellows were examining Red much as town dogs take a look at a stray; but their looks kept going on by him toward the front of the general store, then would snap back and seem to size him up with some symptoms of derision. The blue eyes made him look much more like a kid than he was; and he was weighted down with two big guns and a lot of cartridges.

Red stared back at them with much the air of asking, "Well, just what is there about me that you fellows don't like?"

He stared longest at a tall man with hatchet-thin face, squinty-tight eyes, very small hands, and a white scar on the side of his cheek, as if he had been kicked by a horse or hit by knucks. This fellow seemed to be the leader. He squinted beadily at Red, as if wanting to make him a little uneasy by being stared at so hard. But it didn't work out that way. Red sort of bristled up and stared back.

The squinty man slouched forward and asked, in a cold, mean way, "Was you lookin' for some-body—in particklar?"

"Yes. I come to town to find Judge Trowbridge. You happen to know where he is?"

The squinty-eyed man frowned. Red had a soft, sassy sound, just as if he hadn't noticed that he was being stared at by a man who wasn't used to being stared back at.

Then the spider-shaped saloonkeeper, with the apron about his belly, thrust out his short neck from beside the doorway. He had a smooth voice with a throaty rumble, and said, a little hurried, "The Judge is three or four doors down and upstairs." The dead cigar waggled in a pointing hand, showing that the Judge's place was down the street, beyond the store.

There was urgency in the gesture, as if bidding Red be on his way. Rather like being shooed. Red didn't shoo easily. He didn't like this greasy, spider-shaped man anyhow. And anybody that bossed Red had to pay him wages or be pretty.

Just then one of the slouching fellows said, in a kind of startled, quick way, as if giving a signal, "There he is!"

The four fellows stiffened, moved, changing position a little and doing it quick. One man showed that he had a game knee by the limpy jump he made to get to the edge of the narrow board sidewalk, his hand going toward the butt of his gun. But it was plain that they weren't making a dead set for Red. Their eyes were fixed on the platform before the general store.

10

A big man in a big gray hat had come out. He wore high boots without spurs and dark corduroy pants. Red couldn't see the man's face, for his back was turned as he held open the screen door with far reach of thick arm.

Just as a girl was following him through the door, shots were fired.

The girl faced about, screamed; then she jumped back.

The big man turned, staggered into more bullets, and his broken right arm groped uselessly for the gun on his hip. He fell to his knees, jerked left-handedly to get at the gun, but sagged over, thumped down with the dull heaviness of a big-bodied man whose legs have given way, his face toward the fellows who were trying to kill him. It was a big, dark bulldog face with bulging jaws.

The girl had jumped back inside the door, then out she came with a rush that hit the screen with all her weight, banging it wide. She cried "Daddy!" and threw herself down protectively before the wounded man, who lay still, as if dead.

At the first shot Red had jumped aside. It wasn't his fight, and he had been through enough smoke to know that bystanders are unlucky. One look, and he saw the big man go down, shot in the back, heard the girl's screams; then Red's hands moved like darting shadows toward his guns.

"Why, damn your souls!" he yelled, and his lean body snapped back to the backward jerk of his hands. The right-hand gun barely cleared the top of its holster when it threw a slug into the stiff-kneed man's belly, right above the belt buckle.

The man pitched forward with both hands up, as if in a futile gesture of surrender, then sprawled, with sidelong lurch, face down, in the dust beside the narrow boardwalk.

Red had gone into a point-blank fight with four men who had their guns out and smoking; but he was the gun-trained son of a man who had been one of the West's great sheriffs. And he had the advantage of surprising these killers by jumping them so sudden; the greater advantage of being cool and quick and so good a shot that when he had fired three times two men were down.

The second to go was a chunky fellow that laid his back against the 'dobe front of the saloon and slid down with an air of drunken sleepiness.

Dust from bullets splattered in the street behind Red as if hit by hailstones, but he leaned into the smoke, a gun in each hand. His right elbow was pressed against his side, hip-shooting; and the long-barreled .45 in his left hand was up and balanced, ready to go the moment the other was empty. There weren't many men anywhere who could shoot a single-action as fast as Red. His father had nearly worn off the boy's thumbs teaching him to snap back that hammer the instant it fell.

The horses were tossing their heads, the whites in their eyes gleaming with a half-angered fear as they sidled about, scuffing the dust, but they stood to their reins. That is, all the horses but Red's Black Devil showed excitement, and he threw up his head and poked out his ears, with a kind of anxious look. Red had used up a lot of powder training the black horse to think that there really wasn't much difference between flies and bullets.

Both of the other men were backing up, as if blown by the muzzle blasts of the long-barreled .45, toward the shelter of the Silver Dollar's doorway. The tall, squinty-eyed man had an amazed and pretty much scared look on his hatchet-thin face, and he was sagging over, as if trying to ease a pain in his side. Twice he pulled the trigger after his gun was empty; then he dropped it and made a lurching, hobbling jump, as if crippled, toward the horses at the hitch rack.

A heavy door swung from the shadows inside the Silver Dollar and closed with a jar, shutting out the other man, who was backing into shelter. However fast Red shot—and he had a thumb and finger that could spin a cylinder—he always knew when a gun was empty and never snapped on a dead shell. It wasn't that he exactly counted his shots, but something inside of him kept track; and now the second gun was up and ready to go. His first left-handed shot slapped into the third man's breast, and down he came, with his gun out at arm's length. He fired along the level of the sidewalk, knocking splinters from one of the hitching rack's uprights. Then he slumped over, quiet.

Red leaned forward, watching for tricks. Bad men had a way of playing possum. Suddenly Red staggered and fell to a knee as a horse almost struck against him. The squinty-eyed man, hugging the saddle drunkenly, rode across the sidewalk and spurred down the five-foot space between the walls of the saloon and the general store.

II

There was a lot of silence when the guns stopped. Red stood with a rather surprised and slightly uncertain air of wondering what he had got himself into. Shooting down men that he didn't know anything about was a ticklish thing in a town where he didn't have friends, at least more of a friend than old Judge Trowbridge.

But Red looked toward the front of the store where the girl was on her knees, hovering over the big man, and he felt satisfied. If anybody didn't like what he had done he was willing to carry on the "argyment." To his way of thinking, these men sure needed killing.

Knocked over three and hurt the fourth, he

thought grimly, but he was satisfied—almost. He wished he had got the fourth, who had run, crippled. It happened that Red was a fellow who would carry a sick calf ten miles over the neck of his horse and talk to it all the way, not because it might grow into a twenty-five dollar steer, but because he had a soft heart. Yet he had been raised to think that killers, outlaws, rustlers, horse thieves and such were not a bit better than four-legged wolves; and when it came to "bad men" of any shape, size or age, he felt that it was right and proper to knock them over. His own father had been killed by one that shot from the back.

Red stayed in his tracks and began to reload his guns. There was no telling what might happen next—in a strange town; and an unloaded gun wasn't of much use, except as a club, and some people had heads that might hurt the barrel. As he deftly prodded out the empty shells and replaced them with bullets from his belt, he looked all about, and his glance went to one after another of the men who were dead.

Red fastened his look on something in the board sidewalk and took a step toward it. He half grinned, as if he didn't want to grin, then rapidly looked at the boots of the men who lay sprawled out. The fourth man that Red thought he had crippled must not have been hit at all. He had lost his high boot heel in a knothole, and that had made him sag, caused him to limp. Red muttered, with some disgust, "Well, I'll be damned!"

The twenty-seconds' crash of guns had stirred up the town. Heads were coming out of doorways, turning loose inquiring shouts, excitedly loud. Two fright-faced men in shirt sleeves edged out of the general store, looked to make sure that the shooting was all over, then rushed to where the pretty girl was down on her knees. The older man, with frizzled gray hair and a storekeeper's bib apron about his neck, cried brokenly, "They killed Mr Clayton!"

Red spun about, with hand dangling backward toward a holstered gun, as a man with a rifle in his hands ran at him from across the street. His blue eyes narrowed in a hard look, although he guessed that this tall, broad-shouldered fellow was not unfriendly, else he would have stayed in the bootmaker's shop across the way and used his rifle from the doorway.

He was a big fellow with a hard face, but had a rather rollicking, handsome look to him; and when he stopped stock-still in front of Red he smiled soberly and asked, "Who in hell are you?" But he looked away, glancing at the three dead men, then toward the narrow passage between store and saloon walls through which the horseman had galloped. He stared at the crowd gathering on the store's front platform.

Red was not sure that he quite liked this man. He didn't like so much finery on a man. It wasn't cheap finery, and it looked worn. There was a silver-studded band about the wide hat, stamped-leather holster, long chased spurs, and the sort of soft-leather chaps, lined with silver, that didn't belong in a proper cowboy's outfit. He, too, wore two revolvers—walnut-handled. Red noticed that particularly. Real gun fighters shied usually from ivory handles. Also, he carried a rifle.

"Who in hell are you?" he asked again, and sounded mighty approving.

Red said, "Who are they?"

The man didn't blink, but seemed about to blink. "I don't know." He spoke quickly. He didn't have a hard voice. It was sort of smooth, like the voice of a man who knows how to talk to women easily. "I don't know who the hell they are. But I knew they were up to something. I followed them to town and watched from over there."

Red almost said, "I think you are lyin'!" He was pretty uppish and blunt when he thought folks were lying. He did say, "If you was so ready, why didn't you chip in?"

"I couldn't. The horses were in the way—and you! You were the only one in plain sight!"

"There was a man on horseback out plain enough!"

"God, yes! I'd have given an arm to knock

17

him out of the saddle. But I watched *you*. When you nearly fell I thought you had been shot. That fellow was away and had angled in between the buildings before I could turn loose. But you hit him, didn't you?"

"No." Red pointed. "He lost his boot heel in a knothole. Maybe thought he was crippled. Acted like it!"

The man laughed jerkily, as if somehow he thought it was a better joke than he could let on. It was a short, quick laugh; then he looked worried as he turned again toward the store. He faced Red and asked, "Are you one of Mr Clayton's men?"

"Me? No. I'm Red Clark of Tulluco, an' I just rode in."

The man had brown eyes. They glowed at Red. "I've seen men shoot. You are the fastest ever! And accurate!"

"I sure try to be," Red admitted, sort of absently, still trying to size up this fellow.

"How'd you come to get into the fight—when it wasn't your affair?"

"Lissen, you!" Red scowled, as if the man were putting a hint of blame on him. "Any time some men—any men, an' I don't care who—shoot a gun on purpose toward where a woman is, it's my affair, an' I figger on takin' part to make 'em wish they hadn't!"

The man's good-looking face broke into an openmouthed grin. He poked out a hand impulsively. "We are friends!" Somehow he seemed trying to make Red think that being friends with him was an honor not offered to everybody.

"Maybe," said Red, "I'll need me some friends if these fellers are mourned like they ortn't be!"

"My name's Brady. You done a good job. I wish I'd helped. You'll need friends, though, if you stay in this country. That was Mell Barber that got away!"

Red snapped, "Thought you didn't know 'em?"

The grin on Brady's handsome face changed into a startled expression, as if he had been caught with an ace up his sleeve. All of a sudden he looked slightly mean. It took more than a hard look to put a friz in Red's tousled hair. But the look now changed again to a smile, and Brady shook his head. "I know who he is. That's all." He pulled at Red's arm. "Come along and let's see if the old man is dead."

III

Townspeople had gathered fast, talking loud and in wonderment, with something of the muddled confusion of movement of ants when their nest is poked by a stick. They didn't quite know what had happened.

Brady pushed through to where the girl was. She was on her knees, dipping a handkerchief

19

into a bucket of water that had been brought, and was sopping the unconscious man's face.

Brady stooped. "Is he dead, Kate?"

The girl gave a jump as if scared, turned up her face, said, "Oh, Jim!" Something about him had scared her, but Red was pretty sure that she wanted to throw her arms about this Brady and have him throw his arms about her. Then she stood up and pushed at Brady, said in a low, hurried way, "You mustn't stay here!" Then: "Did you shoot them—did you?"

She was a pretty girl, with something more than prettiness about her. Her eyes were bright and her hair was yellow and curly, and there was a look about her that made Red think of a princess. He had never seen a princess, but he had his own ideas of what a princess ought to look like: it was about the same for a woman as for a thoroughbred horse.

Brady looked regretful, as if he wanted to lie a little, and moved his head. "It wasn't me, Kate. It was—"

Red could tell that Brady was getting ready to speak up and tell just how it happened, but the girl looked scared again. "You must go, Jim!" Her voice was low and urgent. "You must!" She pushed hard. She was small and dainty—or not small exactly, but so dainty that she looked small; and he was a big fellow, but he yielded as if she were strong.

Men—and women, too—were shoving about Red, and he let himself be jostled aside. Nelplaid was a dinky one-horse town of probably two or three hundred people; but to Red it seemed that they were all there, yelping questions—mostly, "Who done it?"—and all talking at once.

The fight had happened out on Main Street, but all in less than a half-minute from the time of the first shot at Mr Clayton to the last from the dying man near Red's feet; and nobody—at least nobody that was doing the talking—had a clear idea of what was what. Scarcely anybody, except Red, Brady and the fat saloonkeeper, who had crawled into his hole and shut the door, had seen a thing.

People didn't even seem sure of who the dead men were. There was also confused guess-talk that old Sam Clayton had downed the fellows after they had shot him. To Red's ears it sounded as if people thought that Mr Clayton was just the kind of man who would do that sort of thing; yet somehow there was more respect than liking in the way they used Sam Clayton's name. Some were even so far wrong that they were saying that the man with the rifle had knocked the fellows over, but nobody appeared to know even his name.

Red stood on tiptoes and craned his neck to get another look at this Brady and the girl—especially at the girl, because he liked her; not so much merely because she was a pretty girl as because of the way she had come out of that door and flung herself down protectively across the wounded man.

As far as Red was concerned, a girl who would do that could do no wrong, ever.

Red was bumped by a short, fat, bald man in a long-tailed coat, a white shirt and no collar, who was pressing in with an air of authority. Red called, "Judge!" but the bareheaded man didn't hear and shoved his way through close to where Mr Clayton was and took charge.

The Judge was a queer sort of fellow, but he had a way of taking charge when he wanted to. He was short and fat, with a red bald head, and always wore a long black coat even in midsummer. Red suspected that when he got up at night he slipped the long-tailed black coat over his nightshirt. The Judge played lots of poker, drank lots of good whisky, read lots of books, especially poetry; but he was a fine, honest man, and nobody could scare him, although he never went armed—not even when he had been judge up at Tulluco and the friends of convicted men threatened, and sometimes tried, to kill him. Red liked the Judge a lot, but the Judge did have a generous weakness for hesitating to believe in the downright meanness of people. People could lie out of things easily, unless there were a lot of contradictory witnesses, when the Judge had

22

been on the bench up at Tulluco. Anybody had the devil of a time lying out of anything when Red suspected them. He was stubborn, sassy and suspicious, too; also impetuous.

Red could hear the Judge's powerful, resonant voice above all the chatter, calling upon people to stand back. The Judge had the kind of voice that made a wonderful Fourth of July oration, and ordinarily he was plain-spoken; but when he unlimbered, he hitched words up together that made them roll and sway and sound fine, and Red sometimes wondered what they meant.

The Judge was telling the mild gray owner of the store to have some blankets spread on the floor to lay Mr Clayton on until he could be moved. He told somebody else to ride out of town to where the doctor had gone to see a sick woman.

Red was tired and dusty, and there didn't seem anything better to do than find the Judge's office, go in and sit down. Pretty soon the crowd would begin to get the straight of the story, and men would stare and ask questions. Red didn't like to be gawked at and asked questions. "Three or four doors down and upstairs," the fat saloonkeeper had said, "An' how he acted was as if he knowed what was coming," Red reflected.

There was only one two-story building in the block. Red went upstairs with jingle of spurs and clump of heels on the uncarpeted boards. It was dark from lack of windows in the hall, and there was nothing to show which was the Judge's room. He knocked on two or three doors, then tried the one at the front, found it unlocked, looked in.

Books—more than two or three men could read in a lifetime, Red thought—were on shelves, and others were stacked on a table. The dusty windows looked down on the street. A bottle of whisky and a tumbler were on the table, with pipes and a stone jar of tobacco. This was where the Judge lived, all right. The books weren't lawbooks, and the whisky wasn't rye.

Red unbuckled his guns and took a second drink. He sat down in the old worn chair with the headrest tilted back. After a long day's ride it was fine to sit and rest, so he put his hat on his knee, took a deep breath, relaxed drowsily.

"Sure looks like a princess orta look," he mused. "I mean . . . acts that way, too."

He closed his eyes.

IV

Red awoke with a start, found himself in darkness and for a second or two couldn't quite figure where he was as the door opened and a slow, heavy tread moved into the room; then: " 'Lo, Judge!"

"Eh? Well, and who are you?"

"Now ain't that a nice way for to do! Write a

feller a letter to come an' see you, then you ask his name! When I was a kid I seen ever'body have to do like you said, even when you said for 'em to go get hung! So here I am."

The Judge puffed a few chuckles. The stairs had made him breathe hard.

"I never thought of your being here, although I have inquired and wondered where you had gone." A match flared, a pudgy hand moved above the flame and took off a lamp chimney. The flame touched the wick. Judge Trowbridge gazed at Red with benign severity. "I knew you were in town."

"Who told you? That Brady feller?"

"Brady? I don't know anyone by the name of Brady."

"Then how you know? I told only him who I was."

The Judge plucked a red bandanna from the tail pocket of his long coat. He wiped his face, bald head, and gouged in under the collarless shirt. All the while he scrutinized Red, as if looking for changes in the lean brown muscular face between the last time he had seen him and now. He shook his head, as if he didn't see any changes worth commenting on.

"How did I know? There was a horse at the hitch rack branded with the Arrowhead. There were three dead men—most deservedly dead!—and a slender redheaded stranger in town, so—"

"That makes me think. I got to go 'tend to my horse. His name is Devil, the which he ain't, bein' the best horse the Lord ever let a plain, ornery puncher like me set on!"

"I sent him down to the stable, son." The Judge took a deep breath, parted the tails of his coat, sat down, rested his plump hands on his knees, looked very dignified as he gazed at Red. He shook his head solemnly. "Red, my boy, I dread to think of the results if your hasty impulsiveness ever makes a mistake in judgment!"

"I made me one mistake. I let one feller get away!"

"The three of them that didn't get away were laid out on the floor of Dave Gridger's saloon and their wounds inspected." The Judge wiped about his collarless neck, where the fat lay in folds. He cleared his throat. "You are uncommonly spry with a gun, Red."

Red grunted, not wanting to be lectured.

"And lucky," the Judge added.

"Course, Judge, they is allus some luck if you don't get hit. But hittin' what you shoot at ain't much luck. I," Red explained gravely, "don't jerk my trigger, the which took a lot of practice not to do, specially when you're in a hurry."

The Judge picked up a pipe, examined it thoughtfully, lifted the lid of the stone jar. "Mr Clayton is a big cattleman of Nelplaid. *The* big cattleman. He has many enemies. Some people complain that he is overbearing. Of late years he has become suspicious—even lately, I understand—of his own son. And disagreeable toward his neighbors. Rustlers have preyed on his herds, and he has found it impossible to check them. There has never been a conviction for rustling in Nelplaid County. The public's sympathy is not with the big cattlemen."

Red leaned forward, poked out a finger. "Why don't Mr Clayton hire hisself some good men an' burn them rustlers' tails with a little powder smoke?"

The Judge sighed. "Old Sam Clayton is a hard man to get on with. Men don't stay with him long. Of late years he has lacked ability to inspire the kind of loyalty that I remember the boys were accustomed to give the cattlemen of Tulluco and adjacent counties." The Judge sighed again. "I like old Sam." As he meditated he sent a cloud of smoke like a misty halo about his big round bald head.

"Who was them fellers that shot 'im?"

"Nobody knows for certain. It is said that they are members of the Kilco bunch, and Dave Gridger declares that he never saw them before, and Dave knows more than almost anybody."

"An' probably tells more lies," Red suggested. He looks fat an' ornery. Did you by happen-chance send for me to work for Mr Clayton?"

"Oh no, no, no." The Judge drew with *plop-*

plop of lips on his pipe. "I sent for you to come and take charge of a little ranch called the Lazy Z. It was owned by a man named Alvord. Much to my discomfort and peace of mind, I am administrator of the Alvord estate, which consists of this little ranch." The Judge frowned, spoke with a rumbling, troubled voice. "I don't know just what the trouble is out there. For some reason the men I put in charge won't stay. Now I have a man named Frank Knox in charge. I am not quite satisfied about Knox. Perhaps I misjudge the man. He appears willing enough to stay, but I fear his reputation isn't just what it ought to be. So, sitting here one day, I said to myself, 'I know one boy that I would like to have in charge out there.' And I wrote you. And you hadn't been in town ten minutes before— Just how did you come to get into that fight, Red?"

Red hunched forward with the cigarette smoldering in his fingers. "You know where I was hatched an' how I growed up, Judge. You know that since I was fourteen I drawed man-sized wages from outfits, that, in a way of speaking, rode with a gun in their hands. Well. They shot this Mr Clayton in the back with some of his womenfolks lookin' on. They needed a first-class lesson in some good manners an' got 'er!"

The Judge didn't smile. He knew that Red had

28

a way of sounding flippant and being earnest, and that most of the time he didn't even know that he sounded flippant; he let go with words just about as he let go with his guns. The Judge took up another pipe, filled it from the stone jar.

"Old Sam himself says that he doesn't know those men, and so can't understand why they—"

"That man Brady knows 'em."

"Brady? Who is Brady?"

"He said his name was Brady. He told me he follered 'em to town. He was across the street, watchin' an' ready to help, but me an' the horses was in the way. So he said."

"Brady? Brady?" The Judge raised his eyebrows, reflecting. "I don't know him."

"That daughter of Mr Clayton sure knowed him an'—"

"She is Mr Clayton's granddaughter."

"She called him 'Daddy.' "

"She is his granddaughter, and for all of her dainty appearance she is more of a Clayton than Mr Clayton's own son. But she is exceedingly—um—well, what you know as 'stuck up.' She was educated in the East, and that is seldom good for anybody that comes into the West to live."

"She is all right," said Red. "She can be stuck up. I don't care if she never even says 'Howdy' to me. I like her. Education ain't spoiled her so that she is easy scairt. She is purty. She has got more grit than a man, but then most women has when

29

you go monkeyin' with their menfolks. I like her fine!"

The old Judge puffed contemplatively, wondering if this wild-headed boy had fallen in love suddenly with the aloof, chilly, slightly arrogant and presumably vain Miss Clayton. Such foolishness came to every boy on his way up to manhood—and sometimes after he had attained manhood and ought to know better.

"What," asked Red, "about this ranch of yourn?"

"The heir is one J. C. Alvord, who lives in Boston. He has written me that the ranch is not for sale. Some of the old Alvord stubbornness, it appears, is in him, too. And he has written that just as soon as he can put his affairs in order, he will come out and take charge."

"What he know about cows?"

"Nothing, of course." The Judge puckered his brow with a discouraged frown. "His handwriting is very precise and small."

"What that mean?" Red had a way of often clipping his sentences to an ungrammatical nakedness, as well as often padding his remarks with a roundabout gabbiness.

"It is symptomatic of a certain overrefinedness, scarcely suitable to ranch life."

"That 'sympto' thingumajig—it is something like 'simpleton,' um?"

"Very likely to be in this case, I am afraid. In fact, I have detected even a lavenderish sachet fragrance about the letter paper."

"Perfume? Me, I won't ride for no man that uses perfume. I just won't. I think it fine on girls. But a man that tries to make himself stink nice—he can go hunt himself another cowboy!"

"But I am not asking you to ride for *him*. I am asking you to ride for *me*. I am responsible for the ranch until the owner comes. And the fact is, Red, that I have reasons for believing that rustlers are making away with Alvord cattle."

"How many cows you run?"

"Between eight hundred and a thousand."

Red snorted. "That ain't a big corralful. Hell, a one-legged man on foot orta be able to keep them on their range. How many men you got out there?"

"Four. But one—"

"Four?"

"Well, really three. But even two of those are youngsters whose parents I used to know. They drifted into Nelplaid looking for jobs, and I sent them out there. And Frank Knox. I put him in charge after two other men had quit. I thought that a man who had cattle of his own in the hills and knew the country ought to be able to handle things. But I don't believe Knox is suitable. In fact, Mr Clayton himself told me that Knox was not to be trusted. True, Sam is very suspicious. But I have heard other things. I sent for you. I want you to go out there as boss."

"What's mostly wrong?"

"It is mountainous country and filled with rustlers."

"You said four men?"

"One is the cook. He doesn't get wages, but stays on. He and Alvord batched together for years. If you don't want him, run him off."

"If he cooks good, I won't."

"Will you go, Red?"

"I don't know about mountain ranches."

"It is a beautiful ranch."

"Um. I don't care about that. Only when I ride for an outfit, it just the same as belongs to me as far as makin' other people keep their hands off. An' if the owner don't back me up, I quit."

"I don't know what the owner is like, but until he comes I will back you up."

"How much wages do I get?"

"How much do you think you ought to get?"

"Well," said Red, studying the ceiling, "when I was range boss up in Tahzo I got me forty, an' they throwed in that colt that turned into the horse you saw when I quit. Of course, a big part of my job up there was gettin' shot at. Rustlers was mighty peevish on account of so many range bosses havin' a way of going in cahoots with 'em."

"Some of my managers have been shot at. Knox, also, I understand. But *he* stays on."

"Me," Red explained, "I won't be friends with rustlers an' such. I just won't. So up in Tahzo, old Jake Dunham paid me purty good wages on account of tangling horns with fellers that thought they was bad men. But I never yet seen a bad man that wouldn't curl up an' be quit if you plugged him in the belly. I don't reckon this Nelplaid country can stack up alongside of how bad Tahzo was. An' me, not knowin' the country a-tall, I can't be as good to start as I orta. So as for wages—I'll leave it to you. Work ortn't be very hard."

"But it is a mountain ranch. There is a rich watered valley, but the cows wander off into the mountains."

"Oh, they do, do they?" Red asked, sitting up. "They must be funny cows." The Judge frowned inquiringly. "To go roaming up among trees an' rocks when they've got grass and water under their noses."

"As for pay"—the Judge pursed his lips about the pipe stem, plopped them a few times—"it will be fifty a month. And if you stay there, you will earn it, son."

CHAPTER TWO

The Judge put on his celluloid collar, poked in a little store-tied black bow, brushed his long-tailed coat and black hat. "Now, Red, we will go eat."

They were late in the Saginaw Restaurant and had the small, dimly lighted dining room to themselves, being waited on by a scrawny man whose broad suspenders tugged at his too big pants. He was a widower with a small son and a Chinese cook, waiting on table himself and helping in the kitchen. By way of keeping them company, he took a chair at the table and leaned on his elbows. "B. Blanton, Prop.," as the crooked lettering said on the front. B. Blanton, Prop., was recently from Michigan and did not like the hot, dry West.

Red went on eating after the Judge had had enough. B. Blanton stared at Red in respectful curiosity. It was now known that Red had knocked over the three men and sent a fourth riding out of town.

"I don't see how you done it," Blanton droned. "I don't see how you missed gettin' kilt!"

Talk made Red uncomfortable, and it irritated him almost as much to be made out a hero as to be made out a bad man. He poked into his mouth a piece of steak that would have done very well to resole a boot, and mumbled, "Oh me, bein' skinny, I'm as hard to hit as a card edgeways."

"Them fellers' friends'll lay for you, mister," said Blanton, gazing at Red as if picturing him laid out for burial. "Ain't you scairt they'll maybe get you?"

"Oh yeah, you bet. Sure." Red drank deep of black coffee into which he had stirred four spoonfuls of gritty sugar.

"Then I reckon you'll git outa town soon?"

"Me? Sure. That's right. First thing in the mornin'."

A small, freckled, barefoot boy dashed in as if blown by a whirlwind. He was saying "Bang! Bang! Bang!" and a corncob in his hand was the gun. When he saw that there were customers he stopped with an embarrassed look, as if he had swallowed his tongue; then, with shy friendliness, said, "Hello, Judge," and stood with a saucer-eyed stare at Red. He asked in an awed whisper, "Is that *him?*"

"Red," said the Judge gravely, "this is my small friend, Jody Blanton, who came West from Saginaw, Michigan, to grow into a cowboy."

Red grinned at the kid. Jody snuggled in under the Judge's arm, with an elfin stare at Red. "Dave, he says that Mr Clayton was shot by accident while them men was fightin' you!"

"Eh?" asked the Judge.

"He, says," Jody went on breathlessly,

encouraged because the grown-ups looked so interested, "that you rode in and the shootin' started all of a sudden."

Red grunted and took a piece of dried-apple pie in his fingers, bit into it, spoke as he chewed: "Is that Dave the feller with the black mustache an' big belly?"

"To whom was he telling that, Jody?" asked the Judge.

"To the sher'ff."

"How did you happen to hear?"

"He is the dangest boy to hear things!" said Mr Blanton, with an intimation of pride.

"Me, I play I'm scout and Injun fighter," Jody explained. "Sometimes I sneak in the back of Dave's place and hide there under a table where it is dark, and I play like I am—"

"Jody," Red told him, "you are goin' to be a great cowboy. A cowboy, he has to have ears funnel-shaped, like mine. One of these days, when I buy me a cow, I'll hire you to ride herd on 'im. Most likely you'll be well growed before I get me that cow, because nearly ever'-body I know plays poker better 'n I do."

After supper, on the way back to the Judge's rooms, Red shortened his stride, with stumble of high heels and dragging rattle of spurs, to the Judge's short legs.

"No, no, Red, I can't believe that Dave Gridger knew what those men were up to. He is a man of—Well, his brother-in-law is the sheriff, and—"

"I seen how he acted. The kid told you how he talked. This Dave is a liar an' not smart."

"He is regarded as a very smart man in Nelplaid County. Very smart!"

"No man gets shot three times in the back, like Mr Clayton was, accidental. Nobody is smart as says so!"

"Jody is only a child and perhaps misunderstood when he overheard them talking."

Red grunted, skeptically. "Next, maybe he'll be sayin' I shot Mr Clayton my own self an' them fellers lit into me for doin' it!"

"Old Sam saw you go into action, Red."

"An' this sheriff can't be much good his own self."

"Why, son, I believe that Sheriff Mattern is a thoroughly honest man, although he is lacking in certain qualities that are desirable in a sheriff."

"Like courage, maybe? An' not catchin' outlaws an' such?"

"He is very careful not to offend voters, I must admit."

"He your friend?"

"We aren't unfriendly. But I am not in politics. I am satisfied with a little private practice, my books, and a friendly game of poker in the evening. A few of us play in the back of the general store. Would you care to take a hand? You will find my friends there."

"Me, poker with you old longhorns? I'll go up an' sleep in your place like you said I could. I'm lightin' out for the ranch at sunup. An' sleep is one of the things I am a tophand at doin'."

II

Red went up the stairs, lit the lamp, put his hat on the floor, rolled a cigarette and sat down. He laid the cigarette aside, pulled off his boots, stretched his toes and lay back, wondering what it was going to be like at the Lazy Z; wondered about saving his wages and buying some cows to grow himself a herd; and so mused drowsily, watching the herd grow.

The cows vanished as he grinned at himself: A fellow worked to have money to spend; and if he saved it, it was just the same as if he didn't have it. Besides, a fellow couldn't get mad and quit if he was his own boss!

So Red began to think of other things, especially of the spider-fat Dave Gridger. Said Red to himself, "I orta be as good a scout and Injun fighter as that kid is." He meditated awhile, then picked up his boots and removed the spurs.

Outside, the sky was clear and starry, and lamplight lay in a few open doorways along the street, glowed in some dirty windows. There were not many people on the street, and Red kept to the dark places as he went around back and moved up along behind the buildings.

The rear windows of the general store were lighted and raised. He could hear the rattle of chips, the muffled mumble of amiable voices; but the windows were above his head, and he could not see without going up on the rear platform.

He edged up to the back of the Silver Dollar. The door was open, and a dim coal-oil lamp, the wick turned low, burned against the wall at the back.

Like most cow-town saloons, this was a big room with a long bar, a few tables and many chairs; and most of the year it had a barnlike emptiness. But when the boys swarmed in after the spring and fall roundups, and lined two and three deep at the bar, and stood around, waiting for a chance to sit in a poker game, proprietors wished that their saloons were bigger.

Red had come, hoping to have Jody's luck at overhearing something; but there was nobody in back. The six or seven men lolling against the bar up front talked so quietly that their voices were a broken splatter of sound, with now and then a few stressed words. Brighter lamps were up there, and the yellowish glow threw a bobble of shadows on the wall across the room. The man behind the bar was not the same that Red had seen in the doorway that afternoon.

Red edged into the saloon to be nearer the

men at the bar, whose voices had the dragging listlessness of men who were still talking of what they had been talking of for hours. It would be talked about for days, remembered for years. The biggest liar of an old-timer couldn't top the story of a gun fight in which a lone redheaded young stranger downed three men and ran a fourth out of town. Red wanted to know if they were saying that Mr Clayton had been shot accidentally, but he could not hear much more than a mumble.

He had an ear cocked forward intently when he heard steps in the alleyway back of the saloon; and he realized that if somebody entered through the rear door, he would be found standing there like a prowler, unless he went on up to the bar; and there he would be eyed and talked to by strangers who were full of questions. He had to do something quick, so he copied Injun-fighter Jody by stepping light-toed to a table and scrouging under it, down on his knees.

Somebody came through the back door with scuff of heels and jingle of spurs, but instead of passing along up to the bar, the somebody walked to a table at the back of the saloon where the dim lamp was burning, pulled out a chair and dropped heavily into it.

Red, down awkwardly on his knees, not ten feet away, felt silly. He was more or less caught in a kind of a trap, because he hadn't expected the man to sit down back here; had thought the fellow would just pass on. Now if he tried to get out from under the table and stand up he would be seen and quite properly asked to explain what kind of a game he was up to; which would surely make the new boss of the Lazy Z look foolish. So he crouched as low as he could and peered between the rungs of a chair at the man whose face was lighted by the dim wall lamp.

The man's hat was tipped back. He was pretty good-sized, with muscular shoulders and a thick neck, a somewhat sullen face, not old. The face showed up more clearly when he lit a cigar. The cigar was almost a sure sign of being a cattleman instead of merely a cowboy. The man did not look happy. "Down at the nose," was Red's way of putting it.

Not much of a cattleman, either, in Red's critical eyes, for there was a lumpish gold ring on the man's hand, a heavy watch chain with a heavy doodad of a charm, and the man's gun had ivory butts. Red did not like ivory butts; did not much respect men whose guns had them.

A tall man in a stiff-brimmed hat came through the door up front, moved his hand in a greeting as he passed the men at the bar, spoke affably, but came along back toward the rear, as if he knew who was waiting. There was the glimmer of a silver star on the man's vest. Before he sat down the sullen man who was waiting asked, "Where's Dave?"

"Dave had some little business but will be along." This man with the silver star talked as if he had a little dab of hot mush in his mouth.

The sullen man took the cigar out of his mouth, as if about to say something, then put it back, bit hard.

"Bill, I sure wish I'd been in town when it happened!" said the man with the star.

The sullen man growled. "Yes, I know, Sheriff."

So this was the sheriff. He had straight shoulders, but a rabbit look to his face, which meant not much chin.

"I just been over to see about your father, Bill. I feel all broke up."

Bill said sullenly, "How you think I feel?"

"Course now you feel ter'ble!"

Bill took the cigar in the hand that had the lumpish gold ring and hit the table. "That Red Clark orta be arrested!"

The sheriff made little sounds as if trying to soothe. "Why now, Bill, I'd think you would feel mighty kindly toward this Red feller!"

Bill put the cigar back in his mouth, and his fist hit the table again. "He rode in here and got in a fight with some men and my old man was hit by their bullets! That's how Dave seen it, and he was watching!"

The sheriff pushed up his hat and rubbed his cheek, looked at Bill with an air of wondering. "Well now, Bill—Dave, he was purty excited, I

43

reckon. Nobody but that scrubby boss doctor can get to see your father—him and Miss Kate. But Miss Kate, she told me that she don't know *just* what did happen, but she says that old Sam says that Clark boy pitched into them fellers after they started shootin'. She says that old Sam says he is goin' to have that Clark boy workin' for 'im if he has to give him a herd and free range. So nobody can go arrestin' him, Bill. If old Sam don't die, he would raise hell about it." The sheriff added in a hurt tone, "And your father has sorta got it in for me, anyhow. And Dave too. But you know, Bill, how I never shrink from my duty, now don't you?"

Bill set the cigar in one corner of his mouth, then switched it over to the other corner. He looked sullenly sick, as a man naturally would when his father was, perhaps, about to die. Red did not blame him for misunderstanding about the shooting. Bill's voice sounded a little queer, even a bit shaky, as he asked, "Do folks know yet who them men are?"

The sheriff removed his hat and ran his fingers around the stiff brim, as if looking for something that might be hidden there. "Miss Kate says— and it is purt-near like havin' your nose frostbit to talk to her!—that they were Mell Barber's men. Since him and Kilco had their fallin' out, I reckon Mell Barber wants to show just how bad he can be!"

"That can't be so!" Bill sounded sullenly angered and nervous, too. "How could one man, and a sort of kid at that, I hear, down four hard-shootin' men?"

The sheriff cautiously said, "Um-m. Folks has said that you and Mell Barber ain't teetotal strangers, Bill."

"Folks can keep their damn mouths shut!"

"They don't, though. That's a trouble with folks. And about that Clark boy—the old Judge told me himself that he had give lead poison to a lot of bad men."

Bill's face had a sick-looking glower.

"I don't want to be what they call impert'nent, Bill. But you have now and then bumped into some of them Kilco and Barber fellers, ain't you?"

"Only like other people when there was drinkin' and gamblin' over at Poicoma."

"And you didn't reckernize any of them dead ones?"

"No!" said Bill, sounding angry. "No, I didn't. Never saw 'em before." He stood up in a kind of nervous hurry. "I'm goin' next door where the Judge is and ask him myself about this Red Clark. You tell Dave where I am."

Bill went out of the back door, and the sheriff sat there looking at the door, as if his thoughts were following Bill.

Red felt that the lesson he had taken from

45

Injun-fighter Jody was helping; so he stayed quiet, waiting for Dave to come.

Dave came through the front of the saloon, waddled up for a friendly chat with a man here and there, told the bartender to set up drinks, then waddled on back and took the chair Bill Clayton had just left.

Dave was even fatter than Red had remembered. Hog fat and bulge-bellied. His black mustache was as thick as a pair of thumbs stuck to his lip and looked as shiny as if it had been rubbed with stove blacking. He had a straight-brimmed hat, too, just like the sheriff's—as if they bought their hats together to get a reduction in price.

Dave took off his hat and rubbed his forehead with the heel of his palm.

"Bill, he went to the store to ask the Judge about that Clark fellow. He was askin' me if I was goin' to arrest 'im."

Dave grunted, looked sour. "Don't you try it."

"When my duty calls, I don't get scairt," said the sheriff, straightening his shoulders, as if having a picture taken.

Dave growled, "You poke your fingers in your ears when duty starts talkin' about that hombre, or your widow'll be hanging on my neck. He is a bad un for sure," said Dave, sort of hopeless and mad.

"I told Bill we couldn't arrest him, not after

how old Sam says the boy pitched in to help."

"I know. I know," Dave growled, meditatively and troubled. "But Sam's back was turned, and Kate was in the store when the shootin' started. Old Sam happened to be right in line of fire as they opened up."

"Who started the ruckus, then?"

"That Clark boy!" Dave broke off and turned his head. "What's that?"

The sheriff looked around, startled. Chairs seemed moving in the dimness, and a table shifted as if by itself; then a lanky shadow-shape rose up off the darkness on the floor and a voice said:

"Me, I'm Red Clark, an' you're a liar!"

The sheriff bobbed in his chair a little, as if to jump up, but all he could do was to say, "Here— here now—here, what's the meanin' of this?"

Dave half crooked his thick fat arms, getting his palms up and out. "I ain't armed!"

Red rocked back on his heels. "They opened up on old Sam Clayton, an' you saw 'em. So why you want to lie like that for?"

The sheriff moved his feet but stayed where he was. Dave swallowed a couple of times, as if to get a scared feeling out of his throat.

"Now now, boy! I just told it as it looked to me. And the Claytons are my friends. I haven't a thing in the world against you, boy. So why would I make up a story like that?"

"The which," Red snapped, "is what I come to find out. *Why did you?*"

The sheriff made some hazy sounds, as if he thought that he ought to take part a little on account of his badge; but he ended merely by clearing his throat.

Dave wiped his forehead with a palm, spoke oozy and gutturally: "Now, boy, if I have made a mistake—"

"Big un! Talkin' behind my back like that!"

"Well then, boy, you just set down here and let's talk it over."

"You bet we'll talk it over—only not here! We-all will go next door where the Judge an' some folks is. We'll talk before them an' have us a showdown!"

The sheriff moved his feet some more. "That is a purty good idea, Dave."

Dave said, "I'd rather talk here."

Red's hand moved, and Dave said, quick and anxious, "You wouldn't shoot an unarmed man!"

"Depends on how bad he needs shootin'. Get up an' move. We're going to have that showdown."

The sheriff said judiciously, "You'd better come, Dave." The sheriff began to get up to show his own willingness.

Then Dave got up slowly by pushing the table to make more room for his belly. The table squeaked a little on the splintery floor. "What are you fixin' to do there?"

"Tell my side of the story an' let you tell yourn."

"That is fair, Dave. Yes, fair and square," said the sheriff, helpfully.

III

The sheriff walked out first. Dave followed. They single-filed across to the back of the general store, tramped up the four wooden steps to the loading platform.

"March right along in," said Red.

The sheriff opened the door, pushed it wide. He looked as if this were his show. "Good evenin', gent'men." The poker players turned their heads with puzzle-puckers on their foreheads and blinked a little. "The Clark boy and Dave has come over here to talk about the shootin' today so folks can know what to think." He was making it sound as if he had brought them. "Come along in, Dave. Come in, Clark."

Dave's black eyes had a startled, searching quickness, as if looking for friends, but his thick mouth smiled, as if everybody were his friend. He pushed up his hat and stroked his thick, shiny mustache, looked longest at Bill Clayton; and Bill's eyes, covered with a kind of sullen glaze, were questioning and not at ease.

Red gave the door a swing that slammed it hard, took two steps forward, stopped.

Five men, all middle-aged or more, were playing poker at a round table over which a blanket had been thrown. This was a kind of storeroom, with coils of rope and bins of nails and shelves of canned goods. There were axle grease and singletrees and a clutter of hardware. A lamp swung from a rafter directly above the table. The smell of coal oil was strong.

"Red, what is all this?" The Judge put down his poker hand, laid chips on it.

Dave spoke up, as though there were no unpleasantness at all. "Just a little honest difference of opinion about—"

"You keep still," Red told him. "I'll talk first." Out went a hand, pointing, that almost touched Dave. "He is sayin' on the sly that Mr Clayton was shot accidental today in that gun fight. He is a liar! I think he purtnear knowed what them fellers was waitin' for. An' I brought him here for you-all to hear me tell him so!"

"That is mighty reckless language!" said the Judge. "Why, we all know Dave." He moved his bald head, earnestly reproving Red. However, two or three of the older poker players eyed Red with a kind of admiration, almost with agreement. "Dave," said the Judge, "has been in this country a long, long time and—"

The Judge didn't seem able to go on. He couldn't quite say that Dave was highly thought of, and he couldn't say that some people talked about him pretty harshly. So he wiped his bald head and looked uncomfortable.

"He says," Red explained, "that Mr Clayton ain't a good judge of what happened, because he was shot in the back an' couldn't see. He says Miss Clayton was in the store, so that *she* ain't an eyewitness. He says that me an' the men started shootin'—me first!—an' wild bullets hit Mr Clayton. An' he has made Bill Clayton here"— Red's arm went out as straight as if he held a gun at young Clayton's head—"think maybe I orta be arrested, as if 'twas *my* shots that went wild— the which some dead men can sorta testify they didn't! This Dave figgers, I reckon, that nobody but him seen the fight start, so he can tell it his way. I seen it start, too, an' I'm tellin' it my way. An' there was a fellow named Jim Brady that seen it start and—"

"Who?" The word jumped out of Bill Clayton's mouth, loud and sharp. He looked quickly at Dave, and Dave looked a little as if he had been poked in the belly.

"He wasn't in town!" said Dave, but there was somehow a faint question mark tied to the words.

"He told me his name was Brady, anyhow."

Bill Clayton's sullen face looked as if he were ready to jump nervously at any sudden sound, and Dave sidled to a shelf of canned goods and leaned against it, as if it helped a little to have something to lean on.

Red puckered up his forehead. "An' that man that rode away—the Brady feller said he was Mell Barber!"

The five poker players widened their eyes, nodded at one another.

"Son," said the Judge, "this Barber has the name of being the worst man in the Kilco bunch, and there is a story that he and Kilco have had a falling out over—"

"Not much of a bad man!" said Red, hotly. "He lost his bootheel an' acted crippled. Run—where there was other men's loaded guns on the ground for him to pick up an' use!"

Dave spoke up, loud. He looked excited and earnest. "If that was Mell Barber, then I sure made a mistake about the boy here—and we have all got to get up a big reward for him, dead or alive! Yes, sir!"

One of the old poker players said, " 'Cordin' to what is said, they is already a little reward for him."

"We'll make a big un!" said Dave. "I'll give—give—five hundred dollars myself!"

"I'll add a thousand to it!" said Bill Clayton, standing up and looking angry-earnest.

Red cut in, looked at Dave with a glitter in his bright eyes: "How it come you all of a sudden are whistlin' such another tune? One minute you are makin' Bill here think I maybe orta be arrested, an' the next minute you are posterin' a reward for the only one them fellers I didn't shoot!"

Dave looked sad and glanced friendlily at Red. He took out a handkerchief and wiped his face, as if doing a little something to give him time to get his thoughts lined up.

"It does look a little like I made a mistake," he admitted, with guttural humbleness. "So I will tell just how it was. Them men come into my place and had a drink. I didn't much like their looks. Then they went outside and stood in front. I went to the door and wondered about them.

"When this boy here rode up, he acted and they acted like they had met before and wasn't friends. And I just figgered right there and then they knowed this boy was goin' to ride in and was layin' for 'im.

"The shootin' started sudden. I jumped back and shut the door of my place, and I naturally figgered that the shootin' was all between them. When I learnt that old Sam had been hit, I figgered it was by wild bullets. So I just figgered—"

Red cut in with, "You're lyin' now! You saw how it started, 'cause you been sayin' Mr Clayton had his back turned an' that the girl wasn't even outdoors!"

"No, no," said Dave, sad and humble and sounding honest. "I had just seen Sam come out when the shootin' started. I didn't know who started it. I thought sure it was between you and them men. But I must've made a mistake. I am glad that things have been brought out in the open and we have had this little talk. It sorta clears the air."

Dave even stuck out a hand to Red, but Red hooked his thumbs in his belt and told him: "I got doubts, but maybe you're tellin' the truth. Only you got no business havin' opinions of what goes on under your nose because you can't see straight!"

Dave looked sorrowful that he was so misjudged, and he was a little relieved when Red added, "Me, I'm goin' up to the Judge's place an' go to bed, because I'm ridin' first thing in the mornin'."

He turned, opened the door, tramped out.

Men looked at one another, but mostly they looked at the Judge, and some grinned. One said, "Whew-ee!" The old storekeeper scratched his nose, murmuring, "If ever there was a full-growed wildcat in pants—!"

"Dave," said another, "it has been a long time since I heard you talk so humble-like!"

Dave twisted his black mustache, showed a sickly grin. "The which of you would have sassed him back?"

"You gentlemen," said the Judge, smiling, "may make raucous sounds of scoffing, but the fact is that Red is really chickenhearted in many ways."

The card players did make raucous sounds of scoffing; but the Judge bobbed his head, affirmingly. Then he took the chips off his cards. "All this delay and I've got a pat hand. Any of you boys want to sit in? How about you, Sheriff?"

"I got some business," said Dave.

Bill Clayton said, "I'll go over to the hotel and see how the old man is."

The sheriff took off his hat and put it back on. "I'll just take a hand or two." He went around to sit on the keg where Bill had been.

IV

Dave Gridger and Bill Clayton went out together, not saying good night as they left the room. Outside, Bill stumbled on the platform steps, unsteadily.

They walked off together in the shadows behind the buildings, as if both had it in mind to get to where they could not be overheard.

Bill stopped and hushed his voice to an uneasy whisper: "He said *Brady* was in town!"

Dave peered into the shadows, answered, gutturally cautious: "Maybe he was."

"Layin' for Mell?"

"Or to see Kate," Dave suggested, turning his head and staring suspiciously at one shadow after another. "Why haven't you ever told your old man about him and her?"

"She would tell about me if I did. It was Brady that told her about me. You know what the old man would do to *me!*"

"He won't do nothin' to you ever again, Bill," Dave said, low and encouragingly. "He ain't goin' to get well." Dave puffed, short of breath. "But we purt-near got ourselves in a mess. Hush!" Dave listened, as if about ready to jump. He rubbed his forehead with his palm and kept turning his thick neck uneasily. Then: "How the hell was anybody to know that a redheaded devil who is bulletproof would come ridin' in! But we can't talk here. Too many shadders. 'Magine him bein' under a table! Why, damn his soul, you heard him say he thought I knew what they were waitin' for. He is just too damn smart. But we can't talk here."

They walked on, across to the blacksmith shop, and went under the cottonwood. "We'd better talk low, even here," said Dave.

Bill sat down and chewed a cigar. Dave grunted a little in getting down with his back against the tree. "You know, Bill," he said, in a smooth rumble, "I got mixed up in this out of liking for you."

"You," Bill growled, "got me mixed up in all this because you know my old man hates the sight and smell of you."

"You needed money, Bill."

"And you've made some, too. Hope to make

more. And you made things worse by sayin' the old man was shot accidental thataway."

"Now, Bill, I sorta had to try to take the blame off Mell. I was standin' right there ready to yell, 'They've killed Sam Clayton!' And that would have been all right if they could have hit their horses and rode out of town. Nobody would have knowed who they are. But I was afraid somebody would reckernize them when they was laid out on the floor. I had to sorta take the blame off Mell as well as I could. There is some, Bill, that know how well you know Mell Barber. And that feller that calls himself Brady is one of 'em!"

"You are in this as deep as me!" said Bill, sullenly mean.

"Yeah. Sure. Course I am. And it will all come out all right."

"If the old man don't die and ever finds out—"

"Don't worry, Bill. That horse doctor don't know nothin'. And he is plenty bad hurt."

"Something is goin' to have to be done about that Red!"

"Something, you bet your life!" said Dave, angrily.

"He will spoil things out there at the Lazy Z."

"I know. I am thinking."

"We ought to send out word to Frank Knox," Bill suggested.

"Frank ain't the man to tackle that hombre."

Bill threw away his cigar. "You act scairt of him."

Dave said, solemn-quiet, "I'm not exactly what you call scairt, but he is such a crazy damn fool— why, look how he hauled me and the sheriff over there to the store and had a showdown that I purt-near lost!"

"Then why don't you send word out to Frank Knox?"

"I'm thinkin'. I'm goin' to send word. But I've got to tell Knox how to be careful."

"There's lots of rocks and trees!"

Dave nodded. "That is so. But it won't do to have this Red shot from behind a rock, Bill. There are some folks that would be likely to suspect me. And maybe you. Your old man, if he don't die, would wonder a lot. He don't like me, Bill. So we can't have no mystery about who kills this Red. It has got to be open and aboveboard— if we can work it that way. So I've got to set and think."

CHAPTER THREE

Red jogged out of town at sunrise with the Judge's letter to Frank Knox in his pocket. The morning air was not cool, but it was fresh and clear, and he looked about at the unfamiliar landscape with just about as much interest as an Eastern man would have looked at the streets of a city where he was a stranger.

He was riding north toward the wooded hogbacks that came down from the mountains like baby hills wandering off a little way from their big mamas. He talked to the horse and whistled a little, sang some; but he couldn't sing very well, and nearly everybody who ever heard him said so.

As soon as he was out of town Red noticed the tracks of a horse that had galloped that way through the night. That was not anything to wonder about, for lots of men rode out of town at a lope; but after some miles, when he saw that the horse had been forced on at a gallop, Red said, "Damn fool," and let it go at that.

In about two hours he reached a windmill and old small 'dobe, called Manning Springs after the old man who for years had been there alone with his gray dog. He stopped to let his horse drink, said, " 'Lo, dad," to the old man and found that the springs and mill belonged to the Clayton outfit. Manning was a sociable old fellow, with broken teeth and scrubby beard, always glad to have folks stop and chat. He looked at Red's guns, looked at the thoroughbred black, solemnly whittled a chew from a hard black plug.

"Why you look at me thataway, dad?"

The old fellow scratched up under his battered hat, showed the broken teeth. "I'm an old man. One reason I've growed old is because I keep my mouth shut."

"You've guessed wrong, dad. I'm not on the dodge. I'm not friends with them that are. I'm ridin' out to boss the Lazy Z."

The old man closed one eye, studied, then chewed awhile as solemnly as a cow chews her cud. He spit, opened the eye, rubbed his chin. "I hear tell they is some good money to be made in packin' snowballs to hell."

"What's so wrong out to the Lazy Z?"

"Nuthin'. Oh, nuthin' a-tall. Purty ranch. Oh, you bet!" He grinned knowingly and jerked his head forward. "Me, I understand that folks enjoy the best health when they keep their mouths shet. Luck, son." He waved an arm in a wide sweep and had a friendly look, but Red knew that he had been given a warning.

The road parted three ways at the Springs. Red kept to the north, taking the least-traveled road, which began to wind over rolling hills that some miles farther on grew into small, wooded mountains.

He saw that the galloping horse had also taken this road.

Red pulled up and got off, examining tracks. Three of the shoes were worn; the right rear was new, at least newer than the others, with calks that left a sharp imprint. He was not a sign reader like some he knew; but he was onto the A,B,C's of trailing; and he could tell by the drag of lizards' tails and dab of quail tracks in the dust that crossed the hoofmarks just about how long ago the horse had traveled this way. This horse, he judged, had come along since midnight and in a hurry.

Red jogged on, thinking it over, suspiciously. This was the road to the Lazy Z, no doubt also the road to other small ranches and nesters' places; but if these tracks turned in to the Lazy Z ranch house they would mean something. Mean that somebody had come out from town with some kind of news. He said, "Um-m. Most dead men have some friends!"

A mile or farther along the road he met a young Mexican coming at a walk, with reins loose, the horse's head down. It was a tired horse, with dried sweat on the flanks.

There were a lot of Mexicans in Tulluco, and Red, after his young mother's death, had been cared for by an old Mexican vaquero, and nearly all the Mexicans that Red knew were gentle and polite.

So Red said in Spanish, "Good day, señor."

The young Mexican peered through slitted eyes and mumbled, but touched his hat and pulled a little to one side to give Red the road. Red guessed that perhaps Mexicans and gringos didn't get on well up here in this Nelplaid country.

He went on about fifty feet before his eyes looked into the dust ahead of him. Then Red wheeled his horse with sweep of reins, touch of spur, and in two bounds he reined up alongside of the frightened Mexican boy.

"Señor," said Red politely, "one question, please." It was ever so much easier to be polite in Spanish. "The Lazy Z ranch, it is not far?"

"It is not far, señor."

"Another question, if you please!"

"Certainly, señor."

"Do you by chance come from there this morning?"

"Yes, señor."

"And to reach the ranch, you rode fast last night?"

"But señor!"

"And what message did you take, if you please?"

"Message, señor?"

Red snapped in English, not politely, "You got ears! Unfold 'em!"

The young Mexican wrinkled his face in uncomfortable puzzlement. "But how could you know, señor?"

"Never you mind. I want to know who sent you. Come on, talk!"

"The Señor Gridger," said the Mexican uneasily.

"What's he tell you to say?"

"It was a letter, señor."

"Who for?"

"Señor Knox."

Red grinned, went back to Spanish: "You have a charming face and a pleasant voice, my friend. Please be agreeable enough to tell me what questions this Señor Knox asked you about a certain unworthy fellow by the name of Red Clark!"

"Who is yourself, señor," said the Mexican boy, bowing.

"If you knew me, why were you so unfriendly just now when I spoke to you in passing?"

"Ah, but I was not unfriendly, señor. I was afraid. You are—" He stopped, embarrassed, not wanting to accuse Red of being a desperado that might shoot with no reason at all.

"A hard-workin', honest cowboy—that's me! What-all did this Knox want to know about me?"

He heard that Knox had wanted to know what he looked like, where he was from, had he really stood up to four men and downed three; and had

Mell Barber been shot, as Dave Gridger seemed to think; and was it true that the man Jim Brady had been in town?

"Peace go with you, señor," said Red, lifting his hat, very politely.

The Mexican's horse, returning from the ranch, had of course made the same shoe tracks in the dust as in going.

II

An hour later Red sat in the saddle and looked about, not pleased. He was unused to mountain ranches. Pine trees were in the way, although they had long ago been cut down near the house and corral. The ranch house was of mud and logs, with a wide door. The sheds and corrals were old, in need of repair.

He rode up to the house and hallooed.

A frowzy, sour man, with a strip of buckskin for a suspender over his gray undershirt, shuffled out of the dimness. He had a long, straggling mustache, and his cheeks were covered with gray fuzz, as if once in a while he shaved. A burned corncob pipe drooped from his mouth. His hands were white and soft, and that meant that he was the cook.

He looked Red over with watery eyes, ran a hand through his tangled hair. "Air you that feller?"

64

"What feller, pop?"

"Knox, he said this mornin' that he had sent the Judge word that he was quittin' and the Judge was sendin' out a new boss."

"I'm him."

Cook snorted. "Not in my end of the house, you ain't."

"That goes if you're a good cook. You go if you ain't!"

Cook looked at the guns, looked at Red's face, gazed at the fine black horse. "He is a-wearin' two guns and a-wearin' 'em low down, and he is a-packin' a rifle! Yes'ir, I bet old Jesse James hisself would turn pale as a sick woman if he was to see you!"

"I bet you'd better be one mighty fine cook if you don't want to have to keep your mouth shut a little. If you are, you can say what you damn please!"

Cook waggled the pipe between his teeth, hitched up his lone gallus, stared without batting an eye and spoke: "We got enough fool kids around here. You ain't no more 'n one yourself. Me, I'm tired of havin' to wipe babies' noses and tuck 'em in their bunks. How long do you think *you* are stayin'?"

"Depends, pop. If you are a good cook, I may stay a long time."

"Sorta sassy-like, ain't you?" Cook pulled at his long mustache. "I been on this ranch for twelve year. No flop-eared kid is a-goin' to tell me when to leave. You get too gosh blame sassy with me, and I'll give you a spankin'. I mean 'er!"

"I been spanked and larruped and tanned good when I was a little shaver, the which makes me so polite to old wore-out fossils about the size an' shape of you. So you pull a steak out of the skillet. I'm goin' to water an' feed my horse. When I come back, if it's a good steak, maybe I'll let you look at a bottle I brung along in case some snakes jumped out an' bit me."

The cook grinned, pulled at a mustache end, raising it in the air, said, "You don't look so much damn fool as I first thought."

The big room had a beaten earth floor, a half-dozen bunks, some stools, a bench or two and a table. At one end was the kitchen, with no partition. The stove was an old cast-iron contraption, and its waggling legs were supported by up-ended chunks of logs. The big room was in the untidy state that bespeaks halfhearted attempts at cleanliness by careless men living together, and it was redolent with the man smell of sweat and tobacco.

The cook put a hot, brown, thick steak on the table, with pickles, cold biscuits and warmed-over coffee, and Red brought out the bottle of whisky. They had a drink, man-sized. Red cut into the steak, chewed. "I guess you've got a right to be ornery," Red acknowledged, heaping sugar into his coffee. "This is good grub."

A half-hour later the bottle was nearly empty, the cook full. He was talking to Red as to a long-lost brother, called Red "son" and told him not to stay. He said that it was all right for the other boys to stay, because they were just kids and didn't do anything but ride around. It was going to be bad for Red if he tried to boss the ranch.

"How so, h'm?"

"Russlers own this country."

"They friends of yourn, pop?"

Cook grinned foolishly. "They ain't en'mies. An' they was friends of Al's."

"Who is Al?"

"Alvord. I told him he was a damn fool. Anyhow, any man is that's been married twict!"

"What about him, pop?"

"Cantankerous of coyote, Al was. An' mean."

"How it come you got on with him so long?"

"I'd make 'im so mad he wouldn't talk for days. Not open his mouth. You ain't no idee how peac'ble that is 'less you been married!"

"I'm listenin', pop."

Cook up-ended the bottle. "I told Al he was a damn fool. He throwed in with russlers an' worse. Al allus liked me. I halfway liked him. So we got on. Al had it in for old Sam Clayton. An' fellers—you'd be surprised what fellers—helped 'emselves to Clayton cows. An' sometimes Al—

67

no harm in sayin' so now, because pore ol' Al, he is dead—he rode with Kilco's bunch. Oh, he was a no-good old wolf!" Cook smacked the table with bottom of the bottle. "But I liked 'im."

Cook drained the last drop from the bottle, teetered woozily on his stool, then sank forward drowsily, face down on his arms. In a few minutes he was dead to the world.

Red rolled a cigarette, lighted it, scratched behind an ear, looked at the cook. "So I've come to be boss of a rustler's ranch!"

A few minutes later he heaved the cook up, carried him to a bunk, rolled him into it, gave the pillow a twist to make the cook's head more comfortable.

"You may not know it, feller, but I sorta like you!" he said.

III

Along late in the afternoon two boys rode in.

Red introduced himself, and they all looked one another over. Red sized them up as good kids, scarcely halfway through their teens. Bobby's nose was upturned a little, as if sniffing impudently, and he had a wide mouth, filled with grins. Pete was of stronger stuff, had more thoughtful eyes, more of a resolute look.

They examined Red with shy stares, their thoughts very close to the surface of their brown faces: Red didn't look much older than they, and he grinned and talked as if not much older.

A little later Frank Knox came. A slim man with straight black hair and straight black brows that joined when he scowled. He scowled a little at Red, but said:

"I'm glad you come. I told the Judge I had more 'n I could do, me with my own ranch just up the valley."

He was making his throaty voice as pleasant as he could, but all the while his black eyes stared coldly at Red, sizing him up. Knox had something of the Injun look about him, as if he could hide his feelings. The Injun look increased when he took off his hat with the rattlesnake band and showed the straight black, grease-shiny hair.

Red didn't say much of anything.

Knox fished around with, "How's things in town?"

"All right, I reckon."

"Any excitement a-tall?"

"I went to bed early an' got up in the dark."

"There is usually some little shootin' in Nelplaid," said Knox, smoothing down the back of his hair with stroke of palm.

"Oh, there was some guns goin' off a little. But at times like that, strangers orta keep their noses under cover. It's safer," said Red, mild and innocent.

Knox's face had a funny look. He didn't want

to admit that he had got word out from town and so had reason to question Red directly. And it was hard for him to believe that this lanky young fellow had made any such gun fight as Dave Gridger wrote about; harder to believe that he would keep his mouth shut if he had made it.

Knox reread the Judge's letter and smiled a little. He looked as if he would be pretty good at poker; at least, at stealing aces in a poker game.

"The Judge, he asks me to give you all the help I can, and I sure will."

"That there is fine," said Red, adding modestly, "I purt-near allus can use some help."

Knox told him, "There uster be a lot of rustlers up here, but we cleaned 'em out. Us little cowmen, we all stick together."

"That," Red agreed, "is mighty fine."

Knox looked thoughtful and explained, "It is nesters and such who are worst. They is one over yonder across the valley who makes his brag, or uster, that he kept fat on Lazy Z beef."

Red looked interested, not speaking.

"He's groomed sorta leanlike since I been in charge," said Knox.

"I bet you kinda explained how it was bad for a feller's health to eat Lazy Z beef, h'm?"

"You are right. 'Twas him as run off the two bosses the Judge sent out before I took charge.

But I made him tuck his tail between his legs and go back up in the hills where he b'longs. Yet he musta heard I was fixin' to quit."

"Um?" Red was mild and interested.

" 'Cause just this afternoon," said Knox, running a palm down over the back of his slick hair, "I met a feller as said old Backman had killed another cow. I was meanin' to ride over in the mornin' and give him hell. But since you come, I think I'll light out for my ranch tonight. You are the new boss now. You can use your own judgment about lettin' Backman eat Lazy Z beef." Knox went on from behind a crooked smile: "Only if he ain't set on, he'll strut around and say how scairt you are of him. He is a windy old shypoke and bellers loud. I'm just tellin' you, and you can do as you please. He knows I'm quittin', because he knows if I wasn't I'd stick my spurs in his neck."

"Some nesters," Red admitted, "are like that."

"Folks'll size you up purty much on how you call old Backman's bluff," said Knox, looking helpful.

Knox would not stay to supper. He was in a hurry to get to his ranch and give it a little care, because, he said, he had been putting in all of his time keeping the Lazy Z straight. "But any time you want to know something, or need help, just you come over and ask me."

"Sure," said Red.

Knox rode off through the evening twilight, and Red sat on a stump, smoked a cigarette.

Bobby and Pete were in the house, noisily messing about, getting supper. Red could hear them squabbling and teasing. He went in and stood by the door. When they saw him they quieted down, self-consciously, not knowing yet just what this boss was like.

"Did you kids see a Mexican talkin' to Knox this mornin'?"

They said, "Yes."

"Did he say anythin' about what the Mexican told him?"

Both shook their heads.

Red went to the kitchen stove and looked at the fried potatoes that were burning, at the warmed-over beans that were drying out, at the steaks that were getting hard and black and filling the room with smoke.

"This here," he said, "is like what I call home cookin'. Least, it is the same kind of cookin' I do when I make myself to home. Let's eat!"

The kids loosened up, and as they ate they explained that their work was riding the hogbacks and running cattle down out of the timber. They gave no hint of liking Knox or of not liking him. They had heard of that old Backman but had never seen him; and he had a bad name.

"In the mornin'," said Red, "you can show me which is the way to his place. I think I'll ride over an' have me a look. I got to get acquainted around here."

In the morning the cook was up long before daylight, as a cook ought to be; and he made the sort of banging and clattering noises that a cook does when he has to get up while other people are still asleep. His head hurt, and he was as cross as a sore-tailed bear.

He went out to the wash bench, where Red was splashing like a duck in a mud puddle. "What-all did we talk about while I was drunk?" The cook had a frowzy, suspicious air.

Red blinked wet eyes and laughed, "About you bein' married, or not bein' married. I forget which."

He gazed with rheumy eyes at Red and twiddled the edge of his drooping mustache. "Did I talk about folks up in this country a-tall?"

"You talked about what a handsome feller I am an' how you liked me."

"That just goes to show how whisky makes a fool of a feller. Don't you go bringin' any more up here, ever again. Only,"—he leaned a little closer—"sick as I am, there ain't nothin' that does as much good as another little snifter before breakfust. Have you got some more?"

Red laughed at him. "Say, pop, Knox, he was tellin' me about a nester named Backman that sorta helps hisself to a cow now an' then. What about 'im, anyhow?"

Cook fished in his hip pocket for his old corncob pipe, stuck it into his mouth, cocked a watery eye. "Knox told you?"

"Right."

"I reckon old Backman would put a kid of about your shape and size into his skillet if he had him a hankerin' for some redheaded meat. You let that old devil alone, son. Al did. And Al didn't back up from nobody—much."

"And Knox? Did Knox ask this old Backman to please not eat our cows?"

"Did Knox say so?"

"A little."

"Me, I ain't goin' to call Frank Knox a liar. He is a purty bad man to argy with. For your own good," said the cook, with a kind of bleary earnestness, "you wanta be p'lite to Frank. He is easy to get on with if you don't rile 'im. But he is pizen on legs if he takes some dislike to you."

IV

After breakfast, which was finished long before the sun climbed above the wooded hogbacks, Pete rode down across the valley with Red and pointed out the way to the rough trail that led back up to where Backman had squatted down.

Pete reined up, ready to turn and leave Red. He spoke slowly and looked as if he really wanted to do Red a favor: "I hear tell that this old Backman

74

don't much like to have people pokin' around up where he has his stampin' ground."

"How you mean, Pete?"

Pete ran his fingers into the horse's mane as if after cockleburrs. "I sorta have heard that *nobody* up in this neck of the woods, from old Alvord hisself on down, monkeys much with that old long-hair."

"Um. Pete, you have got some batwing ears. Tell me, have you ever heard much about Mr Alvord maybe bein' in with a bunch that used to use this valley to sorta coax Clayton cows to come an' hide?"

Pete looked steadily at Red and shook his head a little. "Folks wear tight-cinched mouths up in this country, Red. We don't meet many people. Us kids, I mean. Knox kept me and Bob combin' the hogbacks on account of cows driftin' into the timber." He swept an arm vaguely. "It is mighty rough country. Mighty rough."

"Um."

Pete leaned over and looked down at the ground, then his eyes came up slantwise-shy from under the hatbrim and hovered on Red's face. His boyish mouth smiled cautiously. "You look like a purty good feller, Red."

"I try to be with nice kids."

"Me and Bob was all set to quit."

"How so?"

"They is something been funny. We don't earn

our salt huntin' cows. And cows that used to be thick here in the valley ain't no more. Knox said they went wanderin' back up in the mountains, an' he kept us ridin' to hunt 'em out."

"I sorta see what you mean, Pete. Did you by happenchance mention a little something about it to the Judge awhile back?"

Pete nodded. "He knowed our folks. If we'd kept still, he might have come to think sometime that we kept our mouths shut on purpose."

"Is there anythin' you can put your finger on?"

"No, only you tell me why would cows leave a valley like this for to wear their legs off climbin' hogbacks?"

Red grinned. "Maybe this old Backman puts 'em in his skillet. I'll ride over an' ask him."

V

Red rode on into steep country over a rocky trail. It was pretty, but he wasn't much of a nature lover—except as nature had fitted the scenery to fatten cows. He gave the horse its head, rested his hands on the horn, thought things over, grunted reflectively. It was maybe a big waste of time to come over here to talk to this old Backman, but having said that he would do it, and having made a start, Red could not turn back. The kids might think he was afraid.

It was still and drowsy on the pine-covered

76

hillside, and hot. The horse tipped forward its ears and raised its head.

Red alertly looked up, and a rifle blazed at him from across the top of a boulder about fifty yards ahead. Red saw the smoke—then he was bareheaded. His hat had been shot off.

He threw away the reins, jerked his feet from the stirrups and flung himself out of the saddle to take what cover he could before the rifle went off again; but as he left the horse with reckless sidelong fling, a spur raked the Devil's rump, and the horse jumped, its shod feet rattling on the loose rock. After a few jumps the horse stood to the dragging reins, head up, ears forward.

Red, down on the ground, with one arm under him and the other hand already at the butt of a gun, peered into a leveled rifle in the hands of a tall, shaggy old long-haired, long-bearded man in a fringed buckskin shirt who rose up from behind the boulder.

The old fellow cocked his head and called out, "So *you* are that there bad man what was comin' to run me off my place, are ye?"

Red didn't move. His hand was on the revolver, and the revolver was clear of the holster, but he lay motionless on a bent elbow and just looked. Old Backman had a kind of serenity, no bad temper; just the calm assurance of a man who has always been able to take care of himself and felt that he always would. Red guessed that here was a genuine leftover from the frontier days.

Red lifted his head a little, shouted, "Damn poor shootin', dad! Why didn't you wait till I got a little closter? Maybe you could've hit me!"

Mr Backman held the rifle one-handedly and stroked his beard with the other hand, bent forward a little, peering. "You fuzzy-eared cub, you! I took off your hat 'cause I wanted to see the color of your hair." He called it "har." His voice was slow, deep and smooth. "You looked so danged young, I didn't think you could be that feller. But it is red, like Knox said it would be. Well, here I am, waitin' for to be run off!"

Red poked the nose of the revolver into its holster and sat up.

Old Backman didn't say anything about Red putting up his hands or not touching his guns; and Red, who had known old-timers, many of them his father's best friends, knew what that meant. This tall, shaggy old fellow with the slow, almost gentle voice was willing for Red to try all the fast shooting that he wanted to.

Red got to his feet. "So Frank Knox told you a redheaded bad man was comin' to run you off?"

"Purty smart young un. You understand English." The old fellow had a good-natured mockery. "How it come a cub like you what ain't quite dry behind the ears"—he called them

78

"airs"—"sets hisself up for to be a bad man, anyhow? Two guns and all. With a rifle under his leg. I was mighty skeered."

Red grinned. He knew what he was up against and didn't mind. He had come over, expecting to find a morose old nester who was soured on cowmen, and he had run into an old-timer who didn't give a damn about cowmen.

"Dad, I ain't very smart someways, sometimes, but I never set myself up as a bad man."

"Ho, no?"

"No!"

"That is plumb queer, ain't it? Knox, he come a-rarin' over here yestiddy afternoon a-sayin' as how I was to pull stakes and git or he'd have his special red-haired hellfire-eatin' bad man, that had been fetched all the way from Tulluco on purpose to run off folks, pay me a visit. Bein' sorta lonely-like up here, I allus welcome vis'tors. So I set here on the trail for to say 'Howdy.' You looked so dang much like a fool kid that I thought I'd best have a look at your hair before I got real ser'us. And you got two guns tied to you. Why?"

"I'd rather lose a leg than one of them guns. You sorta keep a leg tied to you so it won't get lost or something. I keep them guns thataway. They was my dad's."

"Well, either you or Frank Knox is a-lyin'. And accordin' to all of what I hear, Frank he is honest and truthful and mighty full of courage. Leastwise, that is how he tells it."

Red felt hot and itchy, but kept on grinning. "So far, dad, the joke is on me. But have you got some time and a good horse, and will you kinda poke my nose in the direction of where this Frank Knox has got his ranch?"

"I got all the time in the world and a good horse. Also legs that has tramped farther than any horse alive. What you aimin' at?"

"Do you know the way to Frank Knox's place?"

"So far I allus been able to find my way to wherever I wanted to git to."

"Well, dad, I'd like for you to sorta show me the way. I want to have a little talk with this Mr Knox. I'd like for you to hear what I say."

Old Backman cocked his head to one side. He had bright eyes. Unlike most of the grizzly old-timers who had lived lonely lives, he was not sour and sullen, but had a sparkle of good nature. "You mean maybe Knox has been up to one of his cute tricks?"

"Purty cute, dad."

"Why he want me to shoot you, you reckon?"

"Judge Trowbridge there in town sent me out to be new boss of the Lazy Z, and Knox took it friendly-like, seeming. But he said you had a habit of eatin' Lazy Z beef an' that I'd better ride over an' ask you not to. So I come."

The old fellow chuckled. "Mosey along up

80

closter, son, where I can look at you good. I got a sorta liking for young uns."

Red went up, walking with pegleg stiffness on high heels over the rocky trail. He stopped before the tall old man, whose rifle lay on his forearm with no menace, except such menace as was in the readiness of a man who knew what he could do with a rifle. Then Red saw that Mr Backman was even wearing moccasins.

"Now why would I want to eat beef when deer come right down to my door so thick I have to throw rocks and say 'Scat!'?"

"I only come up here yesterday, dad. I don't know anything about this country."

"Frank Knox he is a purty hard man," said Mr Backman.

Red snapped, "He ain't! Hard men don't work cute tricks for to get somebody they don't like shot!"

Mr Backman thought it over, stroked his beard, nodded a little. "I reckon you can think straight. Lots of folks can't. That is sure a nice horse. Get your hat, bring your horse, and we'll go along up here to my place and have a snack and git a little acquainted."

The cabin was square, of rough-hewn logs, chinked with mud and moss, with a mud-and-stick chimney. It was clean and snug and in order. He had built the cabin and furniture himself, which wasn't unusual; but he had built it with a care and neatness that was. He took off the pine-needle mattress to show, proudly, his bunk springs of interlaced rawhide.

"I sleep outdoors, mostly—except in the rain." He chuckled deep in his beard. "I did onct in the rain last spring when a purty girl come to see me. I ain't yit so old that I don't like for purty girls to like me!"

He was straight as a rugged old pine, and had been trapper, buffalo hunter, used to loneliness.

"I allus liked kids and women," he said simply. "Nice little shavers that sorta worship you, and women—any size." He shook his head, smiling. "I uster think that when I got me some gray hairs I would have some sense. But they can still tie me around their little finger. This one has shore done it proper. Or maybe not proper a-tall, h'm?"

"Me, I like women fine, too," Red admitted. "They is one in this country that I sure like. Her name is Miss Clayton."

Mr Backman gave him a keen look. "How you come to know her if you are new to the country?"

"I seen her in town."

The old fellow scratched his head and, in an amused voice, said, "Son, let's you and me pitch in together and lick a big handsome feller. She likes him too good for us to have a chance."

"You mean Jim Brady?"

"How you come to know him, too?" Mr Backman

82

was getting doubtful about Red's being so new to the country.

"Who is he, dad?"

"Oh, Jim is just a feller. What do you think of him?"

"Seems all right."

"Seems. H'm. I wonder sometimes. How you come to know him?"

"I don't. Only it was thisaway: There in town some men was shootin' at old Sam Clayton. They shot him in the back before the general store."

"Sam?"

"An' when he went down, that girl, she jumped right out of the store door an' throwed herself down on top of him, like she would rather be hit than him. So I know she is all right."

"They kilt Sam?"

"Purt-near, I reckon."

"Who done it?"

"They was four of 'em an'—"

"What happened to 'em?"

"There was quite some shootin' for a spell, an' only one rode off. The other three was buried. A goodlookin' feller, he come up an' shook hands with me an' he said his name was Brady, an' that the man who rode off was Mell Barber."

Mr Backman eyed Red keenly. "He come up to you and said his name was Jim Brady?" That was hard to believe.

"Right, dad."

"Why?"

"My gun, it had sorta joined in the argyment."

"Oh," said Mr Backman. "But Mell Barber, he got away?"

"You know him, dad?"

"Know about him some." He tossed back his long hair, scowled. "Why you reckon they shot Sam thataway?"

"Some say they are a bunch of outlaws. I 'magine a man like Mr Clayton sorta thinks that the scenery is allus made purtier by some little piles of dirt on an outlaw's belly. Me, I do!"

"Humph," said Mr Backman.

They had their snack of bits of venison roasted on the tip of green sticks held over coals; and it was good. They drank cool spring water. Mr Backman smoked a pipe and Red a couple of cigarettes.

"So you want to go have a talk with Frank Knox?"

"Um. He said for me to come an' see him any time."

" 'Tain't far. 'Bout seven miles or a little more."

"You got a horse, you said."

"Legs is better. I use a horse mostly only for to pack."

The old man's long legs and moccasined feet took the trail easily, much to Red's amazement. Red hated walking, thought other people should. And he didn't like the timber, with its perpetual shade, as if night were coming, and the denseness that kept him from seeing far. He did not like the rough wooded country, for it was hard on horses and the men on the horses.

VI

The trail Mr Backman was using came to an old road, not much used, that wound its way up the valley; and Red at once noticed that quite a few cows had come that way recently.

"See 'em?" asked Red, pointing to the tracks.

Mr Backman looked at him in mild disgust. It was just about like asking a school teacher if she could read the alphabet in big letters.

"How many you figger, dad?"

" 'Bout twenty."

"Are you thinkin' what I'm thinkin', dad?"

"Mebbe so."

"From other things you know about the lay of the land an' folks as live hereabouts, does it surprise you any?"

"Not a great much."

"Then mebbe my visit over here to this Mr Knox is sorta business instead of just personal, h'm?"

"Knox is a hard man to do business with, some ways. Still, if Jim Brady shook hands with you there in town, I got me a notion of why Knox sicked me onto you. He don't like me. He don't like you. He figgered that whatever happened between us would make him feel purty good."

"Yeah, but ain't he goin' to be surprised!"

A half-hour later, when they looked from the timber toward a small clearing where there was a cabin, a shed that was used as a stable, and a small corral, Mr Backman said softly, "This here is the place," and looked up, as if to see how Red felt now, face to face maybe with some trouble.

"An' there," said Red, poking out an arm, "are *cows* in that horse corral!"

"They do look a wee bit like some cows. Only you can never tell. Mebbe Knox has stuck some horns on horses."

"If they're wearin' Lazy Zs, this Knox is a'ready halfway to hell!"

"Careful, son. He may be layin' for you!"

Red's idea of being careful was to kick the spurs into the Devil's flanks. The horse threw back its ears and leaped forward, bound on bound, then, under high pull of reins, skittered haunch down to a stop alongside of the corral. Red rose in his stirrups, peered over the top rail and saw about twenty cows. Those broadside to him were branded Lazy Z.

Again he put spurs into the horse's flanks and rode headlong for the cabin.

The door was open, and Knox's bare head came poking out. His black hair was slicked down, giving him the Injun-blooded look. His face had a silly sort of scared expression when he saw that it was Red. It was just as if he had been sure that only somebody friendly would come riding up at full gallop; but Red's eyes had a glitter that wasn't friendly.

Knox was half minded to jerk his head back inside the house; but the Devil's head flew up under the pull of the reins, and he settled on his haunches, with forefeet braced right at the door. Red flung away the reins and piled out of the saddle, his eyes on Knox; and Knox could see that Red meant to come on right into the house after him; so he stepped out with his hand well away from the gun.

"Hello, kid!" he said, showing his teeth friendlily, but his black eyes were staring. He talked fast. "I was just comin' over to the ranch with that bunch of drifters I found wanderin' over here and shut up in the corral. Us little cowmen has to help one another." Knox had fine white teeth, and he seemed trying to show them all.

Red's words cracked with the sound of a whiplash: "You're lyin'!"

That set Knox's head back as if he had been hit by a fist. His black eyebrows came together in a frown. "You are mighty reckless in how you use words!" His beady eyes fastened on Red's face, as if studying whether or not to risk the draw; but there was something in the blaze of Red's face, the tense, lithe readiness to strike, that seemed to confirm the warning that had been in Dave Gridger's message. So Knox picked out a tune that sounded more hurt than mad: "Here me, I took nearly all mornin' bunchin' them cows that had wandered off their range into the corral so I could drive 'em back over where they belonged, and now you—"

Red let go with, "Feller, you drove 'em from our range last night! You've kept Bobby an' Pete ridin' hogbacks so they'd be out of the way an' not see the goin's on you've done. You are a damn cow thief!"

"No man can call me that and—"

"I'm not wearin' skirts, an' I called you it!"

"Now listen, young feller, I don't want no trouble with a fool kid!"

"I want some with you! An' I ain't no kid. I'm boss of the Lazy Z, an' you stole my cows. You're wearin' a gun. An' if your arm is broke, why don't you put it in a sling!"

Such talk set Knox right back on his heels, as if he had received a flurry of fists in his face. He gulped a little, tried the hurt tune again: "Now see here. You are makin' a big mistake if you think I would drive cows from anybody's ranch! Why, I been workin' myself sick over to the Lazy Z, tryin'—"

Knox broke off. He was too dark-skinned and sunburned to grow pale, but he looked really sick as he caught sight of the tall, shaggy old Mr

Backman coming up toward the cabin door, with a long, easy stride and his rifle in the crook of his arm.

Mr Backman walked up noiselessly in moccasined feet and said coolly, "Why, howdy, Knox."

Knox set his mouth tight and stared uneasily.

"I am beginnin' for to see," said Mr Backman, even as if a little pleased, "just why you wanted somebody to shoot this here boy for you. You don't 'pear to be particklar anxious to do it for yourself!"

Knox sagged against the side of the doorway and scowled. He might have felt that he could talk a young fellow like Red into being off guard for a split second or into halfway believing that there was a mistake about the cows in the corral, but old Backman was too hard to fool.

Red fidgeted, not knowing what to do with a man that would turn belly up and not fight. He frowned at Knox, spoke to Mr Backman:

"Dad, onct I grabbed a mouse. An' the little devil, he scratched an' bit my fingers. He wasn't much bigger'n my thumb, an' he knew he couldn't lick me, but he was willin' to make it a fight. An' he made such a dang good un I was glad to turn him loose. Then I got some cheese an' put it where he could find it, for to show no hard feelin's. A mouse'll fight. Some men won't!"

Mr Backman set his hat back on his head, stroked his beard solemnly. "Mr Knox here has took a lot of trouble for some years now to make folks up in this country think he is a bad man to monkey with. I'm real surprised an' mebbe some disapp'inted!"

"Up in Tahzo and Tulluco," Red explained, "when you cornered a rustler, you had to kill 'im an' do it in the smoke. He never turned up his belly an' waited for to be hung!"

Knox stiffened, and a wild look filled his black eyes.

Red saw the look, but it wasn't his nature to talk and bluff just to make somebody more scared. Readily he said, "Just you an' me, dad, we can't hang 'im like he orta be, 'cause folks might say it was spite. If there was a bunch along to see an' say it was right, I'd be willin' to run him up to a tree." He had kept his eyes on Knox; and now: "You, feller, have been drawin' wages to work for the Lazy Z. An' you have been stealin' Lazy Z cows. It was you, I bet, run off the other bosses just so you could get to be boss yourself an' steal more. But I can't shoot you like I orta, or hang you like you orta be!"

"Then, son, how you figger? You goin' to turn him loose?"

"Hell, no! I'll take him hog-tied clear into Nelplaid an' turn him over to the Judge!"

"H'm," said Mr Backman, meditatively. "I

reckon he'd purt-near rather be shot than took in pris'ner by a kid before all the people that know 'im."

"He can get hisself shot if he wants. He is still wearin' a gun!"

Knox took some deep breaths and set his teeth. His dark eyes had a snakelike glaze, as if he were so full of poison that he would like to bite; but he did not speak.

Red went up and pulled the gun from Knox's holster, stepped back, looked down at the gun. "One, two, three—huh—four. Liars, I bet, can file notches as well as steal cows!" He prodded out the shells and put Knox's 45 into his saddlebag. "Now come along. I'll saddle you a horse."

The old frontiersman, tall and calm, looked on. The rifle lay in the crook of his left arm. He followed Red and Knox on noiseless feet across to the shed where two horses were tied. The fringe of the buckskin shirt stirred in light ripples as he moved.

Red asked, "Which horse you want?"

Knox did not answer. Red gave him a look, then turned one of the horses loose because no one would be left at the ranch to look after it. He threw a saddle on the other horse, but no bridle. Mr Backman looked on critically, but Red seemed to be doing all right without advice.

"Knox, stick your hands out behind you."

Knox sullenly did not stir.

"Suit yourself, feller. But if I have to lay a gun barrel over your head, I'll tie you belly down across your saddle, an' you'll stay there! Put your hands behind you!"

Knox thrust his hands out stiffly behind him, and Red tied the wrists.

"Now come over here to get in this saddle. I'll boost you up. But if you kick or act smart, you won't go to Nelplaid. You'll go straight to hell!"

Red supported Knox's back while he raised a foot up to the stirrup; then Red heaved and Knox swung up, throwing the other leg over the horse. Red hobbled his feet under the horse's belly; then he made a hackamore of the rope that was coiled on Knox's saddle and threw the end to the ground.

The horse stood still while Red opened the corral to let out the Lazy Z cows.

At first they looked about, bellowed a little, as if asking one another questions; but after they were pointed along the road that led down into the valley they began to move as if they knew where they were going and were glad to go.

Red rode back for Knox, and Mr Backman handed up from the ground the rope that was tied to Knox's horse; then he walked along beside Red's horse, not saying a word.

When they came to the trail over which he had brought Red from his cabin, he said, "Son, I'll leave you here." His sharp old eyes twinkled.

"I purt-near think what Knox told me about you bein' a hellfire-eatin' redhead from Tulluco is some nearer the truth than what you told me about yourself."

He flung up his hand in parting, gave Knox a look, and set off along the trail, tall and erect, with an easy stride. His hair was down to his shoulders, his white beard swept his breast. The mountain trail was already darkened by the setting of the sun behind the western hills.

Red had a queer, sad, warm feeling, as if he were watching the last of the old buckskinclad frontiersmen disappearing, not merely from sight, but from the West.

CHAPTER FOUR

It was in the starlight that Red, riding slowly, pushed the cows right along up close to the ranch house. The boys and cook came out to see what was up. They had been wondering for hours what might have happened to Red. Cook took the corncob pipe from his mouth, rubbed his nose on an elbow.

"He ain't alone."

"Where'd he roust out all them cows? Do you reckon from up at old Backman's?" Bobby asked, breathlessly.

The keen-eyed Pete spoke up: "That looks like Frank Knox!"

They were standing outside the door as Red rode around the cows and came up, leading Knox's horse, with Knox stiffly in the saddle, his arms behind him.

Cook stuck out his scrawny neck and sounded anxious: "What does all this mean?"

"These cows was in the corral at Knox's place. I fetched 'em home—an' him along. I'm takin' him to town in the mornin'."

The two kids looked at each other and made whistling sounds, softly. Cook took out a dirty plug, whittled, nervously crumbled the whittlings between his palms. When he lit the pipe he held the match so long that flame nipped his fingers.

Red dismounted, walked to Knox's horse, loosened the hobbles and carefully coiled the rope, laid the coils about the horn of Knox's saddle.

"Light down," said Red.

Knox came off the horse, with awkward kick of leg over the cantle and belly bent over the saddle. His hands being tied behind him, Red steadied him to the ground.

"You boys grain the horses. Cook, we want some supper. Come along, Knox."

Cook's voice cracked, carried mingled reproach and warning: "Red, you are clear crazy mad!"

"I allus am when folks rustle my brand."

"Your brand?"

"She's *my* brand when I draw wages to ride herd on 'er!"

Knox eyed the cook with a sullen, mean stare, somehow expectantly, but the cook was having trouble with his pipe and would not meet Knox's black eyes.

Red took Knox through the house and out behind to wash up. Knox still chafed at his wrists, which were white from the pressure of the rope, for when Red tied a man up, the man stayed tied.

Knox slowly filled a pan from the pump. He thought some about jumping around a corner of the house and trying to dodge away into the night shadows; but he had on high-heeled boots, which slowed down a running man, and also he had the feeling that Red didn't want more than the shadow of an excuse to shoot him.

Red, not saying a word, stood about six feet off, let Knox give himself a long, thoughtful wash, then followed him back into the house. For all of his gabbiness, Red could be silent; and he was satisfied by knowing that Knox was hurt clear down deep at being a prisoner before these men whose boss he had been. Red's mind was made up that Knox should have even more humiliation. A rustler that wouldn't fight was about as low as a fellow could get.

When the boys came back from the stable, Knox was sitting on a bunk. His wet black hair was combed sleekly back, the comb's teeth marks showing. He rolled a cigarette, lit it by drawing the match along his pants leg, stared at nothing. Red leaned against the wall, with lamp between him and Knox; and he didn't explain anything more to the cook or boys.

Cook puttered nervously about the stove, getting the warmed-over supper ready, now and then taking a furtive look at Knox and a longer look at Red, as if trying to make up his mind about something.

When supper was ready, Red said, "Move along up, Knox, if you want to eat." Knox looked up from under a black-browed scowl and did not reply. Red said, "Suit yourself. Eat or don't!"

Knox stayed where he was, as if he were so mad that he thought not eating would spite somebody.

Red went to the table, moved the lamp the cook had put there, and sat facing Knox across the long, dim room. He ate like a hungry man. The cook shuffled near, muttered as if giving the best advice he knew: "You're playin' hell, you are!"

"Make about two quarts of coffee—the kind that will take the hair off a green hide. I'm settin' up tonight."

Cook fiddled with his buckskin suspender, dabbed at the ends of his straggling mustache, and he sighed a few times noisily; then he poked wood into the stove, building up the fire to boil water for more coffee.

Red, still at the table, told Knox to pull his boots and pile into the bunk. He told Bobby and Pete to hang their guns on pegs behind the stove, and to set the cook's rifle there. Red wanted all the guns where he could have an eye on them through the night. He had the cook fill one of the lamps with coal oil so that it would burn until morning. He turned the lighted wick low and put the lamp on a stool in a way that cast a glow on Knox's bunk. Then he sat down at the table, with the sugar bowl and coffeepot in front of him, keeping watch.

The kids rolled in and for a while tossed restlessly, unable to doze off. The cook moseyed about, fingering his buckskin suspender, as if wondering what would happen if it broke. Two or three times he looked as if about to say something. He kicked off his loose, too big shoes, dropped his pants, sat on the bunk and scratched himself thoughtfully. He filled his pipe but did not light it. After a time he got up and, looking something like a skinned monkey in his long, tight-fitting underwear, he shuffled barefoot to where Red sat. Cook pulled up a stool, folded his arms on the table.

"Son," said the cook gently, "you are goin' to be sorry."

"You know he's guilty as hell."

Cook lit his pipe and coughed and spluttered as if not used to strong tobacco. He studied awhile and rubbed his fuzzy cheeks, leaned close and said in a slow, solemn mumble, "Take him in, if you want, kid. But don't come back! I sorta like you. You are such a damn fool—but kinda in the way I like to see a feller be! But don't come back out here." He peered at Red with bleary earnestness. "You'll be dry-gulched!"

Red patted the cook's arm, for he believed that the sour old curmudgeon, friend of rustlers or not, was trying to do him a favor. "Toddle to bed, pop," he said.

The cook shambled off, crept into his bunk.

Red sat in semidarkness, smoking and watching. Time dragged. The cook snored. Red drank coffee that was half sugar, rolled cigarettes. He could have tied Knox up and probably have found him there in the morning after a fair night's sleep; but more probably the cook would have turned him loose.

The night silence was filled with a mournful stir of wind, squeak and creak of tiny night creatures. Some field mice pattered about faintly, looking for crumbs. Red kept his eyes open. Sometimes he paced back and forth to rest his legs, tired of sitting; sometimes he leaned against the wall. He was pretty sure that Knox was not sleeping, but lying there, hopefully watching for a chance to do something.

Somewhere near midnight Bobby got up, yawned, rubbed his eyes, asked, "Can I get a drink?" He went in a sleepy stagger out to the pump, drank, came back and sat down beside Red, used Red's papers and tobacco.

"Listen, Red. I think you are all right."

"Thanks, kid."

"You ain't so much of not a kid yourself!"

Red grinned. "Hope I never ain't!"

Bobby went back to his bunk. The cook sizzled and spluttered, as if being choked in his sleep. Far off, some coyotes yap-yapped shrilly, as if screaming. Red drank more coffee. A low voice called. It was Knox.

"What you want?"

Knox sat up. "I want to have a talk."

"Go ahead."

"Can I come up to where you are?"

"Do no good."

"I wanta say something confidential."

"What about?"

"I want to tell you something."

"Come if you want, but act careful. I'd hate to have to get up a sweat in the mornin' diggin' you a grave."

Knox swung his feet over the edge of the bunk, looked to where Red was. He half raised his hands, to show that he was peaceable, and stood up. He walked slowly, watched where he stepped, and stopped at the edge of the table across from Red.

"Don't take me to town!"

Red looked at him steadily. He could not see Knox's face very well. The low-burning lamp was behind him, but Red knew that the shame of going into town before people as a prisoner had broken down his sullenness. He had put in some hours studying how best to talk, and now he sat down, leaned his cheek on a fist.

"Red," he went on in a careful, half-friendly tone, "I've got friends."

"Sure. Gridger an' maybe the sheriff, an' a bad bunch some'ers back in the hills that rebrand cows an' run 'em out from your ranch!"

Knox didn't say anything for a time. He had to wonder how the devil Red knew so much; then made the guess: "Old Backman was lyin' to you!"

"Old Mr Backman didn't tell me. You fixed it cute, didn't you, to have him shoot me? An' he purt-near did. You ain't the first rustler I've locked horns with. I know you don't eat them cows you run off. An' I know how stole cows are handled. I know that Gridger an' the sheriff are related by marriage. I know Gridger sent you out a letter about me even before I got here. Them was your friends that tried to kill old Sam Clayton, else why was Gridger in such a sweat to have you know what happened?"

Knox thought it over. Red had tried to knock the breath out of him, but it didn't work that way, for Knox said in a sort of crafty, low tone, "If you know so much as all that, then you know I won't ever be convicted for rustlin', don't you?"

"I bet my neck you won't!"

"Then will you listen to a bargain?"

"I don't make no bargain with a man I don't trust."

"I can show you how to get some money and make yourself talked about. Be real famous!"

"All the what you call fame I want is for the man I ride for to say I sure earn my wages. All the money I want is them same wages."

"You ain't been here long, but have you heard of the Kilco bunch?"

"Um. A little. Why?"

"They is a big reward for that Kilco. Wouldn't you rather take in an outlaw like Kilco and collect two or three thousand dollars than me? Wouldn't you?"

"If he starts stealin' my cows, I'll take him in!"

Knox sneered a little. "You sure do talk mighty big!"

" 'Longside of how you act, that mouse that bit me was purty big!"

"I can tell you where to find this Kilco—tell you how to catch him!"

"You," said Red, "can lie like hell, too."

"I know him. Know where he goes. Know how you—"

"Then why ain't you got yourself some honest money an' some of what you call fame? Why try to help a feller like me that you'd shoot in a minute—if I wasn't lookin'?"

Knox leaned forward. "I am tellin' you honest, Red!"

"Go back to your bunk. First place, you'd tell me anything you could think of that might get me not to take you in. So I don't believe you. Next place, if I did believe you, I wouldn't make a bargain. So go on, git!" Red waved a hand.

Knox stood up, with hands on the table, and braced himself as if to jump right across it; then he said, between clenched teeth, "You'll be goddamned sorry!"

He turned and walked back as if a little drunk, threw himself down heavily on the bunk. He turned and twisted and bumped the wall.

Red drank sugared coffee and wished for morning. He could have taken Knox over the road as safely and more comfortably during the night, but he wanted to take him into Nelplaid in broad daylight so that people could see what happened to rustlers that fooled with the Lazy Z brand.

II

It was near noontime and the day was hot when Red rode into Nelplaid at a walk with the lead rope of Knox's unbridled horse in his hand, and Knox was in the saddle, arms turned up behind his back, feet hobbled under the horse's belly, and his holster was empty. Knox must have reasoned that he couldn't hide himself behind his lowered hatbrim, so he sat straight, with head up.

People said, "Gosh A'mighty!" Some called out, questioning. There was a movement of people running about, in and out of doors and up and down the street, telling other people to come and look. Red kept at a walk.

Dave Gridger, with his apron on and a half-smoked cigar in his puffy mouth, was at the door of the saloon, looking spider-fat and watchful. He and Knox exchanged long looks.

A team and wagon stood before the general store. A lanky nester and his skinny, sunbonneted wife were carrying provisions to the wagon. The woman screeched, "Why, that there is Frank Knox!"

The sheriff and some other people who had been eating at the Saginaw Restaurant came bursting out of the door and trotted down the rickety board sidewalk. Small Jody Blanton ran faster than the men.

The sheriff, out of breath, came up to where Red was and stopped before the Judge's place. "What's all this? What's all this?" said the sheriff, puffing. He liked to look well before a crowd and had his shoulders back.

Red turned in the saddle, looked at the sheriff, looked at other people, too. Then the Judge's bald, red round head came out of an upstairs window to see what was going on. "Red!" The Judge had half of his short, pudgy body through the window, seemed in danger of falling out. "What's the meaning of this, Red?"

Red lifted his voice so everybody could hear: "I found twenty-two Lazy Z cows in Knox's horse corral. I drove 'em home an' brought Knox here along into town. He is going to say they strayed over to his range an' he rounded 'em up to shove 'em back, but he is a liar. They was drove in a bunch off our range. I seen the trail!"

The Judge rubbed the top of his head with a pudgy palm. "I—why—I—I can hardly believe—" He broke off uncomfortably.

Red lashed out with, "If you don't, I'm quittin'!"

"No, no, Red. I believe—believe—but since when did *you* take to arresting rustlers?"

"When they turn belly up an' won't fight!"

The crowd hummed and murmured, gazed at Knox; and Knox looked just about as if he were being jabbed with splinters all over.

"They are your cows," Red told the Judge. "I've told you what is what. Here he is!"

The Judge rubbed his head with the other hand. He did not look happy; his eyes searched the crowd, fell on the sheriff's upturned rabbit-shaped face. The Judge said with dignity, "Sheriff, you take the prisoner. We'll prefer charges. And Red, you come up here. I want to talk to you."

Red pitched the lead rope into the sheriff's outstretched hand:

"He's all yourn. But I give notice here an' now that if the law don't take care of him, I've brung in my last rustler—alive! The others are comin' in belly down under a diamond hitch!"

Among the crowd that looked on was a tall man, a stranger to Nelplaid, whose lean face was weather-wrinkled and sun-blackened. He had deep-set eyes, and they had the look of polished steel. He was straight as a ramrod, tight-mouthed, with some gray in his hair. He wore a suit of store clothes and had his coat on, and there was a bulge at the hip under the coat.

He kept well back and looked up at Knox, looked at Red, looked at the Judge, at the sheriff, again looked at Red. His lean, weather-wrinkled face did not move a muscle.

When Red disappeared up the stairway to the Judge's rooms and other people were bunching around the sheriff, and Knox, who had been untied and helped off his horse, was being taken away, the lean, hard-faced man stepped to the other side of Red's black horse, gave it a long scrutiny and rubbed his chin with a forefinger, as if wondering a little about something.

III

Upstairs the Judge had forgot to put on his long-tailed coat. He wore the white hard-boiled shirt, without a collar, and stood flat-footed before Red. An old book of calfbound poetry was open on the table beside the bottle of whisky.

"Son," he said reproachfully, "there has never been a conviction for rustling in the history of this county, and you have only made Knox and his friends mad!"

"There was only me an' old Mr Backman, an' I was afraid we'd be accused of spite if we strung 'im up—elsewise I would've!"

The Judge rattled the pipes on his desk but did not select one. "Knox will be loose on straw bail in twenty minutes!"

"Let 'im!"

"He'll lay for you, Red!"

"Bein' laid for is a part of why you pay me wages."

The Judge looked blandly confused. He shook his head, as if clearing his eyes, and though he did not have on the long-tailed coat he reached absently for the tail pocket to get his bandanna and wipe his forehead. "I," he said quietly, "am for law and order. Yes. I deprecate the use of violence, but—but—"

Red scowled. "Deprecate" didn't mean a thing to him, but it had a pretty good cuss-word sound.

The Judge used his thumb and forefinger to purse his lips together reflectively. Then his fat palm stroked his round chin. His bright, mild eyes stared at Red; then, impulsively: "You ought to have killed Frank Knox!"

"Honest, I tried to coax 'im to reach for a gun!"

"I know that he will try to assassinate you. I don't want you hurt, son."

Red said, "Shucks!" and grinned. "You don't understand about me, Judge. I've stood off an' sorta looked at myself ever since I was a fool kid, an' I find it is thisaway: I've never yet been much hurt doin' what I orta do, no matter what. But you just let me start somethin' crazy-foolish, an' I'll sprain a leg, or fall off my horse, or get bunged up. Why, sir, Judge, onct I was in town on an old slow poke of a cow pony when a purty girl come out of a store an' looked at me. An' me, all of a sudden I wanted to show her what a top-hand buster I was, so I reached over an' thumbed that bone rack with some hide on it—an' the next thing I knowed, I was settin' in the dust an' she was laughin'. Me, that's topped off bad broncs just as fast as the boys could switch saddles! If that pony had started ripsnortin' on his own hook, I could have rode 'im bareback an' sung a song. But tryin' to ac' smart—I was served right. That's how it goes, allus. Me, I figger it's just the same in a gun fight. If it was me that needed killin' an' I knowed it—why, Judge, I'd be all trembly an' scairt. But I ain't never been so far!"

An amused, affectionate smile warmed the Judge's round face. "You may not realize it, but that is a pretty sound religious faith. It has sustained martyrs. It sustained our Puritan Fathers. It has turned many a hopeless battle into a brilliant victory. Well, well! I regret that I haven't any such sustaining faith, but I *am* certain that it must be something of the kind that inspires your—um—oh, have a drink?"

"Sure."

"This old Backman—I have heard of him. He isn't well liked by cowmen."

Red took his drink, wiped his mouth with a backhand swipe. "He sure is by this cowhand!"

There was a light tap on the door, and the Judge made a startled grab for his coat. He was huddling into it as the door opened and a blue-eyed, silken-headed girl, with much the dainty prettiness of a picture-book girl, looked in and asked sweetly, "May I come in?"

Red pulled off his hat, stepped back with stumble of long-shanked spurs, found his hands hanging to his wrists without in the least knowing what to do with them as Kate Clayton looked at him with large, bright eyes. She looked at him so steadily that she did not hear the Judge saying how welcome she was, and wouldn't she sit down; or see that he moved a chair for her and gestured with invitational sweep of hand.

Kate certainly had the princess-girl look, with head up like a thoroughbred and the thin, aristocratic, proud face. The look made Red uncomfortable, as if he had done something he oughtn't and was about to be told about it; then, all of a sudden, Miss Kate put out her slim gloved hand and smiled. Her voice made Red's ears ring with music:

"So *you* are Red? I think you are the dearest, bravest boy in the world, Red!"

It was so simple-honest and sweet that Red turned all hot and fidgety in delighted awkwardness. Right then and there she had a slave, a lean, redheaded, fierce-hearted, even if good-natured, slave. His dark-tanned face reddened, and he stood tongue-tied in pleasurable bewilderment. The friendliness of such a haughty, proud-looking girl dazed him. She had hold of his hand and was keeping hold of it, and there was tenderness in her bright eyes.

"Daddy wants to see and thank you, Red. And I want to thank you! Words are very inadequate things with which to thank you, Red. Daddy says that you are as brave as any man he ever saw. And good, honest bravery is the finest quality a man can have, isn't it?"

Red helplessly mumbled something very like, "Aw, shucks."

Then she took hold of his hand with both of her hands and patted it, and kept holding it, and went on looking at him and smiled a little. The Judge rubbed his head with his bandanna and wondered at the strangeness of women; for here was the girl that frostily looked down her thin nose at every man, now holding onto an awkward and certainly not handsome boy, and smiling as warmly and tenderly as if she loved him.

"Will you come with me, Red?"

"Sure. You bet."

The Judge bowed them out. They went down the stairs and on to the street. Miss Kate held up her long skirt in a gloved hand, kept close at Red's side, talked lively and smiled, with her eyes on his face as if she liked looking at him. To people who passed them and raised their hats she nodded almost as if she didn't see them.

They paused at the corner across from the hotel

while two men rode by, splattering dust, and she put a hand on Red's arm, asked softly, "Do you know Jim Brady, Red?"

"I seen him onct. 'Pears like a nice feller."

Her face sobered a little, and she took a breath like a quick little sigh. "Yes, doesn't he?" She sounded as if she had a little doubt about it; yet Red knew, because he had seen, that she loved Jim Brady.

IV

The Nelplaid Hotel was a small, old, two-story building with a narrow balcony across the upstairs front. The stairs and hall were uncarpeted, and footsteps had the sound of being in an empty building. Miss Kate's small, dainty feet did not make more than the shadow of a sound, but Red's heels and spurs clattered.

Behind her, on the stairs, Red looked at her slim, straight little body and thought that this Jim Brady had better be a pretty fine fellow or he, Red, would ride his neck with rowels.

Kate opened the door and went in ahead of Red.

Old Sam Clayton, bulking under the sheet, lay on his side in bed, with a hand under his cheek. His other arm was in a sling. His big face had the sagged look of a man who is in pain and doesn't want to talk about it.

Young Bill Clayton and another man were

sitting in the room. Kate pushed by them, stooped and kissed Mr Clayton on the cheek and said with quiet glee, "Here is Red, Daddy!"

Red had bobbed his head at Bill Clayton, who did not look comfortable and who had nodded back at Red without speaking. The other man stood up as Kate came in. He was in store clothes, with a bulge at the hip under his coat. A good deal of gray was in his hair, and he had hard eyes, a tight mouth, and the weather-worn complexion of a plainsman. After Kate had kissed her grandfather, the man said, "I'll come up again this evening, Sam."

Mr Clayton said huskily, "So long, George."

The man stood still and eyed Red for a moment, then he went to the door. Bill Clayton's look sullenly followed him, as if he did not like this straight, leathery-faced old-timer.

Kate said, "Come here, Red," and Red went up close to the bed.

Mr Clayton kept a hand under his cheek, but he straightened the wrist of the arm that was in a sling and waggled the fingers for Red to shake hands. "How are you, boy?"

Red shook hands lightly, then twiddled the brim of his hat. "Oh me, I'm fine, Mr Clayton. Allus!"

Mr Clayton was taking short breaths, as if tired from running, and he stared with a trace of a smile at Red. He saw the rawhide leanness, the litheness that was easy, even graceful on horseback but gawkily awkward in a hotel room. He saw the tousled cowlick of brick-red hair, the clear, straight blue eyes that had honesty in their lupine color.

Mr Clayton moved his head a little on the pillow. After a pause he said, low and huskily, "You look like him, too—like your father when he was a young man."

"You knowed my dad?"

"Before you were born."

Red grinned, pleased. Lots and lots of old-timers had known Red's father. Twenty and more years before, when the country was half Indian-owned and only a handful of men were holding the frontier range, men scattered over wide areas had known one another and knew the qualities of one another.

Kate put her ungloved fingers on Mr Clayton's cheeks, stroked them gently and explained, "It is hard for Daddy to talk."

Mr Clayton smiled a little and widened his eyes. "I hear you fetched in Frank Knox for rustlin'. Why didn't you kill him?"

"He laid down an' wouldn't draw."

Mr Clayton grunted. "My advice, son, is to find him and kill him before you leave town. Otherwise, he'll lay for you in the hills."

Young Bill stood up. "I'll be goin' along, Dad." He went abruptly and did not look back.

Mr Clayton's eyes followed him, with a stare

hat was sad and wistful. Bill shut the door, and Mr Clayton shut his eyes.

Kate said, "Sit down, Red."

Red sat, twiddled his hatbrim, looked at Mr Clayton, knew that he was a hard old fellow who rode roughshod and had made it a fight all of his life. Red thought men like that were great to work for. They would never send a man where they wouldn't go themselves; and they backed a fellow up till hell froze hard enough to skate on.

Mr Clayton lay quiet, his hand under his cheek, and looked steadily at Red. The short, quick breathing made him seem very sick. He was a long, long way from being out of danger, but he was tough-bodied and meant not to die. A doctor had been brought from Poicoma, the railroad town thirty miles away, but he had not been able to get the bullets out of Mr Clayton and was coming back to try again when Mr Clayton seemed a little stronger.

Nobody said anything for a while. Red poked a crease in his hat crown, then pushed it out and made another, as if very particular about creases in that old hat. Mr Clayton stirred, coughed a little.

"Alvord and Knox and some others—Dave Gridger for one!"

"Daddy! You mustn't get excited!"

"They used that Lazy Z valley to run out cows.

Mostly mine. Some of my men threw in with them. You ought've killed Knox."

"I reckon."

"And those men you wiped out that day here in town, Red—do you know who they were?"

"Sorta."

Kate's lips trembled strangely, then set hard There was a quick, hurt look in her eyes.

"Some of Kilco's bunch," said Mr Clayton calmly. "Why they jumped me thataway, I don't know."

"I hear tell," said Red, "they was led by a feller named Mell Barber—the one that got away. I hear tell him an' Kilco had had a fallin' out. I don't—"

"Red, have you heard of a man named Jim Brady?"

Red looked toward Miss Kate. She was staring down at her fingernails, and Red felt unhappy because she looked so hurt about something. He said, "Um, sorta."

"I've found out only since I've been here in bed that Jim Brady is Jim Kilco."

Red said solemnly, "Gosh A'mighty!" His quick look struck Miss Kate's pale face. Now her fingers were tangled together in pained writhing, and she stared at them. Then Red blurted, "Why, Mr Clayton, if that is so, then it wasn't him that tried to kill you. I sure know that!"

Miss Kate's lips parted in a noiseless gasp, and

116

she stared at Red with perplexed thankfulness.

His tongue was untied now and he spoke earnestly: "I hate outlaws an' such, Mr Clayton, as the devil hates a preacher—if he's any shakes of a good preacher! But Jim Brady never wanted to hurt you that day. Why, the smoke hadn't quite blowed away before a man come a-runnin' at me from across the street with a rifle in his hand, an' he said that I had done right, an' he was sorry he hadn't been standin' where he could pitch in and help—on account of the horses an' me bein' in the way, he didn't dare shoot. If it was Jim Brady, like he said to me he was, he didn't want to hurt you, Mr Clayton. Why, he could have picked me off from across the street as easy as crackin' a whip!"

Mr Clayton stared so hard-bright that Red added hastily, "I'm just tellin' what happened, and I'm not tryin' to say that Jim Brady is a bit better 'n you think—except I know from how he acted that he was glad them men was killed."

Mr Clayton moved as if he wanted to sit up, but the effort was too much for him. His quick breath rattled, and he said in a loud, angry voice, "That whole bunch is mixed up in rustlin', Red! The next time you see Jim Brady, you shoot him as you would a rattler!"

Red kept twitching the hatbrim in his fingers, and not a word would come. He wanted to look up at Miss Kate, but just couldn't, because he

knew how bad she was feeling. He stammered
a little, then stood up. "I'll go now, Mr Clayton.
An' I sure hope that you'll be fine."

Miss Kate went with him to the door, and he
tried to avoid looking at her, but he had to when
she put out her hand and said, "Good-by, Red."
Her hurt, pale face seemed saying, "Thank you,
Red!" even though she didn't know that he knew
her secret.

CHAPTER FIVE

Red went off by himself over near the livery stable and squatted in a strip of shade beside a freight wagon to think. He was not getting on very well with his thoughts when a long-tailed, lean, black-and-white dog nosed up, twitched floppy ears, cocked its head.

"Go away," Red said. "I don't like dogs. Git, you!"

The dog wagged its tail and came nearer.

"What do you mean, feller, callin' me a liar— like you don't believe what I say?"

The dog wriggled up and swiped Red's face with a long, moist tongue. Red took the dog by the neck, turned it over in the dust, tickled the lean ribs. "You go get some skirts on if you wanta kiss me. An' I got troubles enough without you hornin' in. Go on off an' leave me to weep alone."

The dog scrouged around until it got its head on Red's knee, looked up steadily, with mouth parted in a triumphant dog smile. Red scratched behind the dog's ears and tried to go on with his thinking.

Jody came along. He had a stick for a sword and made swipes all about him as if cutting off the heads of enemies. When he saw some enemies too far off to be reached by the sword, he put the stick to his shoulder for a rifle and said, "Bang!"

He edged up. " 'Lo, Red."

"Howdy, big feller."

Jody sat down in the dust and patted the dog, put his head down on the dog's head. "You goin' to keep him, Red?"

"I'll tie your ears behind your head in a hard knot if you go suspicionin' me thataway. I don't keep nothin' that ain't mine."

"Aw, he don't b'long to anybody. He follered a wagon in last week and just stayed. He ain't nobody's."

"Then why ain't he yourn? Here is a nice dog lost in the same town as a freckle-nosed kid, an' they ain't in cahoots!"

"Paw won't let me. But he is a nice dog, ain't he?"

"All dogs is. Four-legged ones, I mean."

"You are funny. Whoever seen a two-legged dog?"

"How old are you, Jody?"

"Purt-near eight. Then I'll be goin' on nine."

"You are just the next thing to growed up, ain't you? But you will see some two-legged dogs an' such things plenty by the time you are as old as me."

Jody put his head down against the dog's again. "Why are you settin' here? Waitin' for the stage?"

"Thinkin'."

" 'Bout Knox and them?"

"Not much, no. I got worse worries."

"They are up there to the Silver Dollar. Laughin' at you."

"So Knox is laughin' a little, h'm?"

"Yes."

"The sheriff, too?"

Jody shook his head. "He ain't there. But Bill Clayton is—drinkin'. I mean he ain't laughin'. Knox is. He is sayin' you and an old man snuck up on 'im while he was asleep."

Red moodily drew a finger about in the dust. 'That old man is a real old Injun fighter, Jody. Sometime, mebbe, I'll interduce you. He hankers for a boy of about your size to set an' listen to him." Red fished down in his pocket, pulled out a dollar. "Here. You tell your paw this is to pay for that dog's keep till I come to town again. You tell him me an' you are sorta pardners in that dog. Now you trot. I got to do some more thinkin'."

II

Fifteen minutes later Red's thinking was interrupted by the arrival of the stage that stopped to change horses. A man or two who belonged to Nelplaid got out and hurried off. A woman got down, too. The driver climbed up and uncorded a trunk and some boxes that he slammed off into the dust, all the while arguing with the livery-stable man who was changing horses. Nobody paid attention to the woman, and the violence of the language she heard shocked her.

She came over to where Red squatted. He was the only one in sight who was not grinning at the argument between the driver and the livery man. "Young man!" she said sharply.

"Yes'm?" Red rose, pulling off his hat.

Red thought she was a sour old woman; then he saw that she wasn't very old, but she did look sour; or maybe not sour so much as sharp and set. She stood stiffly erect; her elbows were stiffly at her sides, with one gloved hand in the palm of the other before her. The high-collared tight waist was of some black stuff, and her long dress looked heavy and was black, too. Her mouth was tightly drawn together. She looked Red up and down, as if a cowboy were something out of the zoo.

"Young man, can you direct me to a person known as Judge Trowbridge?"

"Yes'm. You bet. I'll take you to where he is."

"And my luggage?"

"Your what?"

"Trunk and bags."

"You mean 'traps.' You can have the hotel come an' get 'em."

"I thought Western men were chivalrous!" She turned with rebuking stare toward the coach, where the argument still went on, profanely.

"Lady, them fellers are no more mad than two pups. They are playin'."

"Playing?"

"Sure. In this country real quarrels are short an' quick-spoken. You just call a man a liar, then shoot 'im—or he shoots you," said Red, as simply as if giving directions.

She eyed him severely and with doubt. "I do not believe you."

"All right, lady. That's how 'tis. I ain't tryin' to pull your leg."

Lady's face flushed a little at Red's mention of her leg, but she let it pass. "If you will be kind enough to direct me to Judge Trowbridge—" She gathered up the long, heavy skirt, ready to go with him.

They walked along in silence, with Red sneaking a look at her face. It was easy, because she kept her eyes straight before her, as if uncomfortable and trying not to let anybody see just how uncomfortable. She wasn't old at all, but her face was hard-set. Red bet himself that something would crack if she smiled. She looked pretty thin and sort of underfed.

The Judge was dozing in his deep worn chair. The day was hot; he was sweating and had his mouth open. The odor of whisky and tobacco were strong. Red and the woman were in the room before the Judge awakened with confused splutter and dazed look. He got out of the chair quickly, but didn't have on his coat, and his manner was just about as confused as if he had been caught without his pants.

The woman said crisply, "Are you Judge Trowbridge?"

"Yes, madam." He reached for his coat.

"I am Miss"—she gave a good deal of stress to the *Miss*—"Jane C. Alvord, Judge Trowbridge?"

The coat dropped from his hand. He blinked, raised his eyebrows, looked accusingly at Red, as if expecting some joke. "My, my!" he said weakly. "I—I thought you were a man, miss!"

"I deceived you purposely, sir."

The Judge vaguely said, "Oh." He got into his coat, brought out a bandanna, wiped his head. "Purposely?"

"You would have tried to oppose my coming to take possession of my ranch."

"I? Oh no, no. It is your ranch, whether you are Miss or Mister."

"But I mean to live there and run it." Miss Alvord looked defiant.

"But you can't do that," said the Judge. "A lady alone on—a cow ranch!"

"Certainly I can! It is *my* ranch, isn't it? I have always wanted to live in the West." Miss Alvord spoke rapidly, with feeling. "I have been smothered and stifled. Do you know what it is to be a school teacher in Boston?"

The Judge regarded her with benign sympathy,

bobbed his large head. "I can imagine. But, my dear young lady, you can't imagine what a ranch is like—what it will be like for a person of your refinement!"

"My refinement, as you call it," said Miss Alvord severely, with impatience, "is the one quality that it will give me the least regret to lose! I have been made miserable during the past few years by trying to be the sort of person fitted to instruct *refined* young ladies." There was a sound of almost desperate pleading in Miss Alvord's insistence.

The Judge blinked and sighed and rattled the pipes on his table, as if trying to select the one he wanted. "But you can have no understanding of—of living conditions, Miss Alvord."

"I will get an understanding of them very readily, sir." Now she was defiant again.

Again the Judge mopped his head vigorously and looked about, as if trying to find something to say to this sharp-featured girl. "Ah. Well. But here, Miss Alvord, is the manager of your ranch, Mr Red Clark."

She faced about, eyed Red as if she hadn't seen him before. He was leaning against the wall, rather weakly, as if his spine were broken, and watched her, thinking things, none of them approving.

"This boy? Manager? Manager of a ranch!"

"No'm," said Red, "I ain't. I quit just now. I

took the job till the owner come. You're him—her, I mean. So I quit. Yes'm."

The Judge made little, flustered movements with a pudgy hand. "That isn't fair, Red. You can't quit. This lady would be helpless without—"

"I was never helpless in my life!" said Miss Alvord, with spirit. "I am going to live at the ranch. If Mr Clark doesn't like his situation, surely there are other gentlemen who—"

The Judge put out both hands, begged: "Miss Alvord, please! Please listen! You don't in the least understand the conditions. Do sit down. Let me explain."

Ten minutes later Red still had a shoulder slumped against the wall and gazed with slant-eyed curiosity at the owner of the Lazy Z. She had repeatedly looked at Red with an incredulous, astounded expression. Judge Trowbridge took his third drink of whisky, wiped his lips and concluded:

"So you see why we can't hope to replace Red. And also why it is impossible for a lady of your quality to live on the ranch. It is dangerous—positively, physically, dangerous!"

Jane Alvord turned toward Red. Her mouth was slightly open, and with her mouth open she didn't look nearly as hard-set and severe. The Judge's recital had jarred some of the tightness out of her. Her elbows were not against her sides, her back was bent forward a little, the better to peer, and her eyes were bright, rather amazed.

"I—I don't feel sure that I understand," she said, in a low voice that was not crisp. "Do you mean that this boy—*killed?*"

"Yes, miss."

"And risked his life also to defend *my* property?"

The Judge poured another drink and held it, as if about to propose a toast. "Lady," he began in his best Fourth of July manner, "the knights of old in their glittering armor, with plumes waving, never showed more gallantry, loyalty and courage than do the cowboys of this Western kingdom to those to whom they pledge fealty!"

The Judge, being well warmed with enthusiasm and whisky, encouraged, too, by Miss Alvord's interest and softened manner, would have gone on; but Red spoke up:

"Shucks. All a cowboy wants is wages."

"And haven't you been receiving suitable wages, Mr Clark?" she asked.

"Sure."

Jane Alvord arose and went to him; and, just like any other woman when she wants something, she smiled with a sad, coaxing look and asked, "Then why are you deserting me, Mr Clark?"

"You're a woman an' don't know anything about cows."

"I am a woman, and by that I suppose you mean that you think I am helpless?"

"Sorta."

"And I do not know about cows, therefore I am in need of assistance. So for the reason that I need assistance, you are deserting me?"

Red stiffened and flushed.

"And Judge Trowbridge has just compared your chivalry to that of the old knights!"

Red didn't know anything about the word "chivalry" or about "knights"; but he knew what Miss Alvord meant. He blurted, "I mean you won't let me run the ranch like it orta be!"

"But, Mr Clark, I do want it run as it ought to be. Of course I do!"

"Will you fight rustlers an' them?"

"Do you mean persons that steal cattle?"

"Yeah."

"Of course I want to fight them! I do not approve of anything weak and cowardly!" She was earnest, and the heightened color in her pale face made her almost good-looking, certainly bold and strong-looking.

Red stuck out his hand, "Lady, I'll ride for you!"

"Thank you, Mr Clark."

"My name's Red."

"Thank you, R-Red." She went on staring at him, shook her head slowly, murmured, "It seems incredible." She was thinking of what she had heard about the gun fight in town, and of how he had brought in Knox, hog-tied. Then quickly, as if he might misunderstand, she added: "But I approve, R-Red. Really I do!"

The Judge's face was flushed with pleasure and whisky. "Now, Miss Alvord, you can turn the ranch over to Red and settle down in town here."

"But I am going to live at the ranch."

Red said, "You can't live out there. They is four men an' only one room, an' all of us snore."

Miss Alvord caught her breath, as if some ice water had been tossed into her face; but her face set, her mouth took on its tight look, and when she moved her tight lips, she said, "But I *will* live out there. We can make arrangements of some kind. They will have to be made, because I am going there to live. It is my ranch!"

"Your ranch," Red admitted, "but you won't like it much. You ever been on a horse?"

"Never. But I mean to learn."

"Then we'll have to have a buckboard to take you out. Only—When do you want to go?"

"Immediately."

"You mean right now?"

"Yes, please."

"A'right, *now* she is. An' do you want all your duds took along?"

"All my what?"

"Duds. Traps. Trunk an' things."

"Of course."

"Then they'll be took."

III

When Red drove the buckboard back from the livery stable, he hitched the team before the general store, loosened his guns in their holsters and moved over to the Silver Dollar.

Frank Knox was with a half-dozen men at the bar. The sheriff was not there, but Bill Clayton was. All were well liquored, and all, excepting Bill, sounded happy.

When somebody noticed Red in the doorway, there were nudges and lowered voices, then silence, except for the scuffle of feet as men, expecting trouble, moved and stood well away from Knox. Bill Clayton sullenly did not move.

There was somebody's borrowed gun in Knox's holster. He drew his black brows together and glared at Red. "What do you want?"

"I wanta know who turned you loose."

Dave Gridger spoke smoothly from behind the bar: "Some men went his bail, Red."

"I am interested for to know *who*."

"Me, for one!" said Bill Clayton sullenly and took a step forward, his hand moving a little toward his hip, but not quite enough to make it a threat.

"That's shore callin' 'im!" some fellow squeaked nervously, bucking Bill up with a little soft soap. Then he wished that he hadn't said

130

anything, for Red's eyes picked him out, just the same as asking, "Do you want some trouble?"

It was quiet, hushed to breathlessness. Gridger's arm was half raised, as if to reach across the bar and get hold of Bill; but Gridger let his arm drop.

Red and Bill eyed each other, and it certainly looked as if Red had been invited into a fight and wasn't accepting. Bill's lumpish face had a sullen scowl, faintly glowing with triumph. He wore an ivory-handled, silver-plated gun in a stamped-leather holster, and his hand was set to jerk. The lump of a gold ring was like a big wart on his middle finger.

Gridger said softly, "Now you boys don't want to have no hard feelin's! Bill, you just calm down!"

Knox looked mean and defiant, too, as if he were anxious to uphold his end of the fight if it came. There was so much silence that Knox couldn't keep still any longer, so he said, mean and snappish, showing off some because he thought Red looked a little bluffed, "Well, what are you goin' to do about it?"

He got his answer. It came cold and quiet and quick: "I'm goin' to kill you—unless you turn belly up here before all your friends an' show 'em just how you won't fight!"

Knox tightened his black brows and glared. He was mean, but he was afraid. He frowned as hard

131

as he could, trying not to look afraid. He hated Red as a snake hates a dog that has snapped it up and shaken it. He acted tensely, as if about to draw; but he didn't.

Red slapped him with words: "Now maybe folks won't think anybody snuck up on you while you was asleep! An' as for you, Bill Clayton, go ahead an' be a damn fool if you want. You are backin' a cow thief—an' a fourflusher!"

Pause and silence. Men's nervous breathing could be heard. Red waited to see if anybody wanted to speak up. Nobody did.

"What I come in here for to say," Red explained, "is that the Lazy Z ain't goin' to be used no more by rustlers. It used to be used by Knox an' them to run off folks' cows. Then Knox an' them started in stealin' Lazy Z cows. I'm servin' notice that the healthfulest place rustlers can find is as far off my range as they can git to.

"And you, Bill Clayton—you ain't overbright to go even straw bail for a man that run off Clayton cows through the valley an'—"

Bill said, "How do you think you know so damn much?"

"Your father told me!"

Bill looked sullenly unhappy. His glance twitched toward Dave Gridger, but the fat saloon man was eying Red and trying not to seem astounded.

Everybody sensed that Red had come in there

looking for a fight, and it was pretty plain that he wasn't going to get it. The way he had knocked over Mell Barber's men was just a little too much for anybody to want to walk into him.

Red waited until it was plain that Knox wasn't going to do anything—or Bill, either. Then he said, "This'll be about all for today."

He backed from the doorway, and when he was out of sight nobody said anything for almost a full minute. Men looked at Knox as if at something who had turned into a stranger. He saw how they looked, knew how they felt.

Bill said, "You are yaller!"

Knox said, "Boys, I'm not." He put out his right hand. "I know how it looks, but my wrist is so sore from the way that . . ." he called Red all kinds of ugly names—"tied me up that it is stiff. I just would have been clumsy. But I am going to kill him. I swear to God that I'm goin' to kill him!" He added, with hasty afterthought, "And in a fair fight, too." He rubbed at his wrist. "Just as soon as this wrist is all limber again, I am going to find him and have it out!"

Gridger put out glasses and bottles, invitationally. "Step along up, boys. On the house!" he said.

IV

The buckboard had gone only a few miles when Jane Alvord's bones and joints seemed shaken to pieces by the jolting of the rutty road. She asked, "How much farther?"

"We ain't halfway."

"Is the road all like this?"

"Worse."

"Worse?"

"You want me to take you back to town?"

She sighed, and her tight lips smiled a little at Red. "I never turn back."

"You set too stiff an' straight, miss. You orta sorta slump an' take it easy-like—like you was a little drunk."

"I am afraid I can't comply. I am totally ignorant of the condition that you suggest. And I never slumped in my life. As a young girl I wore a board strapped to my back to keep my shoulders straight. I hated it, but it kept my shoulders straight. And now," with a faint hint of teasing, "you tell me that is all wrong!"

"For ridin' a buckboard on a rough road. Maybe all right for school teachin'."

"I am not interested in school teaching. And never was."

"Then why'd you do it?"

"There are two ways that a lady can procure

her livelihood. One is by marrying. The other is teaching."

"Why didn't you marry?"

"I preferred to teach."

"But you just said you didn't like it."

"I didn't."

"Then why didn't you marry?"

"I told you that I preferred to teach!"

Red clucked to the horses, thought it over, asked, "Ain't they no nice fellers a-tall back East?"

"Of course."

"Then why didn't you catch yourself one?"

Jane laughed a little. They were in the open country, with not a place of habitation or sign of man, other than the road, in sight. That in itself gave a sense of freedom, and Red's simple directness was almost like a new language to her. Her ears flinched at his "ain'ts," "ortas" and "sortas," but she found his frankness amusing. There was a good deal of the repressed tease in the prematurely severe Miss Alvord. She asked, "How does one go about catching a man?"

"You women was born knowin' how!"

"I am afraid that enlightenment was left out of my heritage."

"Shucks. When you see one you want, I bet you get 'im all right!"

Jane laughed quietly. It may have been the air,

the scenery, the freedom and the relief of not feeling that she had to be on guard against critical misinterpretation; but she soon found herself talking quite freely.

When her parents died, she had become a teacher in a girls' school; and because she was young, she had to be that much more grave. All the teachers in the seminary were erect and grave. Her only dream had been to escape. She knew of an uncle in the West and thought better of him because he had been a black sheep! Somehow she had learned that he was near the town of Nelplaid and had written, but no reply came. Yet it must have affected him a little, because he told Judge Trowbridge that he had a relative in Boston. "But he didn't say that I was a girl. I suppose he was ashamed of having an old-maid school teacher as his only relative."

Red turned on the seat, faced her. "You don't look so much like an old maid when you smile."

She looked startled for an instant, then she smiled. "Thank you, Red."

Because Red had driven slowly and stopped often, it was long after supper and in the starlight when they came to the ranch. For some time Jane had been tired and silent. The deepening shadows and loneliness of the pine-covered hills, all strange, and her own weariness gave her rather a large apprehensiveness about venturing among unknown men in a one-room house. But anything, she thought, was better than being an old-maid school teacher.

The boys and cook came out, saw the buckboard, recognized Red's black horse, unsaddled and tied behind the buckboard; and they saw a woman on the front seat.

Cook peered and grumbled in a kind of awestruck voice, "Now what's that fool Red gone and done?"

"Married 'er, I bet!" Pete guessed.

"Stole 'er!" said Bobby.

"I'm leavin' if that's a woman!" said the cook.

"I reckon it's a woman," Bobby explained, " 'less he put Knox in skirts and drug him back out here to help you cook."

They didn't say a word as the buckboard came up and stopped. They merely stood and stared in the clear starlight, stared quite as hard at Red as at the woman.

Red calmly wrapped the lines around the whip, got out, held up his hand to help her down. Her long skirts were very much in the way.

Red took off his hat. "Boys, this here is our boss. She owns the ranch. Miss, this here is cook, Bobby an' Pete. Cook don't like women, so he says. But he's an awful liar. All cooks is!"

Jane said, "How do you do?" Cook mumbled. Bobby and Pete marched up closer, stuck out their hands, said, "Howdy."

137

"I told her," said Red, "they was four men an only one room."

For a long minute nobody said anything. The boys were confused by the implication, and Jane felt herself blushing. Red's matter-of-fact frankness was not altogether amusing.

"It'll be all right, miss," Bobby told her. "We'll fix somehow so you'll be fine. And we'll gag the cook here. He snores like sawin' through a barrel."

"Or drown him for you, like he was a blind kitten!" Pete exclaimed.

They were very young, and she was a woman, and all women are lovely to lonely boys on the range; and besides, in the bright starlight she smiled at them. Then she stepped up to the frowzy cook whose corncob dangled in his mouth, and she held out her hand. "Red has told me what a wonderful cook you are!"

Cook straightened, took the corncob from his mouth, shook hands and, running a thumb under his lone suspender, said solemnly, "You can sure count on whatever Red tells you, miss."

Cook, who "didn't like women" for much the same reason that most sensible males "don't like" them—that is, because he had such a helpless weakness for them that they could make a big fool out of him without any trouble at all—stuck the pipe into a hip pocket and began to unlash the trunk. He nearly broke his lone suspender in eagerness to carry in more than the two kids, who also wanted to make Jane think that they were nice boys.

Red had brought along two bottles of whisky. He kept one out of sight, let the other go into the house with groceries. He rolled a cigarette and looked on while cook and the boys did all the toting; and when they were in the house, he said slowly, "Miss, if you are goin' to be a cowman, you've got to be one."

"What do you mean, Red?" He was a puzzle to Jane. She could not at all reconcile his frank good nature and cheeriness with what she had heard the Judge tell; it seemed incredible.

"Eat our grub, don't be finicky about our talk, an' purt-near pertend you ain't a woman."

"But, Red, please, *how* can I sleep in one room with f-four men?"

"By shuttin' your eyes an' forgettin' us. I told you before you come how it was—an' you come."

"I couldn't quite visualize the circumstances. I was so eager to get away from people—all people that huddle together in even a small town. I wanted to be free. But isn't there any other possible arrangement—here?"

"No'm. An' now you lissen. Me, I like women fine; an' I like you. Nobody's goin' to hurt a hair of your head. All us will eat anybody alive that does. But this is a ranch, an' we're cowhands. We

139

sleep in our underwear an' we snore. We get up
at night to get a drink from the pump. We cuss
some in fun, an' sometimes when cook needs a
dressin' down. I didn't want you out here, but
here you are, an' as owner you are boss. But I'm
your foreman, an' you'll do like I say or you'll
get another foreman. I think you're much nicer
now than I thought when I first seen you; but if
you was ten times nicer, you'd still have to do
like I say, 'cause when I run an outfit I run it!"

Jane Alvord looked at him steadily, with a good
deal of the old maid sticking out, but she didn't
say a word. Something deep within her, some of
the black-sheep blood that had made her uncle a
strong, if not an entirely honorable, man among
strong men, made her respect the lanky, blue-
eyed redhead that fought four men at a time and
carried hog-tied rustlers into town. She herself,
both by nature and training, was pretty bossy; but
there was also something within her, as within
most bossy women, that made her reluctantly
admire anybody who could boss her.

The boys and cook came back, with Bobby
carrying a lantern, and he swung it up the better
to see her face. Jane, perhaps remembering what
Red had said about the old-maid look, smiled.
After all, they were just eager youngsters and
showed their delight in having a lady boss; and
she was a very lonely-hearted person, pleased at
being admired.

" 'Nother thing," Red explained, dropping the cigarette and squishing it into the dust with twist of the toe, "you've got to learn to ride. You can't ride in skirts. So you might as well begin to be nice to Bobby, who is about your size, so he will loan you some of his pants."

When things were out of the wagon, Red drove over to the stable sheds, unharnessed, watered the horses. He rubbed the black Devil's velvety nose and confided, "Son, how it come that all of a sudden on the same day we run into two nice ladies? Only bein' nice don't keep our lady boss from bein' just so much extra weight to carry, an' not a damn bit of use—does it?"

He buried his extra bottle of whisky in the litter at the bottom of a manger and went back into the house, where he found the boys bustling and sweating with ropes and poles and blankets, trying to rig up a little private place for Jane to bunk in. She looked doubtful and slightly forlorn as she held up a lantern so the cook could see to drive nails.

"What's all this monkey-doodlin'?" Red demanded.

"We are fixin' Miss some privacy," said Bobby.

"You are fixin' up for her to purt-near smother, too. Cook, you go get something to eat. I'll finish this up. An' open that bottle of whisky."

When they learned about Knox being turned loose on straw bail, cook looked solemnly down his nose, and Bobby and Pete chimed a warning:

"You'll have to look out, Red!"

"He makes his brag that nobody ever got the best of him!"

"He knows this country like I know the inside of my hat!"

"He'll sure lay for you, Red!"

Red told them, "You pups have got to learn about folks an' things. First off, anybody that is doin' something sneaky is scairt. An' anybody that is scairt is unsure an' easy rattled. I've seen some real bad men in my time, an' Knox ain't got their earmarks. He," said Red, hammering away, "is yaller from the bottom tip of his skunk-shaped tail to the tip-top end of his Injun-black hair."

Red was very tired and very sleepy, but he was a bit handy at rough carpentry from having to build and repair corrals and such. He nailed the poles, braced them with ropes, rigged a sort of small clothesline arrangement, took blankets and fastened them to the clothesline.

When supper was ready the bottle of whisky, opened but untouched, was on the table. Cook might have been tempted, but he had not fallen. Whisky was poured into cups, and Jane, not admitting that she had never in her life tasted whisky, tried a sip, made a face and was astonished that anybody could enjoy the stuff.

Bobby and Pete, with the appetite of young wolves, helped themselves to another supper and chewed noisily, with their eyes on Jane's face. Having a nice lady boss made them warm, excited, adoring. And as they were merely kids, their eagerness didn't make Jane uncomfortable.

After supper, Red said abruptly, "I can't stand this cook's snorin'." He took up his bedding and went outdoors. Pete and Bobby decided that they preferred to sleep out in the fresh air. Cook hurried through with the dishes and in a mumble explained that he always slept outdoors this time of year.

So Jane Alvord was left alone in the big, dim room with her trunk and boxes and blanket-partitioned bunk. She sat thoughtfully by the lamplight and was lonely, a little nervous, but not afraid. She even felt like crying, half happily. The awkward courtesy of these boys, their frank, slightly worshipful eagerness to please her, stirred bewildering emotions. She smiled, too, because Red, after laying down the law about having to sleep in the same room with them, had been the first to move out. She made the pleasing guess that Red and the others were really quite as helpless with women as a woman liked men to be. But she decided that she couldn't, really could not, have them sleeping out of doors. Tonight, yes; but not tomorrow night.

V

During the next few days Red and the boys worked almost as if it were roundup time in bunching Lazy Z cows in the valley so as to have some idea of how much of a herd was left.

Red rode with rifle in a saddle scabbard, a supply of cartridges in his belt. He rode alone most of the time and was alert but not anxious.

When Jane mentioned to the cook how Red had fought with four men and killed three during his first ten minutes in town, cook dropped his arms, opened his mouth, slowly gasped, "Wha-at?"

"Didn't you know?"

"Know? Gosh A'mighty, no! You mean that boy is a killer like that?" Cook forgot himself and swore in amazement. "And me, I sassed 'im for a wet-nosed kid the day he rode in, and he didn't git mad! No wonder he rode down on Knox and snaked 'im outa his house like a bogged-down dogie outa a mudhole!"

When cook imparted the story to the kids and they tried to question Red, he shuffled his feet and told them, "Figger it out anyway you like, but when you get done all you can say is that me, I'm lucky. Sorta allus was. Sorta mean to stay that way."

And when Jane asked him why he had not told of the fight, Red gave her a solemn stare.

'Miss, my dad brought me up that when you done what you orta, keep your mouth shut. If you don't, it means that doin' what you orta is kinda exceptional an' has turned your head a little."

Jane could not bring herself to wear Bobby's pants, but she meant to learn to ride. She took one of her heavy skirts, shortened it, split it, sewed it into a divided skirt. Cook, from day to day, put a rope on a gentle horse and led it about with her in the saddle, until she began to get the feel and balance of being on horseback.

Her face became tanned. Her hair, which she had worn since girlhood tightly drawn back into a knot, began to squirm from under hairpins and try to curl. She was soon eating in a way that made cook proud of himself. She had made the boys return to their bunks; and even though cook did snore like a saw going through a split plank, she slept so well that she did not hear him—much.

Soon she was riding about alone. The horse was old and gentle, but she did not go far, then only at a walk. Trotting jiggled her so that she could not breathe, and she was too unsure of her seat to gallop. Cook said, if she ever got lost, to give the horse his head and he would bring her home.

She was four or five miles from home one afternoon when she saw three men gallop out of a clump of trees toward her. Jane's heart flew up into her mouth and beat frantically. She wanted to turn and run, but she could not ride well enough, so she pulled the horse about and faced them, waiting with lips tightly set.

They were rough-looking men, or so she thought. To her, all Western men looked rough. The one in the lead was straight in the saddle, hard-faced, hard-eyed, not young. His coat was tied on the saddle behind him, but he wore a vest. The horsemen pulled up, pulled off their hats.

"You are Miss Alvord?"

"I am."

"Miss Alvord, we are having a look at the country. Thinking of buying a little ranch."

"Mine is not for sale."

They were polite in a restrained, hard-staring way, but she felt that the man was lying about wanting to buy a ranch. She thought that he had a harder face than the other men, who were a bit bulky, with a kind of perpetually frozen stare. All of them wore revolvers and carried rifles.

"Miss Alvord, can you tell us where the Knox ranch is?"

"No, I can't. It is near here, but I do not know the country very well."

"If you don't mind, we'll just ride home with you and have one of your boys tell us. I believe that Red Clark is your foreman."

Jane was frightened. She thought that they had come to find Red, and they looked dangerous. "No one is at home," she said, "excepting the cook."

"We will go with you and wait for Red."

That made her more frightened. They rode with her, keeping at a slow walk and not even talking among themselves. She didn't know what to do; there was nothing to do. Her gentle horse bobbed his head at every step, plodding homeward. Jane sat stiffly erect and tight-mouthed and felt that she was a coward, because she knew that she was afraid.

Cook appeared in the doorway, a hand shading his eyes. He knew nearly everybody in the country, but he did not know these men. He went to where his rifle lay on pegs in the kitchen part of the room, slapped the lever, throwing a shell into the chamber, then put the rifle against the wall at the side of the door. He waited in the doorway, pulled at the ends of his long, rat-tail mustache and peered with a blear-eyed scowl.

Jane rode up close to the door. "These men want to know the way to the Knox ranch."

Cook kept one hand out of sight, his fingers on the barrel of the rifle, for he could see that she was frightened. "Why, sure." He gestured with the hand that was in sight. "You go right over there south a piece, then—"

The men were getting out of their saddles. "We'll stay for supper," said the tall old hard-eyed man, and walked over to offer his hand to Jane to help her dismount.

Strangers, of course, had a right to stay to supper, and all night, too; but it was the part of good manners for them to hang around without saying why until supper was ready, then be invited and to act a little as if they hadn't expected to be invited.

"We'll water and feed the horses," said one of the bulky men, in a thick voice, as if he had a bad cold.

The leader nodded and watched Jane go indoors. He gave the cook a straight look. "She is afraid of us. From what I hear of the country, I don't blame her. We will wait outside until the menfolks ride in. We are all-right people."

Cook was a broken-down, frowzy old fellow, but he nipped a mustache end between thumb and finger, met the man's straight look, mumbled, "You'd better be, 'cause she is a nice woman!"

He picked up the rifle, letting the man see just how ready he had been and still was. He took it with him over to the stove and up-ended it against the cook table.

The three strangers stayed outdoors, squatting together and talking a little in low voices. Jane remained over at the cook's end of the room and fretted. She was sure that they were waiting to kill Red. The cook puttered at getting supper, mumbled reassuringly, guessed that Red was "sorta able to have something to say about bein' kilt."

". . . But you ortn't be out here to this ranch. It ain't no place for a lady."

"Then I would rather not be a lady!"

"I mean on account of fellers that may try to make trouble."

"If there is trouble," said Jane severely, "I want to be with *my* boys!"

Cook blinked his bleary eyes and grinned. "You are shore all right!"

And Jane Alvord, seminary instructress in history and Latin, flushed with pride. Not many days before she would have drawn her skirts aside from this frowzy old shambling fellow as from something unclean; now she felt like hugging him.

They heard hoofbeats and went to the door, cook bringing along his rifle. Red was riding up, fast. As soon as he had caught sight of the strangers outside of the house, he suspected that they had come for trouble, had perhaps already made some. But when he saw that the tall man who stood up was the stranger who had been in the hotel room with Mr Clayton, Red's feelings changed and he swung out of the saddle with a "Howdy," spoken in a friendly way.

Cook was a little relieved, but nevertheless grumbled to Jane: "Then I guess they are goin' to stay for supper. I was expectin' Red would shoot 'em. Save me so much cookin'."

The tall, strong-faced man was saying, "I am

Mr Vickers, Red—George Vickers. That horse o
yours is one of the Dunham black breed?"

Red rubbed his cheek against the horse's nose
"He is."

"And branded Arrowhead."

"Sure. The Arrowhead is home to me when I'm
in Tulluco."

"When I first saw the horse in town I wondered
Dunham never sells a horse of the black breed
But I heard from Judge Trowbridge how it was. I
am afraid that we made Miss Alvord nervous by
riding down on her the way we did."

After supper Mr Vickers took Red out of the
house, and they went for a little walk down
behind the corral. Mr Vickers stopped, struck
a match, turned back his vest and showed Red
a small gold badge that said, *United States
Marshal.* Then they climbed up on the top pole
of the corral.

"I am after that outlaw Kilco, Red."

"I'd help you catch 'im in a minute."

"The two men with me are Wells, Fargo men.
I am after him because he killed my deputy. Too
bad, Red, that you didn't drop Mell Barber that
day in town. He is wanted, too—dead or alive.
What do you know about Kilco? He's known to
some people, I understand, as Brady."

Red rolled a cigarette but chewed on the
matchstick for a time before lighting it. He
wondered if he ought to tell the marshal that

Kilco was in love with Kate Clayton and she with him. He didn't like to bring her name into it. Red said, "Um-m," thoughtfully. "I sure have got no use at all for outlaws." He felt that he had even less use for this one because of the way a lovely girl like Kate loved him.

The marshal put a hand on Red's knee. "I am trying to keep Kilco—and Barber, too—from knowing that I am up here. Sam Clayton has known me for thirty years. He said that it was all right for me to confide in the Judge—and you, of course.

"This Kilco is a bad one and hard to catch. The Wells, Fargo boys have found out that he comes up in this neighborhood frequently. That's why we are up here pretending to be looking for a ranch. I understand that your rustler friend Knox is thick with the bunch—or used to be."

Red rubbed out the cigarette, put a hand up under his hat, scratched. "Knox, he ain't to home. I rode over to his place yesterday to see. He ain't been home, either."

"If he had been, it might have been bad for you!"

"No more 'n for him."

"The man indoors has the advantage."

"Not over a skinny man behind a tree. Lots of trees up there."

"We won't argue. Knox hasn't been around town, either." The marshal patted Red's knee. "If

you get any news, just send word into the Judge
We'll be in Nelplaid every few days."

"If I hear anything, I'll sure let you know."

"By the way, Red, isn't it a little—well—um—
this young woman living here with you boys?"

"She's owner."

"It's going to be hard on her reputation."

"It's goin' to be harder on anybody as meddles
with her repytation. She is all right."

CHAPTER SIX

The following afternoon Red thought that he would ride over to say hello to old Mr Backman and nose around to find out if he knew that Jim Brady was Kilco. Red didn't want to believe that; but he was almost willing to bet that Kate and Brady-Kilco met over at Mr Backman's cabin. It made him mad to think that a pretty, brave, picture-book girl should be in love with an outlaw.

Red was riding a skittish buckskin that showed lots of white in his feverish eyes. The skittishness irritated Red, because he was trying to think. Thinking didn't seem to do him much good, for he had been awake most of the night, mulling things over and not getting anywhere. Ought he to have told the marshal about Kate and Kilco?

He crossed the valley and was edging up to the steep bluff covered with pines when—*Bang! Bang! Bang!*—rifles cracked at him.

Red struck the skittish horse with spurs, and the horse made a tremendous bound and came down on limber forelegs, falling headlong with a bullet through his heart. Red went out of the saddle and into the air all spraddled out, as if trying to fly. He landed face down, badly jolted and skinned a little. Vaguely he heard an exultant yap, "We got 'im!"

Red raised his head, squirmed about, peering up the steep side of the hogback. For a moment he felt that he couldn't see very well; then he saw three men coming out from among the trees on horses to ride down on him and make sure. They weren't much over a hundred and fifty yards off, but the hogback rose sharply, almost like a bluff, and they would have to zigzag down in a roundabout way. It was a nice place for an ambush. One of the men was Knox.

Red got up, unconsciously reached for his hatbrim to shut out the sun's glare; but he had lost his hat. The horsemen saw him rise, and he could hear echoes of the cussing that they gave him for not being dead. They had rifles in their hands, and all piled out of the saddles to begin shooting. Red, with stride that stumbled partly because he was still a little dizzy and partly because of his boot heels, ran drunkenly back to his dead horse; and they mistook his staggering for a bad wound.

He pulled a revolver, rested his forearm on the horse's rump, raised the front sight well up and let fly. It was a long way for a .45 slug to carry accurately; but some of the bullets came close enough for the fellows up there to think it was best to get in behind trees while one of them hurriedly led the horses back out of sight behind a ledge of rock.

Red's eyes were clear, and his head was clear, and he said to himself, "I ain't got much of a hole to hide in with them up there shootin' down—which is why I'm glad I ain't fat." The horse had fallen on the rifle scabbard, and Red had to stand up and turn his back while he jerked two or three times to free it, and bullets were smacking at him. He was not much of a rifle shot—not as he considered good shooting—but he had plenty of ammunition, providing he didn't burn it up recklessly.

He could not hope to pick them off from behind trees and rocks, but he knew that if he were not hit he could stand them off until night; then he would have to walk four or five miles in the dark to the ranch house. He hated walking so much that he began to dread the trudge as soon as he thought of it.

It was only a little after noon and hot. An hour passed. He watched warily, keeping his face down along the rifle, but not shooting often. Red had the eyes of a hawk, unspoiled by much reading, unstrained by lamplight. The men were hugging the trees, and Red waited for them to get careless; but apparently they didn't mean to get careless. They were not shooting very rapidly now and were doing a good enough job of it to plunk the dead horse with bullets once in a while. Two or three times he got away snap shots as some one of the men changed to another tree to get a better view of Red's sprawled-out body, but he didn't see anybody drop.

From somewhere the flies began to come, attracted by the blood ooze of the horse, and soon had Red slapping at them. "You fellers are gettin' some previous," he growled. "I ain't dead yet awhile." He wiped the dirt from a pebble and put it into his mouth, wishing for water. It seemed to him that the sun had caught on a snag in the heavens and was standing still. "Knox an' them must be Joners!" he guessed, mixing a few scraps of Biblical lore in thinking of the man who had made the sun stand still so that he would have more daylight in which to slaughter enemies.

Two hours went by. Red wanted a drink, but instead took a smoke. His mouth was sticky-dry. Flies hummed in his face, smacked his neck and started biting.

The men up there on the bluff were shooting again, rapidly, pouring down slugs. Smoke popped out from rifle muzzles, swirled as if from a damp fire. Red scrouged, peering. The sun was in his eyes, and his hat was gone. Some of the bullets had the whine of flies; some of the flies the buzz of bullets.

Red thought, "Maybe I am goin' to have to *crawl* home!" as two bullets in a row flicked dirt onto the same leg by a miss of inches.

He opened up rapidly on the man who was

getting his range, just firing away; and the man didn't send more bullets quite so close. There was no way for Red to escape from the line of fire, no better place to scrouge down. He had to lie there and take it, and he meditated reproachfully:

"I orta pertended to be dead in the first place an' let 'em come down clost."

He had a simple-minded faith in close, fast, man-to-man fighting. Sharpshooting was not to his liking. He fingered his belt, counting the rifle cartridges, and decided to hold his fire. Anyhow, there was too much smoke from the guns up there for him to draw a bead. All he could do was to pour in a lot of bullets more or less blindly.

"Next time me an' Knox meet, hell's goin' to be fuller 'n she is on account of him bein' such a big—" Red used what seemed a suitable name.

He wiped his face with the bandanna about his neck, slapped at some flies, thought, "I'm glad one of 'em up there ain't old Mr Backman. I bet he could pick the kernel outa a nut an' not hurt the shell."

Red shaded his eyes, squinted between his fingers at the sky, but the sun seemed hanging right where it had been. His hand swiped the back of his neck, taking off flies. Something tugged at the handkerchief as if fingers had jerked it. "Close!" said Red, but added serenely, "Close is

157

a miss, allus!" He huddled himself to his knees crouching low, took the best aim he could and touched the trigger.

Smoke whirled out in the still air before him like a cloud, and before it cleared Red heard a startled yelping.

"I must've had some luck!" he thought, and confusedly changed the thought because guns were going off up there like the brittle crack of dried sticks in a fire; and bullets were not coming toward him.

He raised himself and saw dim shapes flitting in the timber as men raced for their horses; then he heard the crash of tree limbs as they rode caught glimpses of horses laboring along the hillside. Red straightened up, with the rifle to his shoulder, worked the lever, throwing bullets after them.

When the gun was empty he lowered it, stood peering up. "I owe somebody some thanks," he said, then cupped a hand to his mouth and hallooed.

He guessed that old Mr Backman, attracted by the shooting, had walked in on the men; then he changed his guess with a shake of his head. "Nope. If that old feller had drawed a bead on a man, that man wouldn't be ridin' off."

His next guess was that one of the kids, Bobby or Pete, had from a distance seen what was up and had worked his way around behind the men nd opened fire. "Good kids," said Red and nallooed again, then listened.

His shout rang in dim echoes, as if answering nimself. "Funny!" he thought. He went for his nat and stood with eyes searching the bluff, expecting somebody to appear and have his nanks. In the stillness he thought that he heard a aint shout, so faint that he was not sure whether or not his ears were playing him a trick.

Red cupped both hands to his mouth and yelled, 'Hi—O-o-o!" Echoes flitted like dim shadows of sound; then, nearly as dim as the last echo, a shout reached his straining ears.

"After doin' me a favor," thought Red, "he acts is if hidin'." Suspiciously: "Maybe it is a trick o get me up there." He thought things over. At no time had there been more than three men shooting at him, and he had seen three men riding off. This other unknown man must be a friend.

Red went forward, pausing to shout, wanting an answer. Then, instead of hearing a shout, a gun was fired. That settled any doubts. Nobody who was trying to draw him into a trap would start shooting instead of shouting. He pitched the rifle down and stumbled at a run to the foot of the bluff of the hogback and began a zigzag climb. He had more faith in revolvers than in a rifle, anyhow. It was hard climbing, took his breath, but now and then he shouted, inquiringly. Once more a shot answered his call.

He got to where Knox and the men had stood behind trees. The ground was sprinkled with brass. "Hi—O-o-o!" Red sang out. "Where the hell are you?"

Higher up on the hill and over to the east a little, a voice said, "Here!"

Red clambered up, looked over a fallen half-rotten tree and found Jim Brady-Kilco bareheaded on the ground. He peered up with a pain-twisted smile, and his eyes had a fever bright stare, much like the look Red had seen in the eyes of wounded animals that watched a man come up to kill them. He held the revolver with which he had been answering Red's shouts, but now he dropped it. "Got any water, Red?"

Red climbed over the fallen tree, which crumbled under him like loose clods.

"You bad hurt?"

"My right leg. Busted. High up."

Red stooped over with a sympathetic, "Damn!"

"In the thigh. Doesn't hurt yet—much. But I—I'm helpless!"

"You knowed they was after me?"

"I guessed it was you. I left my horse down over yonder and crept up. When I saw it was Knox I knew it must be you."

"They mustn't have knowed they hit you from the way they run."

"Knox, he happened to see me just as I stood up behind that log. He shot all of a sudden. I went down but kept throwing bullets. I couldn't see, but I made noise."

"They high-tailed like they was carryin' hot coals in their hip pockets. Why did *you* pitch in to help me?"

Red had let an inflectional squeak get into the "you," significantly. Kilco stared at him, and Red stared back. There was something so plain in Red's face that Kilco said, cautious-soft, "You know who I am?"

"I wish I didn't!"

Kilco lifted himself on an elbow, looked toward the fallen revolver.

"You don't need that," Red told him.

"Some three to six thousand dollars . . . I don't quite know myself," said Kilco.

"You ain't very smart!"

"How you mean, Red?"

"I'll never want money bad enough to turn over somebody that got hurt helpin' me. Specially not when I sure as hell needed some help!"

Kilco slumped back down on the dense pine needles, ran his hand delicately down along his thigh. "It's bad. I don't know what to do."

"I'll go find your horse an' take you over to old Backman. He's your friend?"

Kilco nodded. "He isn't home. I was just over there. Sometimes he's away for days."

"Can you set a horse?"

"I'll have to."

Red rolled a cigarette, lighted it, put it in Kilco's mouth, then put his own hat, crown down, under Kilco's face to protect the dry pine needles from the chance of fire. Kilco said, "You are a good kid."

"You lied to me in town, sayin' you didn't know who them fellers was?"

"I had to." Kilco nodded submissively. "But I don't know what made them do it. I think rustlers must have put Mell Barber up to it. I don't know where he is. In hell, I hope!"

"You an' him had a little fallin' out, so folks say."

"We did."

"What over?"

"Something I can't talk about," said Kilco.

"Who was them with Knox here today?"

"I didn't see. They were on the far side. When I looked up, Knox was right there. He let fly and I got hit. Then he yelled and must've run. What are you goin' to do now?"

"With you?"

"Me."

"I got to do what I can. Which way is your horse? Mine is dead."

"Where will you take me?"

"To our ranch. Does the cook there know you?"

"I don't know him."

"Well, ever'body else there will be all right. An' him, too, I think. He is a no-good old feller an' was friends with Alvord. But if he knows you an' knows of the reward—Still, what better can I do? It is for you to say."

"I think my leg is broke up close to the hip."

"It's goin' to be hard ridin', however gentle we go."

"I can't stay here."

"An' you'll need a doctor."

Red took the cigarette from Kilco, rubbed out the fire against a piece of wood held over the hat, dusted out the hat and put it on. "It is steep up here for a horse, but I'll bring him. You're a big fellow, but I'll get you on."

"I can set a saddle if I can get into it."

"I'll get you into it."

"You are a friend, Red."

Red squatted down, bringing his face on a level with Kilco, and stared for a moment. "No. No, I ain't. But I'll do ever'thing for you I can like I was the best friend you've got. Only it has got to be understood I ain't your friend!"

Kilco stared back suspiciously. "How you mean?"

"Just what I said."

"Why did you say it?"

"It was an outlaw shot my dad—in the back. Me and outlaws don't be friends, ever!"

"You don't think—"

"I know you didn't, because I know who did. I killed 'im, right up face to face. Now you pitched in here today an' helped me, so you are goin' to be took as good care of as I can take for as long as the hurt you got doin' it keeps you down. But once you can ride again, we ain't friends."

Kilco studied with a troubled look. He was a handsome fellow with a strong, reckless face. "I don't understand, Red. You mean you want—you don't want the reward that much?"

"Reward be damned! It's just that me an' outlaws don't mix friendly. I'm makin' it plain so there won't be no surprise an' hard feelin's later on."

Kilco was suffering, but he tried to smile. "I don't understand." A troubled look, with fierce suspicion close to the surface, scrutinized Red's face. He forced himself to say, "But I know you are all right." But the man Kilco had been so long hunted for the price on his head that he had doubts about Red and that strange kind of honesty that would take care of a man, as if he were a friend, yet warn him that he wasn't a friend.

Red found Kilco's horse a quarter of a mile down the hill and back near the trail to Mr Backman's place. He led the horse up the steep hill, found the footing hard for his own feet, found thinking harder. He had been friends with fool cowboys on the dodge for this craziness or that, and helped them; and a time or two he had had to light out and duck away himself when people misunderstood about something; but he had never befriended an out-and-out outlaw. He could feel how embarrassed he was going to be when he met the stern-grim old Marshal Vickers again; and he couldn't think of much of anything to say to himself to make it seem all right to take care of Kilco, but he wouldn't try to think of any reason for not taking care of him.

Red said, with troubled muttering, "I *know* it is wrong, but I feel it is right."

He did, or tried to do, what he felt was right, always; and that is what gave him his intrepid assurance and kept his eyes brilliantly honest.

He found Kilco with a pain-twisted mouth, trying not to cry out. He writhed and clutched handfuls of dry pine needles. Agony had begun to come into the wound.

"You're a purty big man. All I can do is help boost you up. It's goin' to be hell. On you, I mean."

"Help me to stand so I can get hold of the horn."

"First I'll shorten this left stirrup so you can put more weight on your good leg."

"Over there at your ranch, maybe they won't like hiding me?"

"If they don't, I'll take you som'ers else. You b'long to me till you can ride."

There was sweat on Kilco's face, and he kept his teeth clenched. He was bleeding a little, and pain screamed in his leg. He raised himself on his hands and left knee, then took hold of Red with one hand, of the stirrup with the other, and pulled himself up, breathing hard. He got his hand on the horn.

"I don't see how you're goin' to get up without hurtin' yourself terrible."

"I have to get up!"

Red locked his fingers together and stooped until his hands were on the ground before Kilco's foot. Kilco held the horn and gave a little hop, inching the ball of his foot onto Red's locked hands. He pulled on the horn and Red lifted, raising him until his foot was even with the stirrup. Kilco squirmed the toe of his foot onto the stirrup, but his right leg dangled helplessly. He could not throw it over the saddle. In a muffled voice, through set teeth, "You'll have to drag that leg over for me."

"It'll purt-near kill you."

"Worse can't be much worse. Do it!"

Kilco raised himself as high as he could in the shortened stirrup and held to the horn with both hands, leaning against the saddle as if he had cramps. The horse swung its head inquiringly at this awkward way of mounting and sagged a shoulder yieldingly to the lopsided weight. Red pushed Kilco's limp leg around the horse's rump, but the high cantle was still in the way.

166

Kilco said almost in a scream, "Go on! Get me nto the saddle!"

Red pulled the leg around, and Kilco cried out n agony; then he said angrily, "Go on! Don't pay ittention to my blubberin'!"

Kilco sat down in the saddle. His hands on the iorn were white from the tenseness with which ie had gripped the horn. It hurt to sit in the saddle, but it was so much relief to sit that he did 1ot mind the hurt.

Red took off his spurs and tied them to his belt. He took the horse up close to the bit and began :o lead him, zigzagging, down the hillside. It was iard going, and the jolting of even the slowest pace was terrible on Kilco.

II

They reached the ranch house about dark. Jane, the two kids and cook came out, wonderingly. Red told them how it was, letting them think that Kilco was a stray cowboy, although any-body, excepting Jane, would have known that not many cowboys wore as much finery as this man.

Kilco was the next thing to unconscious when they helped him out of the saddle and carried him into the house; and he was unconscious when they laid him in a bunk. Cook kept looking at Red in a queer way, but he brought water and clothes. Jane wrung out a cloth and put it on Kilco's forehead. Red cut off Kilco's boot, ripped his pants leg, to get to the wound. The leg was swollen and purple-bruised.

"Oh, he must have a doctor!" Jane said.

"Yes'm," Red agreed. He didn't know much about wounds, but he knew that this was a bad leg.

"The poor fellow is suffering terribly!"

"Nothin' much to what he will be soon. Bobby, you go out to the stable, an' in the manger, second from the north, deep down, you will find a bottle of whisky I have been keepin' hid from the cook. That will have to do for medicine."

"I'll go!" said the cook.

"All right, you go. But you two kids go, too, to see that he comes back sober."

They all went, as if it were some kind of a game. Red solemnly watched until they were well away from the door. He touched Jane's arm and did not say anything for a moment after she looked at him; then he leaned close to her and said:

"Miss, this is bad. Like you say, he orta have a doctor. All I have told you about how he helped me is so. Only I haven't told you all. He is Jim Kilco, the outlaw!"

"Red!" Jane was frightened. "Oh, Red, what shall we do?"

"Take care of 'im till he can ride, of course."

"B-but an *outlaw!*"

"He got hurt helpin' me. I don't give a damn who he is while he's hurt. An' I had to tell you," Red droned softly, seeming to look inwardly at his own thoughts, as if reading them aloud, "because in helpin' me it was the same as helpin' you, too, for the fight was over how I been runnin' your ranch."

Jane stooped a little nearer to Kilco, as if the better to search his face. He was barely breathing, and his eyes were half open, as if he were dead. Kilco had suffered the tortures of the rack during the long ride.

"I," Red went on, softly droning, and looking at her to be sure that she understood, "don't have truck with outlaws; but I stick to my friends, an' he has been one. After he gets cured an' rises again—" Red shrugged a shoulder. "But till he can ride I'll do what I can to keep him from gettin' caught. It all sounds sorta crazy to you maybe, but that is how it is."

"Oh, Red, I am afraid that he will die!"

"That is right, miss. What they call gangrene is purty liable to set in. An old-timer like Mr Backman might know what to do, but he ain't home, which is why I brought him here."

"He must have a doctor."

"If we fetch the doctor from Nelplaid, who is not much good, so I hear tell, he will sure talk to somebody about a wounded man out here. An' if we tell him not to, he will be that much surer to talk."

"*Something* must be done, Red!"

"We can't keep him here without tellin' the boys an' the cook, because we all are goin' to have to act funny about not lettin' people that happen to come get in the house an' see 'im. The boys will be all right, but I don't know about that cook. Some thousands of dollars is a lot of money. They will do more for you than they will for me, because you are a nice woman. The kids an' that cook are plumb silly to please you."

Jane flushed, but she was pleased. "I know the cook is all right."

"I sorta like the old shypoke."

She put her hands against Red's breast. "You *must* get a doctor, Red. I don't care if he *is* an outlaw. We must take care of him. And he doesn't look like an outlaw, does he?"

He almost said, "Some other nice women thinks that, too." But he gazed at her, not smiling.

The cook and the kids came in with the bottle of whisky, and the kids wanted to tell how they had kept the cook from making off with it, but Jane pointed toward the bunk and said, "Shh-hh-h!" and they shut up.

Red opened the bottle and poured a deep drink for the cook in a coffee cup. He gave drinks to the kids and mixed some with water for Jane to give to Kilco when he stirred.

"You'd better have a little, too, miss."

Red had the frontier belief in the beneficial effect of whisky if used moderately. Jane was badly shaken, and she drank a spoonful of whisky and water.

Red sat and thought awhile; then he told the boys to bring in his horse. "An' put on one of your saddles. Bring mine in tomorrow. An' you take that horse I brung in with him on it over to—well, you turn 'im loose so he'll go home. 'm goin' to town to see about a doctor."

Cook had sneaked over to the table and poured more whisky into his cup before Red took away the bottle. Cook grinned as if he had won a big jack pot, tossed the whisky down his throat, rubbed his belly. A moment later he beckoned Red to the back door, and they stepped outside.

Cook put his face up close to Red's and asked, "Will you whack with me if I tell you how to get a pile of money?"

It was dark out back. Red took hold of cook's shoulder and struck a match, holding it near his face. "How do you know who he is, cook?"

"Him and old Al was friends."

"Did he come here?"

"No, but Al told me about him. Sometimes Al rode with the bunch. Sometimes they would be gone for ten days to two weeks to hold up a train som'ers."

"Did he help Alvord rustle cows?" Red sounded

171

as if stealing cows were worse than robbing trains—and he almost felt it. All of Red's life he had drawn wages for riding herd on cows, never for taking care of trains. "Did he?"

"Not as I know of."

Red held the match until the flame nipped his fingers. He dropped it, stepped on it, lit another match.

"Now, cook, you listen to me. You have been kinda friends with a bad bunch for a long time an' kept your mouth shut. You just go right on keepin' it shut. I have told our missus who he is an' that until he can ride again he is to be took care of like a friend. So don't you get any notion of gettin' yourself some reward unless you want to have it spent on a finer coffin than most people are buried in. You hear me?"

The cook grinned. "You are a fool kid. Me, what I wanted to find out was would you turn over a man that got hurt helpin' you for some reward!"

He put out his hand, and Red took it, not with enthusiasm. He was suspicious that the cook had merely said that because it was a nice way to wiggle out of a bad hole; but it was hard to tell about the frowzy old cook, whom Red couldn't quite dislike.

III

Red got into Nelplaid at about eight o'clock in the morning. He had an idea. The idea was that almost anybody would do almost anything that Miss Kate wanted him to do, which included the Nelplaid doctor, who might go out to the Lazy Z and tend the wounded man and not talk of it afterwards. Anyhow, he meant to ask her about it.

He rode straight to the hotel. One of the Wells, Fargo men was straddling a chair on the porch, with his arms across the back, and smoking a cigar. He was the fattish one with the hoarse voice. He came to meet Red and asked in a voice that sounded as if he had a bad cold, "Anything?"

"I come to see Miss Clayton."

"They moved old Clayton out to the ranch yesterday. The doctor they brought up here again from Poicoma said it was bad, but old Clayton was frettin' to get home. Anything about that feller Kilco?"

Red took out papers and tobacco to give himself a little time to think. "Did the city doctor go, too?"

"Yes. Have you heard anything?"

Red lit the cigarette. "Is the marshal in town?"

"Somewhere." Eagerly: "You want to see him?"

Red inhaled deeply, eyed the Wells, Fargo man. "You can tell him that I'll be up to the Judge's office for a little talk."

The man hunched forward, more as if bullying than asking, "You know something?"

"A little, maybe."

"What? Tell me!"

"I'll tell the marshal."

"All right. You be there." The man had a bossy sound. "I'll go find him."

Red went to the Judge's room. The Judge had his feet on the table, a book in his hand, a pipe in his mouth and was in shirt sleeves. It was a hot morning, and the bandanna was in his hand to mop about his neck. He looked quizzically at Red's sober face. "Trouble, son?"

"I'm in a pickle."

"Miss Alvord?"

"No. She is all right."

"Then what is wrong, Red?"

"How far is it out to the Clayton ranch?"

"About fifteen to twenty miles. Why?"

"I sorta wondered."

"You aren't quitting?"

"Me? No."

"The marshal told me that you two had a talk."

"Um. We did, Judge. We're goin' to have another 'n up here purty soon."

"Kilco, Red?"

"Kilco."

The Judge cleared his throat and beamed. "I hope you get the reward!"

Red took off his hat, shook the bottle of whisky, poured a small drink. "What do you know about 'im?"

"Only hearsay. Why?"

"I sorta wondered, like."

"You look a little disturbed."

"Me? Oh, I'm just thinkin'. It's allus trouble-some to have to think when you don't know how to act. It's a pile easier to go right ahead an' do things without havin' to think. Only sometimes you can't. This is like that."

Heavy footsteps marched down the hall with a clatter as of men hurrying eagerly. The marshal and the two heavy-footed Wells, Fargo men came in. The marshal shook hands with Red, as if already thanking him. The marshal was Western from the heart out, calm and hard. He pushed back his hat with a slow movement, looked with approving directness at Red. "You have news for me?"

Red eyed the Wells, Fargo men. One was fattish, the other not thin. They had staring eyes, always staring, as if they had once looked so hard at something that their eyes were fixed in a perpetual stare. They were taking chairs.

"News?" Red asked, looking at the marshal. "Yes. Some. A little."

The Judge placed a chair for the marshal.

"Hot," he said, companionably. "Sit down, Red."

"I talk better on my feet," Red replied moodily. He pulled at the handkerchief about his neck, breathed slowly, lifted his look from the floor to the marshal, who sat straight-backed, waiting. "I'd rather take a beatin' than have this talk. But I'd rather take a harder one than not have it. You can see how I feel. So here goes."

The marshal leaned forward stiffly, rubbed his cheek, frowned a little. The Wells, Fargo men took out cigars, drew a light, with heads together, from one match, settled back in their chairs, stared at Red as if about to be pleased.

Red cleared his throat but didn't speak. He picked his hat from the table, looked at the crown, poked it, put it back on the table. "Yesterday Knox an' a couple of fellers laid for me—right at the edge of the timber across the valley. They knocked over my horse, an' I spilled outa the saddle like I'd been took by the heels an' swung. I snuggled down behind the horse an' played peekaboo—two hours or more. They wouldn't come out from behind the trees, an' they used up a pile of shells. Some come clost. Damn clost!"

The Judge clucked wonderingly. Red's luck seemed to hold against gunfire.

"Then all of a sudden somebody that had heard the shootin' an' crept around up the hill through the timber opened up on them, an' they skedaddled." Red was speaking directly to the marshal, eying him almost as if half angry. "Then went up yonder to say 'Thanks' to whoever it was, an' I found a man with a broke leg layin' here. Knox an' them had run without knowin' they'd hit 'im. It was Kilco. His leg was broke up near the hip."

The two Wells, Fargo men rose out of their chairs. One smacked his hands together, and the other slapped his partner's back. "Good boy!" said one, gleefully. "That is luck!" said the other. "Where is he, Red?"

Red didn't hear them. He was looking steadily at the marshal. The Wells, Fargo men got closer. One said to the Judge, "He is a great boy!"

The Judge examined his pipe, felt in the bowl with a little finger and decided against refilling it. He struck a match, and as he sucked, *plop-plop,* he looked at Red as if wondering about something unpleasant.

Marshal Vickers asked, crisply soft, "So?"

"So," said Red. "An' I hid 'im, careful!"

The Judge pulled in a deep breath, relaxed a little, glanced toward the marshal, whose stern face was poker-set, expressionless.

"Just tell us where," said the hoarse Wells, Fargo man, in an eager hurry. "We'll go get 'im!"

The marshal flicked a glance aside at his companions, hinted at surprise that they had so little understanding of what this meant; then he asked quietly, "Why did he throw in with *you*, Red?"

"I 'magine it's on account of what I done that day in town. I told you he told me that he approved." Red picked up his hat again, poked the crown, watched where he poked.

The marshal thought things over. "So you don't intend to give him up, Red?"

Red's eyes lifted somberly. *"Would you?"*

"Not give him up!" said the hoarse Wells, Fargo man, with a popeyed, astonished stare, as if never in his life had he before heard of such a thing.

"Why, Red," said the other, explaining and warning, "that will make you in with him! We'll have the right to arrest you for protecting him!"

Red paid no attention. He was looking at the marshal, waiting for his answer. The Judge decided that the pipe needed filling and knocked it out against his heel.

"Why, there's some five thousand dollars reward!" said the hoarse man, putting his face up close to Red's. "You'll be fixed for life!"

"And if you don't we'll arrest *you!*" said the other, scowling.

"You can't hide him without getting yourself in with the bunch!"

"And we'll have to hold you, Red! You don't want to be 'rested for—"

They just batted at Red's ears, one after the other saying something, as if they had rehearsed

178

ow to talk fast together, or almost together; but Red went on not looking at them, almost as if he didn't hear. He was watching the marshal.

The Wells, Fargo men got louder and crowded closer, working on Red; then the Judge knocked sharply on the table.

"Gentlemen!" He was using his sonorous courtroom voice. "Gentlemen, you are unquestionably efficient officers or you would not have been assigned to co-operate with Marshal Vickers in a matter of this importance. I am confident that you are skillful at interrogating, influencing and persuading criminals. But here your ordinary methods of procedure are of no value. You are dealing with an honest man! I suggest, gentlemen, that you keep quiet!"

The Wells, Fargo men looked as if they didn't understand. No doubt they really didn't, but after a long look at the Judge, another at the marshal, who ignored them, they edged back and kept quiet.

The marshal asked, "Is he bad hurt, Red?"

" 'Pears to be."

"But he could ride?"

"He stuck in the saddle till I got 'im to where he wanted to go."

"With a broken thigh?"

"I don't know if it is broke, but I think so."

"The bone was shattered by a bullet?"

"I guess so."

The marshal stood up, stood breast to breast with Red, and spoke gentle-voiced: "Red, he i purty sure to die without a doctor. A shattered bone is mighty hard to deal with. If you tell me where he is, I'll see that he gets good care."

"If he dies, I'll tell you where he is."

"You won't give him up?"

Again Red whipped out as if cracking a whip *"Would you?"*

The marshal's eyes were steady, and there was no shadow of expression on his bronze-dark face He looked at Red for a long time. "Why have you told me all this if you don't mean to give him up?"

"I promised to tell you if I heard news. I do what I say, allus. Or try to, allus. 'Nother thing I want you to know how it come about if you ever caught me actin' like Kilco's friend. If I ge caught, I'll be guilty as hell. Only I don't wan you, and the Judge, an' some people I like, ever to think I throwed in with an outlaw because wasn't honest. That's why I made up my mind to tell you just how it was."

The marshal pulled down his hat, turned to the door. "Come along, boys. We may as well go."

The Wells, Fargo men went out, grumbling loudly, trying to tell the marshal that he had made a big mistake, saying they ought to be allowed to work on that fool boy. Halfway down the hall the marshal, exasperated, opened his tight lips

'We'll catch Kilco if we can. But you never could get anything more out of that boy!"

When they had gone, the Judge got up slowly, put out his hand. He was sober about it. "I am not saying that you are doing right, son. But I am saying that you are being honest!"

Red gave his head a troubled shake, spoke as if looking inwardly at his own thoughts, reading them aloud, slowly: "The marshal is going to nose around out there an' see if he can find Kilco. An' if he does, it will look like I give him away. So I'm wonderin' if it was honest of me not to keep my mouth tight shut when I'm helpin' Kilco. I don't like this thing of not knowin' what I orta do!"

CHAPTER SEVEN

Red trotted through the dust to Manning Springs, watered his horse, washed his own face, then squatted in the skeleton shade of the windmill and began to roll a cigarette, still trying to decide whether to go home or turn off toward the Clayton ranch.

He eyed the sun from under his hatbrim, thinking. The city doctor would be out there, and Miss Kate could persuade anybody if she wanted to be sweet. He felt better at having put his cards on the table before Marshal Vickers and the aggressive Wells, Fargo men; but it was not doing Kilco much of a favor merely to keep him hid, let him suffer and most likely die. After all, that fellow Kilco, who most likely was pretty bad in many ways, had grit. Red was not thinking so much of his going up the mountainside alone to jump three men with rifles in their hands as of the way Kilco had not groaned and cussed during the two-hour torture of the ride to the ranch house.

Old man Manning came from the house, bare-headed, at a drowsy shuffle, with the dog at his heels and a wide grin.

"Howdy, pop."

"Howdy, howdy, boy." He cocked his head,

grinned. "Yore name, it is Clark, but air you tha Clark boy from Tulluco?"

"I'm him. Why?"

"Well now, somebody as must've knowed you purty well come by a little while ago, and he pitched a letter up on the shelf, and he said, 'If that Red Clark of Tulluco comes along, you see as how he gits it.' And here you air!" The old fellow looked triumphant.

"For me? A *letter?*"

"That's right," said the old man gleefully. "Come along in. Have a drink and a dish of beans."

"I need 'em. I been so busy thinkin' I forgot to eat."

The old fellow chuckled, swept an arm invitingly and started shuffling back to the 'dobe. "Come along." The dog sniffed at Red's legs.

Before the house Red, who had led his horse along, said, "I may as well take off the saddle if I'm goin' to eat."

The old man stood at the door, looked inside, grinned, furtively gestured. Red uncinched the saddle, pulled it off, spread the blanket. The horse shook himself, gave a long, vibrating snort.

The old man, waiting beside the door, had a funny grin on his face, as if about to play a joke. He stepped aside, put a hand on Red's back. "Go right along in, boy."

Red stepped in, scraping his spurs, frowning purblindly at the dimness.

It was a one-room 'dobe with only two small windows. They were recessed and narrow, and the room was very dim to Red's eyes after the bright sunlight.

The old man paused in the doorway, peering and, knowing where to look, saw something that made him throw up an arm and yell, *"Look out!"*

His screechy voice had a frantic sound, and Red jumped sidelong, keeping his back to the wall. He stumbled over a stool and went down to a hand and knee as a flame-flash cracked at him. His free hand was on the butt of a gun when he stumbled. Falling, he drew the gun. He hit the dirt floor where a table, with legs driven solidly into the ground, was before him. A second gun fired from another dark corner.

The old man was cursing at the top of his lungs. The thought whipped through Red's mind, "I'll kill him last!" and he fired once, twice, again and again, toward the nearest corner from which the flame of a gun struck at him. The only way he could tell if he hit was if the man died; and a vague shape tumbled out of the shadows, sprawled with a soft thud.

Red felt 'dobe dirt splatter on his neck as a bullet smacked into the wall behind him, and he twisted about to face the other corner, from which a .45 was smashing at him. Red fired and thought that his gun had blown up. Something sounded as if it had blown up. A deafening roar, such as never came from any .45, filled the room, and a cloud of smoke swirled densely.

Red saw that the old man stood in the dense smoke haze that sifted outward in the draft of the open doorway. He had emptied both barrels of a ten-gauge shotgun into the other man.

The old fellow cursed in a high, screechy voice. "They seen you outa the winder there, the . . ." He called them names until he was out of breath. "They said they'd rode with you up in Tulluco the . . ." More names, or rather the same. "They said for me to go tell you they was a letter and you'd fall over from surprise when you come in an' saw 'em, the . . ."

"Who are they?"

"I don't know, the . . ." He had a range of cuss words that would have dazzled a mule skinner.

"How they come to be here an' no horses?" If Red had seen horses he would not have walked into the house without knowing who was there.

"They rode in and asked to eat. Said they'd stay till the cool of the evenin'! Put up their hosses the . . ."

The old man followed Red across the room. Red stooped, pulled the man he had shot over on his back, bent down. "I don't know this one."

The old man was rubbing his shoulder, but held to the double-barreled shotgun as if it might come n handy for a club as they went to the second nan.

"I don't know him either, pop. But I got me a ;uspicion they was out in the hills yesterday with ⁷rank Knox."

"They was. That's right. I heard 'em say they'd)een huntin' yestiddy up at Knox's place. Sure, hat's them. How you know?"

" 'Twas me they was huntin'. Laid for me up in he hills."

"An' they used me to git you into the house, he . . ."

"I'm not very smart, pop. I might've known 1obody would be leavin' me a letter."

"You mayn't be smart, but yo're gosh a'mighty]uick!"

Red began to prod out shells. "Very slow, pop. thought I never would get goin'."

"This scatter-gun near busted my shoulder, but wanted 'im to have both ba'ls. And me, I didn't]uite see how it could be done, but now I begin o un'erstand how you, lone-handed, downed hree men that shot Mr Clayton. You don't jus' ;hoot—you jus' ripple 'em out!"

"An' I thought at first that you were in with 'em."

"I knowed it!" the old fellow squawked. 'Course you did! I wuz so mad I'd've bit 'em to Jeath if this old scatter-gun hadn't been on pegs 1ere by the door. I wuz so mad that when I pulled them triggers I give a shove to make the buckshot hit harder, the . . ."

"I suppose the sheriff'll have to come out to look at 'em?"

"No, he won't! No sir! You jus' he'p me load 'em in the wagon and I'll take 'em to town the . . ."

"Take 'em to the Silver Dollar, pop. Tell Dave Gridger I'm goin' to keep on sendin' in his friends!"

"You don't think Dave had anything to do with tryin' to kill you?" The old fellow left his mouth open.

"If I didn't I'd be an awful fool!"

Red helped put chain harness on a couple of worn-out horses, hitched them to a wobbly wagon, drove the wagon around to the front of the house. The old man kept up a screechy complaint about having been used to trap Red while they took one body by the arms and legs, carried it saggingly to the wagon, lifted it in. The dog followed, sniffing the drip of blood. They brought the other body, laid it in beside the first.

Red gathered up the dead men's hats and tossed them into the wagon, and the old man brought out a frayed blanket, spread it over the bodies.

"Son," said the old fellow, with a foot on the front wheel, ready to climb onto the seat, "I wouldn't argy with you. But I don't b'lieve Dave had anything to do with it. Why, him and young

Bill Clayton are clost friends. And young Bill, he orta give you the shirt offen his back, and the hide, too, if you had any use fer it, on account of how you he'ped his dad that day!"

"You tell Dave Gridger what I told you. You tell 'im I bet I got more bullets in my belt than he's got friends!"

As the wagon creaked off, with the old fellow hunched forward in the seat much like a scarecrow that had been brought from a cornfield and stuck up there, all bent over, Red mused, "'Pears like the real old fellers in this country are more all right than the young uns. 'Ceptin' the young women."

II

Red cantered west instead of north, riding through rough, timberless country that skirted the foothills.

It was not far from sundown when he came to the Clayton ranch house, a long, low building with a long veranda that had scarlet runner beans straggling up the posts. Two sycamores, twisted, gnarled veterans of many hot summers and hard winds, locked branches in a kind of affectionate friendship; and under their shade were two or three rough benches.

Bill Clayton was sitting there, his face sullenly masked. His eyes lifted again and again toward the open door of the house, which was as dim within as a cave.

He saw a rider coming with a flurry of dust drifting away from under the trot of a black horse, and he knew from afar that it was Red Clark.

Red pulled down to a walk, came up, stopped, waited from behind a steady look for Bill to speak. Bill stood up and said, "Howdy," in a level, dull voice, as if he wanted to see how Red would take it.

Red's voice was without inflection, returning, "Howdy."

"Light down. I want to have a talk."

Red turned the horse so that he would come out of the saddle facing Bill and dropped the reins, hit the ground. He hitched up his belts with pull of hands and waggle of slim body. "How's your father, Bill?"

"That joltin' was too much for 'im. He's bad off—expected to die. I tried to keep 'im from comin' home, but he just would! Mighty stubborn an' set. Come over here and set." That was a good deal of talking for Bill to do. He was secretive and sullen, nautrally; had grown more so of late.

Red went in under the sycamores and sat on a bench.

"Cigar?"

"No, thanks. I don't like cigars, unless I'm too drunk to taste 'em." Red pulled out tobacco and papers. He thought that Bill looked a good deal like his father, especially in build, but the son had a sullen shrewdness in his eyes that the father did not have, that no old-timer had.

Bill said, "Red, I figger that I owe you an apology."

With paper to his lips ready to be moistened by a tongue tip before the final roll, Red looked up. "Me, I figger the same."

"I listened to a lot of liars."

"More 'n listened. You believed 'em."

"I was upset over the old man gettin' shot that-away."

Red's match burned the tip of the cigarette. He shook out the match, broke the stick between his fingers. "An' also you sorta stuck up for Knox that day, too."

"I couldn't believe Knox meant to steal them cows."

"From what I hear, he stole Clayton cows, too—him an' Alvord an' some more. You've growed up in this country. Me, I'm a stranger. Funny, *you* never heard."

Bill pondered, masklike. "I never believed it. The old man accused 'em. But he never got on well with neighbors. Or his own men." Bill paused, looked fixedly at Red. "But now I'm changin' my mind. And I hear you used to be a foreman for the Dunham outfit?"

"Dunham had a dozen foremen."

"From what I hear, that's a hard-riding, hard-fighting bunch."

"Dunham sure wanted his wages earned."

Bill grinned friendlily and came over to the bench. He sat down, took out a fresh cigar, lit it thoughtfully, then leaned over, elbows to knees, turning his face toward Red. "Do you think that Knox and some more, maybe Dave, have pulled the wool over my eyes?"

Red cuffed the ground with a heel, studying. He looked up. "You heard me speak my piece about this Dave the night after your father was shot."

"I was all too upset to think straight."

"Yeah. An' you was some upset, too, that day I brought Knox into town, hogtied. You so much didn't like it that you waggled some fingers toward that gun of yourn."

Bill chewed awhile on the cigar, his face sullenly thoughtful. Red wasn't an easy fellow to talk to. Bill explained, "You were a stranger. I've known Dave and Knox a long time. I sided with them."

"What's made you change all of a sudden?"

Bill had the sort of face that is good at poker. Red had the sort of nature that made him a poor poker player. He always called; and outside of poker he called, too, liking a showdown. In the one case he had to have the cards to win; in the other, nerve.

"Maybe I have woke up," said Bill. "I've been

192

hinkin' and putting two and two together. Only 'ou have got to remember that even the Judge, vho is your friend, thought that you were wrong ıbout Dave."

Red grudgingly admitted, "That is right. But he eads so much po'try he don't know much about ıuman nature."

Bill nudged closer. "Red, how would you like o work for me when the old man dies?"

"Maybe he won't die."

"Yes, he will." Then Bill added, with a sad hake of head, "I'm afraid he hasn't got a chance. ['hat joltin' was too much. And he was doin' well n town, too. But he just made up his mind to :ome home. So how would you like to work for ne?"

"I got me a job."

"This is a big ranch, and you can boss it."

"I like to work for a man that bosses his own ·anch."

"You are working for a woman now that don't."

"She is all right. Why don't you boss your own ·anch?"

"I want to go away—go on a trip. I've always vanted to go to Europe—a place called Paris 've heard about."

"An' you want to leave *me* as the big boss?"

"That's right. That shows how much I've :hanged my mind about you."

"You," said Red simply, "are a damn fool."

"Why, how you mean?"

"I don't know this country. You've got men tha do. An' nobody is bein' sens'ble that goes off an leaves somebody else to run his ranch."

Bill looked at him steadily. "Are you tryin' t say you won't work for *me?*"

"Listen, you. That wasn't what I had in mind but since you brung it up, I'll say so. I'm cowhand an' a good un. I'm no cattleman. I ca boss a trail herd from here to hell, but I don't lik to dicker an' figger."

"But you were Dunham's range foreman weren't you?"

"My job was chasin' rustlers. I chased 'em, too You don't have to dicker with them! An' you'v been too good friends with Dave Gridger an' thi Knox not to know they are a bad lot. An' if yo didn't, you just ain't smart enough to be a goo man to work for."

Bill looked mad and got up. His face had th hot glow of too much blood rushing to his face and he glowered as if any little puff of an impuls would make him do something reckless.

Red spoke softly: "Don't be so much damn fool. For one thing, I'd purt-near, but not quite maybe, let you shoot me before I'd draw a gur with your father dyin' where he could hear. You asked me some questions, an' I give you some answers. Besides, you've got no business pickin a fight. You get too blind mad instead of keepin

194

ool. For another thing, you've got the wrong kind of a gun to draw real quick. You jerk at ivory grips, an' if your hand is sweaty, an' it is usual in this climate, you are liable to slip a little. An' a little slip of that kind will land you neck deep in hell fire!"

Bill spread his feet as if bracing himself and glowered. He looked mean and ready to do something; but there was an alert steadiness in Red's blue-eyed stare that was different than the look in the eyes of other men that Bill knew.

Red studied awhile, then went on in a thoughtful manner: "I can't see as there has been any call for you to get all het up unless you have been lyin' about not knowin' Dave an' Knox bein' worse than no good. An' if you have, you'd better go to town an' have a look at a couple of fellers I just met at the Springs on my way up here. Maybe they are friends of yourn, too. They was of Knox!"

Bill looked as if he wanted to ask Red what he meant, but looked also as if he were a little afraid of the answer. He glared for a moment or two, then threw down his cigar and walked off, going across toward the bunkhouse.

Red watched soberly, pulled at an ear, frowned, mystified.

III

Red went to the open door of the house and looked through, hesitated, then started in on tiptoes. That was out of respect for Mr Clayton who maybe was dying. A fat Indian woman waddled out of shadows and grunted at him.

"I wanta see Miss Clayton. Tell her Red Clark is here."

The stolid Indian stared, then grunted again. He followed her into a big room that had Indian blankets on the puncheon floor, skins and horns on the wall. There were three or four rocking chairs, and an organ in the corner. The room was dim and became dimmer as the sun sank.

Red sat down with his hands on his knees, his feet drawn awkwardly back along the rockers to brace himself so the chair wouldn't move. The chair squeaked when it rocked. He thought the Indian woman had forgotten to tell Miss Kate, but he sat patiently, not stirring.

Miss Kate came in looking tired and sad. She had a moist handkerchief crushed tightly in her hand. She smiled woefully and without a word took Red's hand, held it as if she liked him very much. He could feel that the handkerchief was as wet as if it had been just wrung out. She pressed her lips tightly, then sighs trembled in a long breath. "Daddy is dead. He just died."

Red cleared his throat, but he couldn't say anything. Kate kept hold of his hand, just as if she had forgotten that she held it, and pressed knuckles against her mouth. It was growing so dark that even the bright-colored patterns of the blankets under her feet lost their color.

"Red . . . almost the last thing he said was for me to trust you—Judge Trowbridge and you. It is strange that you came just as he died."

"How you mean, trust me?"

Kate turned to a window, still holding his hand. They heard a horse galloping. Bill Clayton went by the house. He was leaning forward in the saddle, and the horse was heading down the road over which Red had come.

"Where is he going? He doesn't know that Daddy is dead!"

Red didn't say anything.

Kate let his hand fall and put the handkerchief to her mouth. There was a square beam of evening light coming through the narrow, deep window. Red thought that she was the prettiest girl he had ever seen. He had thought that of lots of girls, but Kate was unlike the others. She was pretty and dainty and proud, yet very sweet to him.

Her long breath trembled in sighs. "Daddy left the ranch to Bill—and me." She was looking straight into the window's light; then she turned to see if Red understood something that was in her mind; but he did not. "Bill and I—" Kate stopped, shook her head. Red understood now.

"Take your half. Let 'im have his," Red advised.

"Oh, Red, if Daddy had stayed in town he would have been all right. The doctor said so. He is a wonderful doctor. But Bill kept saying that things were not being run out here as they ough to be, and Daddy insisted on being brought home. The doctor said that it was dangerous, but I know that Bill never realized that it would be the death of him!"

Red very solemnly said nothing as his face took on a studying look, with a frown tightening his brown forehead; then, impetuously, "Now you see here! You take your half of what's comin' an let him have his. But sell yours!"

"Why, Red?"

"I mean it."

"But I can't do that."

"You do it, quick. If Mr Clayton said you was to trust me, you'd better. I got more 'n a feelin'. I know."

"But, Red, you—you don't understand. I wouldn't say this to anybody else, b-but I can tell you—at least now that Daddy is gone. Bill has drifted into what is called a bad bunch. Oh, Red," she said earnestly, "Jim Kilco quarreled with that awful Mell Barber because for my sake he was trying to keep Bill straight. Daddy, of course, never knew. He never knew half the things that Bill did, but he knew that something was wrong. And Red, you don't, do you, think it is horrid of me to be *friendly* with Jim Kilco?"

"How you come to know 'im in the first place?"

"I met him when I was riding alone. I was really lost, but I didn't mind. I could have found my way back. You know how safe a woman is, always, in the West."

"You wasn't very safe in town that day when I rode in!"

"But they didn't mean to hurt *me!*"

Red said, "Um," feeling that he wasn't sure. "Is that city doctor still here?"

"Yes. Why?"

"I wanta borrer 'im. Somebody is hurt over at our place. You ain't told me yet why you can't sell your share."

Kate sat down in a rocker and put her hand wearily against her cheek. It was now dark in the room, but Red's eyes were accustomed to the gloom, and he looked at her steadily, as if he could see her clearly. "I don't like to talk," she said, and for a time it seemed that she would refuse to do so. Red stood patiently silent. Kate dropped her hand into her lap. "Jim told me that when Daddy died all of Bill's friends would be at him like vultures."

"It generally knowed that you would get half the ranch?"

"Oh yes. Yes. Why?"

"I'm just askin'. An' why'd his friends be at 'im?"

"They're bad friends. They know things about him."

"What kind of things?"

"I can't tell even you, Red. It wouldn't be right to Bill. But he has been what is called 'wild.' "

Red said, "Um." A long pause. "Then if Bill is smart he will hire him somebody as don't like his friends, an' Bill, he will go on a trip off som'ers—like to Europe, maybe. When the smoke has all cleared away, he can come back. Um?"

Kate stood up and took hold of him. "Will you come to work for us?"

"You sell out your share quick an' go on a trip your own self."

"Oh, I can't do that. I have lived most of my life in the East, but the West is like home to me."

"Won't be so much like home with Mr Clayton dead."

"That is true, but—"

"An' Jim Kilco can't take care of you!"

Kate stiffened haughtily, like an offended princess. "Red!"

"You don't need to get your dander up. When folks I like want my advice, they get it. Sometimes folks I don't like, too, when they don't want it."

"B-but why did you say that about J-Jim Kilco?"

" 'Cause he's an outlaw on the dodge. Not only s the law after 'im, but I bet his own men, too, on ccount of bein' in town that day an' not shootin' t me."

"Red! Red, you don't think anything dreadful vill happen to Jim?" The princess was, after all, merely a woman anxiously in love.

"We'll talk some more about him in a minute. Right now I'm tellin' you to sell your share, even t a low price. You can't run a cow ranch. Not ven half one!"

"Miss Alvord is running hers, isn't she?"

"No. Course not. An' besides, if that whole anch of hern was a handkerchief, it wouldn't e big enough to wipe your nose—or at least mine. She's just settin' there sleepin' behind lankets that are hung up for some of what s called privacy. She has got a crazy cook, a ouple of nice kids, an' a fool puncher of about ny size all drawin' bigger wages than they are vorth—even though the cook don't draw none! She don't belong to this country. Neither do ou."

"But, Red, I am not civilized at all. Really I'm iot! I am a wild, raving savage at heart. I must e, because I feel a bitter, exultant joy that you killed those men who murdered Daddy!"

"They was Kilco men."

201

"Oh, they weren't! They—Why, you know he didn't want Daddy killed!"

"I know it. But they was his men—with who he'd quarreled."

"Oh, Red, don't talk that way. You—have you seen him since?"

"Yesterday."

"Where? What did he say? How is he?"

All of Red's notions about breaking the news delicately flew out of his head, and he told her, "That's why I come to you about a doctor. He is bad hurt."

Kate gripped him; her fingers trembled. "Red!"

"He was hurt helpin' me in a fight up there in the hills. It is his leg. I took him to our ranch. Miss Jane—she knows who he is, 'cause I told her, on account of him helpin' me—wants him to get well an' not get caught. He needs a doctor. But if the doctor does any talkin' before folks they are liable to wonder who the wounded man is. So I come to you."

"I can't go home with you, Red. Not with Daddy in the house, dead." She turned around. The stolid Indian was bringing in a lighted lamp and put it on the table. When she had gone, Kate squeezed the handkerchief against her mouth, mumbled, "Badly hurt, Red?"

"Yes'm. He's got to have a doctor. One that will keep his mouth shut, too."

"Wait."

Red was left alone. He sat down, motionless, in the squeaky rocker. The yellow lamplight fell on his face and showed that his lean, weather-whipped features were tensely thoughtful. He was thinking about Bill Clayton.

Miss Kate came in with the doctor. He was a young, tired-looking man with a beard and bright, earnest eyes and a soft voice.

He gave Red a long, thin, delicate hand. "I am indeed glad to meet you, Red." The doctor looked gentle and not strong. He had on a low collar and a little black tie.

"Dr Mills will go with you, Red."

"You know where? I mean about him?"

"Miss Clayton has told me."

"Unless I know you won't talk, I'll have to carry him off som'ers else. How'll I know that?"

"May I offer you my promise, Red?"

Red studied for a while. "They is a big reward."

"Red!" Kate exclaimed and looked quickly to see if the doctor was offended.

"I got to know," said Red stubbornly.

"Red," the doctor told him and touched his own breast, "I have lately been so near to death myself that my sympathy is rather with condemned men."

Red understood that he had come West for his health—and felt better.

He and the doctor left the Clayton ranch about eight o'clock. They paused at Manning Springs.

No one was there, and Red did not tell him what had happened.

The moon came up. Dr Mills said that he was enjoying the ride; that he loved this country; that it was giving health back to him. The air was pleasantly cool, the scenery different than any he had seen, and the tangy smell of the pines was delightfully fragrant. He talked entertainingly of many things. Red got a glimpse of what education meant and wished that he had some.

A lamp threw its pale glow out of the ranch house doorway. Jane came to the door; hearing horses, called uneasily, "Red?"

The cook got up, shuffling barefooted. The two kids, young and tired, lay as if dead.

"Coffee," said Red to the cook. "An' lots of it. keep forgettin' to eat."

"And hot water, please," Dr Mills added.

He took Jane's hand and held it as if there were understanding between them, instantly Whatever he may have thought of dainty Kate Clayton's concern over an outlaw—and she had not admitted more than a humanitarian interest— he had not expected a woman of Jane Alvord's culture to be living in a ranch house with five men, one with a price on his head. And Jane recognized at once that this young doctor was the type of physician accustomed to the homes of cultured persons. The great weariness of her long, distressing vigil had done away with all trace of reserved old-maidishness. She was merely a young and very tired woman who had been nursing a feverish man with all the tenderness of a repressed woman who had found someone in great need of her.

Kilco raised himself on an elbow, stared suspiciously. He had a wounded outlaw's fierce distrust. Red said quietly, "Miss Kate sent him."

Kilco's body relaxed. He forced a smile that was half pain, half grimace, lifted a hand toward Jane. "She is all wore out, Doc. Give *her* something first."

The cook had shuffled to his end of the room and, by the light of a lantern on a shelf, was hacking kindling from a split pine chunk with a hatchet. Red hurried out to the doctor's horse and brought in saddlebags.

"Fortunately," said Dr Mills, "I brought surgical instruments."

"The pain is bad," Kilco told him, "but I'm more afraid of bein' crippled. Will I be?"

"He has suffered terribly and," Jane added, "bravely."

Red held up the lamp. Dr Mills studied Kilco's haggard face, then laid back the wet dressing and found Kilco's leg blue-bruised and red. The skin was swollen tight, as if about to burst.

"Some water, please—in a glass or cup," said the doctor. He was gentle and at ease, as if he knew exactly what to do.

Red gave the lamp to Jane and went for water. In passing the cook, who knelt before the stove and puffed at the flame, Red thumped his shoulders. "Better cook a whole cow an' make a tub of coffee. My appetite's the biggest thing about me."

The doctor took a bottle from his bag, held it to the light, pulled the cork and shook out some black pills. With the cup of water in his hand, he stooped to Kilco. "Take two of these, please."

Kilco raised on an elbow, obediently swallowed the pills with a sip of water.

"You will feel better in a few minutes."

In twenty minutes he was asleep.

"Opium," said Dr Mills. "And exhaustion."

An hour later the cook and Red and Jane and the doctor sat at the table, drinking coffee. Cook leaned forward gnomishly, corncob pipe dangling in his mouth. Red helped himself to sugar. The doctor was very grave. He did not say so, but they understood that Kilco was in danger of losing his life—or leg.

"Well, Doctor," Red told him, "you'd better be makin' a start."

Jane protested, vaguely shocked by Red's abruptness. She liked the doctor. "Red, how can you! He is tired and needs sleep."

"All true, but he ain't goin' to get it here. He's got to be down at the Springs by sunup.

If somebody knows he's been up here, folks'll wonder. People are awful nosy. I'll shake one of the boys outa his bunk an' send 'im along. We didn't bring a doctor up here to fix Kilco so he would be caught an' hung instead of merely dyin' on our hands, maybe."

It was plain to anybody, as Jane and the doctor parted, that they liked each other. "I shall try to arrange to come back soon. He needs attention," said the doctor. Jane stood wearily in the doorway and watched him ride off with Bobby. Red had the feeling that she was wondering how soon he would come riding back.

CHAPTER EIGHT

Mr Backman was sitting in the shadow of a rock near his cabin, with the rifle on his knee, and as soon as Red saw him he took off his hat. "Just so you won't have to waste a bullet, dad!"

The grizzly old fellow stood up and waved a welcoming hand.

Red got down, and they shook hands. "You been away, dad?"

"I went up in the mountains to get a bear." He called it "bar." "There is nothing like bear grease to keep your joints limber in the winter."

"Things has happened. I come to tell you . . ."

Red told the whole story, omitting only that Marshal Vickers was on Kilco's trail. When he finished there was a long silence. The old man twiddled with the bottom fringe on his buckskin shirt.

"I'm not agin law. Not much. But I don't need a sheriff and a judge to tell me who to like. I like Jim Kilco reasonably well. Jim is a bad enough fellow, I reckon, but I don't figger that he is mean. As for Katy Clayton—you would think to look at her that she had more sense than to be in love with a fellow like him.

"I don't know much about folks up in this country, on account of keepin' away from 'em.

I don't think much of that sheriff who com up here onct to ask me questions. I've skinne varmints I thought more of than Frank Knox. sca'cely know Bill Clayton by sight—and Dav Gridger only from seein' him a time 'r two i town. You and me sorta hit it off from the first So you are allus welcome. I like kids.

"Katy Clayton used to ride over here ever once in a while, and by some happenso Jin would ride in. She lied a little to old Clayton b sayin' she went to visit folks over yonder that ha girls, but she was allus careful to visit 'em so i wouldn't be a teetotal lie. She told me she wa tryin' to get Jim to give up bein' an outlaw an' h promised. Sure, he'd promise. A fellow like Jin would promise a girl like her purt-near anythin' Wouldn't you?"

Red grinned but wouldn't agree.

"I'll bet you," said Mr Backman, "that insid of two days Katy will be over for to visit he neighbor, this Miss Alvord." Backman laughed "To see Kilco."

II

Red put in most of the day riding, and whe he got back to the ranch it was late in the after noon. He was unsaddling outside the corral whe he looked around and saw three men comin through the timber, a quarter of a mile off befor hey could reach the clearing about the house. He stared long enough to be sure that he knew hem, and swore a lot as he jerked off the saddle, pulled the bridle and ran his horse into the corral.

As he ran to the house, he tried to think how in he world it would be possible to keep Marshal Vickers and those Wells, Fargo men out of it. If hey got inside—there was Jim Kilco; and Kilco would surely think he had been turned in for the reward.

Red lurched with a clattering stumble through he back door. Cook was kneading dough in a dishpan and turned, with dough stringing down from his fingers. "What bit you?"

"That Mr Vickers an' them two fellers is ridin' in for supper again!"

Cook stood open-mouthed, giving his head an owl-like twist to watch Red as he went on; then cook slowly followed, his hands held out from his body and dough stringing from widespread fingers.

Kilco had heard and, instantly suspicious, tried to sit up. His pain-sunken eyes glittered. "*Vickers!* You—goddamn you—you—"

"If I wanted to give you up, I wouldn't be purtendin' I didn't!"

"He's that marshal!" Kilco looked as if he were about to try to get out of the bunk, fight Red, be ready to fight Vickers.

Cook worked his hands to keep the stringy dough from dripping about the floor and peered through the front doorway. He faced about with a squeaky, "They are comin'!" as if anybody doubted Red.

"Give me a gun!" Kilco snarled. "I won't be taken!"

"You will be if you try to use a gun!"

Jane caught hold of Red. "Can't you keep them out of the house?"

"No'm! The minute we do, their suspicions'll be up like a fire in the wind!"

"You sold me out!" Kilco was half crazy with the pain from twisting about, and he had the fear that is never out of an outlaw's heart—the fear of pretended friends who want to make peace with the law; also get a reward.

He glared at Red murderously. "If it's the last thing I ever do, you—I'll kill you!"

Red cursed him. He cursed in a way that made Jane draw back and shudder. Red's words bit like flame: "You've rode with men you didn't trust so long you don't know about people that keep their word! You're a goddam liar yourself too, I bet, ever' time it gets you what you want Well, I ain't! Now, damn your soul, you do like I say or you'll be drug out of here an' hung! I ain't bein' your friend—I'm just payin' a debt An' if you don't do like I say, I'll lay a gun over your head an' keep you quiet so we can do it

212

You hear me? You cockeyed fool, if I wanted the money, I wouldn't rig up no shenanigan like purtendin' to have men just ride in. You gotta take some of them black pills so you'll lay quiet when me an' cook poke you over here behind the blankets of Miss Jane's bunk. They won't look there unless you start gruntin' an' groanin'!"

"I won't take pills! I want to know what's goin' on! Give me a gun so—"

"You won't get any gun, 'cause if anybody's goin' to get shot, I'd rather it'd be you than Mr Vickers. I'll hide you from him, but I'll kill anybody as tries to hurt 'im!"

Kilco glared, amazed and still suspicious. It was almost as if Red spoke a strange language; but there was a fierce honesty in Red that had to be trusted.

"You orta take pills, 'cause yankin' you over there'll purt-near tear you to pieces, an' if you squeak an' groan, you'll be caught!"

"I'll lay quiet," said Kilco, still distrustful but somehow submissive. Red, when aroused, was as fierce as any outlaw.

Red threw up the curtaining blankets on their rope, revealing some of Jane's garments hung on the wall above the bunk. They were white, frilly things that Red would have blushed to see at any other time.

"We got to hurry! Cook, you an' Jane get that

pan an' them rags outa sight! His boots, too. An that bottle of pills!"

Jane swooped at the bottle, thrust it down inside of her waist. "Oh, hurry!"

Red took hold of Kilco. "This is goin' to hurt."

"Hurt an' be damned! I'm trusting you." There was something almost distrustful in the way he said it.

"I can help," said Jane and reached out, no knowing just how to help lift a big, helpless man

"Cook, dough or no dough, you'll have to carry his good leg! Miss, you hold the other 'n. Now Kilco, put your arms up tight around my neck and hang on. It's goin' to be hard!"

Red heaved. Kilco groaned. He was a big man and all dead weight. Red was slender but rawhide-tough. Kilco had shattered nerves, and the pain was agonizing. He groaned between clenched teeth.

"Shut up!" Red snapped and gasped for breath himself.

They were staggering with Kilco clear of the bunk where he had been lying when the slow *trop trop trop* of horses were heard, then the halloo.

Red was overburdened with Kilco's weight. He held on desperately and tugged, staggered on the peg heels, and the long-shanked spurs jangled against the hard dirt floor. A cry escaped Kilco's clenched teeth. Cook said hopelessly, "Ow, God!" and stared at the doorway. They all staggered

214

near to Jane's bunk. Red breathed anxiously, expecting challenging voices from the doorway. He heard, or thought he heard, booted footsteps. Anxiety struck him like a blast of fear; and, with a desperate last heave from sweating, slipping hands, he got Kilco's shoulder on the edge of the bunk, roughly pushed Jane and the cook aside, gave Kilco a roll and hissed a warning: "Not a peep outa you!" then jerked down the blankets.

Red sucked in a deep breath, looked toward the doorway, knew that he heard footsteps now. He jumped at the cook, caught him by the hair and whispered savagely, "Come on, damn you! We got to make 'em think we're havin' a fight, else they'll be suspicious of how we are flustered!"

Cook put feeling into his response because the pull on his thin hair hurt. He smacked Red's face with a sticky palm. Jane nervously cried out and pressed clenched hands to her cheeks. To her this looked like real anger.

Shadows blocked the door as three men looked in. Cook was striking and scratching and swearing. Red, breathing hard, seemed to be getting the worst of it. The two Wells, Fargo men laughed. Jane backed up against the blanket curtains, instinctively putting herself between these strangers and the concealed outlaw. She looked frightened; she *was* frightened. Kilco was twisting about on the pine needles and gasping. She could hear him—feared the strangers, too,

would hear. But cook and Red were making a lo
of noise.

Cook had found that Red would not hit him
and that made it nice, particularly with the two
Wells, Fargo men looking on and speaking
approval. "I ain't scairt of you!" cook squalled
and came at Red with doughy fingers clawlike
"You ain't nothin' but just another stray cowboy
to me!" He had Red backing up, and cook yelled
like an Indian at a war dance.

Red smacked him hard with an open palm, and
cook shuffled back, reeled, lost his balance, and
sat down, hard.

Red looked around at Marshal Vickers, who
was not smiling, though the Wells, Fargo men
guffawed. "Just a little argyment," said Red
puffing. "Cooks get overimpydent sometimes."

The marshal took off his hat, stepped forward
He said, cool and stern, to Jane, "Miss Alvord, I
am United States Marshal Vickers. I have learned
that the outlaw, Jim Kilco, has been wounded
and is in hiding up near here somewhere. Do you
know anything about him?"

Jane flinched nervously. She could hear
thought she could hear, the pine needles rustling
and the heavy breathing behind the blankets. The
marshal looked almost as accusing as if he knew
that she knew. Jane caught her breath and reached
a hand behind her, gripped a blanket.

Red stepped between her and the marshal.

Dough and flour was on his face, on his clothes, in his hair; but, somehow, Red did not look ridiculous. He knew that Kilco was listening, that Kilco was fiercely suspicious even yet, and that if anything leaked out about Red having met the marshal and talked with him there in town, Kilco would never believe that he had not been betrayed.

Red spoke defiantly, "Kilco was hurt helpin' me in a fight, an' I hid 'im. I hid 'im good, too. I told her I did. I won't tell you where he is, an' you can't make me! Your job is to ride around an' find 'im if you can, but you don't need to try to scare her. For two reasons. One is, she won't care. An' the other 'n is, she ain't ever been more 'n three miles from this ranch, so how can he know where I carried Kilco off to an' fixed it up to have him tended an' fed?"

"And brought a doctor!" said the marshal sternly.

"You're right I did! I don't want anybody to die that I'm tryin' to help. An' I bet you the doctor wouldn't tell you where I brought 'im to, neither!"

"He was seen coming down from this way with that boy Bobby."

"An' Bobby, he will tell you when he rides in that I brought the doctor right here to this house, an' I roused Bobby up to show the doctor the way to the Springs. You-all just set down an' wait

217

for supper, an' when the kids ride in, you ask 'em!" Then Red grinned. "Though this shypoke of a blear-eyed cook'll have to pull some dough outa my hair to make up enough biscuits to feed comp'ny!"

"I think," said the marshal calmly, "as how we'll accept the invitation."

"That'll just be fine. I'll get out my comp'ny manners an' stop tellin' this cook some truths about himself. Only you'll have to put up you horses your own selves if you want 'em fed. I go to scrape myself rid of where I been touched by this cook."

The marshal gazed at Red as if somehow disappointed in him. "We'll put up our horses." The three of them went out, got into their saddles rode over to the stable.

As soon as they were out of hearing, the cook chortled and cut capers.

Jane protested: "Red, you shouldn't have asked them to stay!"

"If I hadn't, they'd suspicioned something." Red pulled the blanket aside. "This cook is lot smarter 'n he looks. We had to make that noise on account of bein' flustered an' breathin' hard. Kilco, now will you take them pills so you can be quiet easy?"

Kilco's face was wet with cold sweat drops and set so tense and hard that he looked as if he were trying not to cry. He gasped soundlessly and

odded. His hands gripped his hurt leg, then flew
way from the leg because it hurt more when he
ripped it; but he couldn't keep his hands away,
nd he couldn't keep his hands there.

Cook brought water, and Jane fished down
leep inside of her waist for the bottle of pills.
She rolled three out on her palm. Red took them
rom her hand, the cup of water from the cook.
Kilco opened his mouth wide, and Red put the
pills back on his tongue, then put an arm under
Kilco's head and raised it a little, holding the cup
o his mouth.

III

t grew dark, and Bobby and Pete had not
ome. The cook, still acting surly, was ready
o put supper on the table. Red had washed up,
hanged his shirt, and stood near the front door
s if wishing to join in the conversation, but the
narshal talked a little to Jane and ignored Red.
The Wells, Fargo men squatted outside and
numbled to each other, one as if he had a bad
old.

Jane was nervous, even jumpy, but she
ightened her muscles and did not show any
motion. It was hard for her not to look toward
he blankets that hung down before her bunk.

The marshal asked, "Isn't it lonely here for
ou?"

She said that it was, a little, sometimes. "But," moving a hand toward the blankets, "I do have privacy."

"Miss Alvord, it is a very serious offense to shelter an outlaw."

Jane flinched, because it was just as if he knew that Kilco was behind the blankets. Before she could answer, Red spoke up:

"It sure is! But before it can be so damn ser'us you've got to prove that he is bein' sheltered. All you got to go on so far is my word, an' maybe I'm a liar!"

The marshal frowned. "Red, you are playing with fire. I thought it mighty fine, the way you used your guns there in town. But someday you are liable to misuse them—then be an outlaw yourself." He went on staring at Red for a while then looked at his watch and began pretending that Red wasn't anywhere around by talking of other things to Jane. "I rode over today to attend Sam Clayton's funeral."

The kids came. They could see through the lighted doorway that company was in the house and rode up, piled off and came in, curious as pups. The marshal faced about solemnly, but before he spoke, Red whipped out:

"Bobby, you was seen ridin' with that doctor—"

"You keep still!" said the marshal.

Red didn't keep still: "—an' you know I had took that doctor to Kilco an' then—"

"Red!" The marshal's voice was stern.

Red went on as if he didn't hear: "—I had you show him the way to Manning Springs from here. So," Red added earnestly, "if now you know where I've got Kilco hid, why, you just up an' say so to the marshal here! An' I mean it!"

The two kids looked about the room. The lamplight carried to the bunk Kilco had been on, but they could see that he was not there. They looked at Jane, and her face was set anxiously. They looked over to where the cook held a long fork and had paused in dishing up steaks. The cook waggled his fork, and they understood they were to keep their mouths shut. They looked at the marshal.

Pete shook his head, and Bobby said, "Cross my heart, I don't know!" He was so mystified and sounded so truthful that the marshal believed him.

But the marshal was not in a good humor. He couldn't put his fingers on anything definite, but he sensed that Red was fooling him. He eyed Red sternly and said nothing.

The boys put up their horses, washed up and came into supper, which the others were already eating. The Wells, Fargo men ate heartily and said that the cook was as good a cook as he was a fighter. Jane wasn't hungry, but dabbed at her food as if eating. The marshal didn't have much of an appetite either; but Red did. He explained:

"I'm so afraid of rat poison when I eat alone. I don't get a good meal only when we have comp'ny, which is why I hope you-all come often."

Jane smiled cautiously and thought Red a wonder to joke and grin. The two kids ate solemnly, with their eyes on their plates, not saying a word.

After they had eaten, the marshal thanked Jane for the supper and said that he would be riding. Red sent the kids to saddle up for the marshal and his men, and when they came with the horses, the marshal turned to Red:

"You had better think over some more what you are doing."

Red told him in a low voice, "An' if Sam Clayton was my friend for thirty years, I would put in some time thinkin' about why he was killed!"

"Kilco's men killed him!"

"It was men Kilco had quarreled with that killed him!"

"Do you know why Sam was killed?"

"I think I do. Only you won't think so, I bet."

"Just how do you mean?"

"Come over here an' I'll tell you."

They walked off some fifty yards, and the marshal stood, tall and silent, listening to Red's suspicion that Sam Clayton had been killed at the instigation of his son and Dave Gridger.

He asked, cold and low-voiced, "Red, will you tell me something straight and true?"

"If I tell you a-tall, it'll be true."

"Do you believe what you've just said, or is it something you have made up to take my mind off Kilco?"

"Marshal—why you callin' yourself *marshal* now after keepin' it secret?"

"I found out that everybody knows. If Bill is like you say, he probably told. He learned from his father."

"I tell you solemn, I know Dave Gridger knowed that day what them men was up to while they waited for Mr Clayton to come out of the store. Then I've told you how Bill Clayton set here outside the house with his father dyin' an' lied about how he'd tried to get him not moved from town. An' he wanted me to work for him, knowin' I'd do my damnedest to kill off his *friends.* Yet just add things up an' see if it don't look like I say."

The marshal studied some more. "This is mighty confidential."

"Yes'r."

"I heard just the other day that Bill and Mell Barber had been seen together down near Poicoma. An officer hears lots of things that ain't so. I just put that down as one of 'em. Now you've made me wonder. If that is true, then you have guessed right."

"Who told you?"

"Dr Mills sent up word that a man who knows Bill and Mell both had told him they were together outside of town at a drinkin' place.

"But now, Red," he went on calmly, "I'm going to catch this Kilco. I'll get him, because I'm no goin' to quit until I do. And then I may arrest you for helpin' him. Most likely I will, because these Wells, Fargo boys are mad about how you have acted, and they will tell folks how you made a monkey out of me and the law, too. So that is understood between us?"

Red stuck out his hand. "I like for a man allus to do what he thinks is right—allus!"

When the marshal and his men rode off, Jane sank weakly to a stool and for a minute looked as if she were about to cry, her nerves were so jangled. Then she began to laugh, but it was almost as if she were laughing so as not to cry. The kids' eyes popped out when the cook told them to peek behind the Miss's blankets.

Red said, "Now we will all pitch in an' help this ornery cook wash his dishes. He is all wore out from his play-actin'—an' he sure done it good. Me an' him are goin' to stand watches so the Miss here can sleep. She is goin' to have to sleep in my bunk. We can't risk movin' Kilco back."

Jane smiled nervously. "It all seems so trivial now—privacy and such things as only a few days ago seemed *so* important. Things now seem o no importance at all that I used to believe were all-important! For instance, I know that it is shameless, but I think that I am even in love with your men!"

She looked from one to another, but longest at the two kids; and they all felt greatly pleased and a little embarrassed.

CHAPTER NINE

The following afternoon Kate came to the Lazy Z ranch, not by way of the Springs, but over the hills and into the valley, following shorter trails that were well worn because rustlers had used them.

Red and the kids found her by Kilco's bunk when they came in; and the kids thought that she was someone out of a picture book. They would loyally have denied that she was prettier than their own lady boss; at least if their lady boss also wore a divided buckskin skirt, and slim boots with dainty silver spurs that sparkled, and a fluttery blouse. Miss Kate, to them, looked like all Western girls ought to look, but she was the first they had ever seen that looked that way.

It was just about dark, and Kate did not want to leave; and Jane did not want her to leave; and Kilco did not want her to leave; and the kids did not want her to leave; but she said that she really had to get back, for it was growing dark and she had promised the servants that she would be home for supper—and here she was some fifteen miles away at suppertime.

Red rolled a cigarette. "You can't go alone."

"I came alone."

"Don't care."

"There are stars, the moon will be up, and I am not afraid!"

"Woman alone has no business traipsin' around Not at night. So don't argy. You're goin' to have comp'ny."

"Let me go!" said Bobby.

"Me too, Red!" Pete urged.

"Kilco here'll be cuttin' off your ears, you are showin' so much eagerness to be ridin' off with his girl!"

Kate blushed at that, pretended not to notice and argued: "There is no sense in making these boys spoil their night's sleep."

"You hear how they're beggin' to spoil it."

"I won't let them!" She tucked curls under her hat, slapped a boot with the quirt.

"Then I'll have to what you call spoil mine No woman rides alone just on account of some man not gettin' a little sleep. That's that, so don' argy." Red flung out a floppy hand. "You kids go saddle up."

They went with peg-heeled scamper.

"Come on out, you," said Red and took the cook by the neck. "We gotta talk."

Outdoors, he sat the cook on a log by the woodpile, sat down beside him.

"What you want, Red?"

"To get you outa the way, so they can say good-by—nice. Ain't you ever been in love?"

Jane came out into the shadows beside the

228

house and, by way of pretending to have something to do, started to pump a cup of water. Red got up and worked the pump for her. She stood and drank a little. She, too, was keeping out of the way.

"I like Miss Clayton." Jane somehow conveyed that she was a little surprised, as if ordinarily she did not like women.

"Me, too. But lots of people don't—so I hear tell. They think she is stuck up."

"I fail to see how they can think that. She kissed this dowdy, hard-faced old maid, Jane Alvord, as soon as we met!"

"You," said Red slowly, looking straight at her, though in the darkness she was dim, "ain't dowdy, you ain't hard-faced, you ain't old-maidish any more. An' if she'd been takin' good care of somebody you like as well as she likes him, you'd kiss her, too. I bet you'd purt-near kiss this old cook even!"

"Red, you are an awful person!"

"No, I ain't. I'm all right. If I wasn't, you wouldn't have me as your range boss."

"But do you really think she may not be safe in riding home at night?"

"If I did, I'd go myself."

A few minutes later Kate rode off, with Pete on one side and Bobby on the other. She set the pace, trotting at first to warm up the horses; then, as they got down into the valley, galloped.

Red, smoking a cigarette on a stump, could hear the hoofs vibrating muffled echoes in the night stillness.

II

The cook roused Red at four o'clock for breakfast. Cook got breakfast noiselessly so Jane could sleep on. The kids were not back yet. Red ate thoughtfully and figured. Three hours to go, three hours to come, and a couple more at most for fooling around in case they got lost, which wasn't likely; and they ought to be home.

There was much riding to do that day, particularly if he had to do it alone; so Red went off but he cut the day short in midafternoon and returned to the ranch.

Jane asked, "Have you seen the boys?"

Red said, "Oh, they piled off som'ers an' went to sleep. I know kids!"

Then he changed horses, took his black and started off along the trail. The tracks were easy to follow. He rode down through the valley, climbed into the barrens, and there among the scrub oaks along a worn, rutty trail he found the kids. They had been filled full of holes, their guns stolen, their horses taken.

Red got down in the lengthened afternoon shadows and bent over Bobby, who lay on his side with a cheek in the dust, as if wearily asleep.

His upturned nose had something impudent even yet in its look. Just a kid, full of fun and the hard-working willingness of an honest range-bred boy. Pete lay sprawled on his back, eyes partly open. His face seemed to retain the troubled, defiant look with which he must have faced the killers.

"You poor kids!" Red mumbled, with a sound as if praying, and squatted beside Pete, looked hazily at the ground, trying to think.

Had they been killed coming or going? Coming home, he thought, for who would shoot them down before a woman? And as the question formed itself, the answer slid right along with it: "Mell Barber would've!"

He stood up and walked about, as if looking for something lost in the dust, noting the marks in the dust, and wished for old Mr Backman's eyes and wisdom. He walked along, head down. His breathing deepened, his stomach felt a little sick. There had been four or five horsemen, and they had met the party, the boys and Kate. Red found where the horses had stood, trampling the ground, while they waited; and the bootprints of men and the cigarette butts.

He went on over the crest of the hill and stared out across the broken country that was Clayton range. The men had taken Kate and gone somewhere out there. It was too near sundown for him to follow the trail for any distance.

He had loved those kids; and he was about

as near to loving Kate Clayton as a man could without being in love.

Red squatted down and smoked solemnly with angry, hurt thoughts swirling about in his head. "Just spite," he said, meaning that the kids had been murdered cold-bloodedly. "They was waitin' for her," he guessed. "Knowed that she'd come."

He squinted grimly at the evening haze that was gathering in the distance and asked himself, "Bill Clayton?" and left the question hanging up unanswered. He said, "Knox?" and shook his head. As rotten mean as Knox was, why would he murder the kids he had eaten with, bunked with, never quarreled with? From somewhere deep inside of him a silent voice spoke up, "Because they knowed him?" Red absently brushed at a swarm of gnats. There had been four or five men in the party, all mean enough to hurt a woman. Up again jumped the name, "Mel Barber." Then Bill Clayton's name. The silent voice, just as if it were another person speaking, suggested, "Bill Clayton killed his father to get half the ranch. Wouldn't he kill Kate to get it all?"

Night came, and Red squatted solemnly, with a dead cigarette in his fingers, thinking. The boys had to be packed back to the ranch. That would mean tearing Jane's heart to pieces. She loved the kids. And the old cook loved them, too. Old

Backman would have to be told. Old Backman would take the trail.

Red stood up. His leg bones ached from long squatting. He rubbed at his knee hinges. Twilight had gone, and the stars were flittering in the clear blue-black, sky. It was just quite not light enough to see clearly. The very night silence had weight, and from far off was the soft breath-sound of wind in the trees. Somewhere, away off, a coyote yip-yipped with that peculiar ventriloquistic effect that made one coyote sound like a half-dozen scattered about on the hills. Red swore softly, again with the sound of praying.

It was then that he saw a blob of shadow move along a low, round hill below him. His eyes had a range-trained keenness. He could not quite see any outline, but he knew it was a horse, and his straining ears heard the clink of iron shoe on flinty pebbles; then another shadow appeared.

Two horsemen, riding in the darkness. Were they going to come up the trail where he was? They were not. They were angling south; and when they reached the top of the low, round hill they trotted as if pushing on purposefully.

Red did not know this country at all, but he knew that they were not heading toward the Clayton ranch house. He guessed right off that they were Clayton cowboys, scouring the hills for some trace of Kate. At least he knew that cowboys on any ranch where he had ever worked would be scouring the country, day and night and he was so sure that these were friendly persons that he ran to his horse, rode at a gallop out through the scrub, and raised his head in a long call of "Hi—O-o-o-o!"

The shadow blots that were riders reined up. One called in a thin, shrill scream, strangely anxious, "Who are you?"

"Red Clark of the Lazy Z!"

Such was his confidence that he had met with honest men who eagerly searched for the missing girl; but two red spurts whipped through the starlight; then another, and others, and rifle echoes pounded the hills.

"That," Red told himself fiercely, "is all I need to know!"

Firing upon him at the mention of his name seemed the same as confessing guiltily their part in the murder of the kids and the seizing of Kate Clayton.

With long reach of arm he drew the rifle from its scabbard. He knew that shooting from a running horse was foolish, at least for him; but he dropped the reins on the Devil's neck and rode on, firing at a gallop.

One of the horsemen plunged forward, running away, disappearing over the round hill, and faintly his shrill voice reached Red's ears. "Come on, Knox!" Then the second rider, who vould be Knox, disappeared over the hill.

Red threw up his rifle, jiggled the barrel back
nto the scabbard, pressed it home, and urged
his horse at a gallop down the rough slope, but
carefully gave him a steadying pull on the reins.

When he reached low ground, Red did not start
up the low hill before him. He turned, circling
t. The riders had been heading south when
hey went over the hill, and Red circled south,
knowing that he could make faster time the long
vay round and not tire his horse so much.

He laid his spurs almost gently in the black,
ean flanks, and the powerful horse buckled its
body with lunging bound on bound, and the reins
swung lax, for Red trusted the Devil's eyes and
slim feet. He lay low along the flying mane to
balance his weight and ease air pressure.

Red knew that if he could get those fellows out
nto open country he could ride them down. The
Dunham black breed were small-footed, sure-
footed and tireless. The horse sprang with nice
footing over small boulders, cleared hummocks,
hen with a bound that made Red feel the
muscles tense in powerful effort went across the
crumbling banks of a deep arroyo as if flying.
The hoofs struck gravel that crumbled, beat
with the pawing rapidity of drumsticks, holding
heir own in the rubble until they got an instant's
footing—then leaped on.

"Good boy!" said Red, stroking the sleek black

neck, and a moment later, again almost gently touched the flanks with blunted rowels, and the Devil swept around the foot of the hill. And there within a hundred yards or so, were the two men looking back over their shoulders, expecting the pursuing horseman, or horsemen rather—for the idea of Red alone giving chase was not yet clearly in their heads—to come down over the hill. By rounding it, Red had angled in almost upon them before they realized that the flying hoofs were not drumming softly on account of distance but because the horse was running over hard, grassy sand.

Both, with rifles in readiness, fired, but with no better luck than men bobbing in saddles usually have. Red had been in too many chases to waste many bullets at long range; but to let them know how ready he was to talk back, he drew a revolver, shot once or twice just to show what he meant.

The man in the lead had the better horse and was spurring hard with rifle upthrown to balance himself; and the man in the rear, falling farther behind, with Red's bullets singing about his ears, began to yell, "Knox! Knox!" It was a cry for help. He was pleading for Knox to pull up so that they could make a stand together. At that, Red whipped up the revolver, let go in Knox's general direction, and Knox leaned low and spurred harder.

The fellow in the rear had dropped his rifle and was laboring his horse, his face turned backward. The black Devil was rapidly coming up. The fellow suddenly jerked his horse aside as if to pull down and surrender, so as not to be shot out of the saddle. The frantic pull threw the running horse off balance, and it stumbled, fell as if horse and rider had been splattered on the ground.

Red straightened and, as he flashed by, fired twice and did not look back. His face was set toward the dim, flying shadow on ahead. It was Knox that he wanted.

Twice Knox turned in the saddle for snap shots and missed by a mile. It was too late now for Knox to pull down, pile out of the saddle, stand broadside to his horse and aim over the saddle. Red was thundering at his heels. Knox flung away his rifle, drew his revolver. Red prodded cautiously until he felt the muzzle of his empty revolver slip into the bobbing holster, then rammed it home. Then he crowded the Devil a little closer, drawing Knox's fire. *Crack! Crack!* Red smiled grimly, pulled the reins a bit; and Knox, evidently thinking he had scared Red, fired again and beat his horse in the desperate effort to hold the lead.

Soon Red was crowding him again, edging closer, well within pistolshot; but Knox seemed determined to save his last bullets for close quarters. Red yelled; it was like a panther's scream, and too much for Knox's nerves. He jerked about and fired again and again.

No man could reload on a galloping horse. Red had kept count. That emptied Knox's gun.

Red loosened his rope, straightened, flung out the limber rope and let it drag for a moment to make sure that all the kinks were cleared. Then he gathered it into slack coils in his left hand and shook out the loop and began swinging as he drove the spurs hard into the tender black flanks.

The Devil leaped with back-bending bound on bound. Red rose in his stirrups, let go with forward-thrusting swirl of arm, and the loop sailed ahead as accurately as pouncing hawk's claws, dropped over Knox's hunched body.

Instantly, Red spun a snub around the horn, jerked the reins with high lift of arm. The Devil, a champion roper, squatted haunches down, forefeet braced into a skitter that showered dust. The rope snapped taut, and Knox came backward out of the saddle as if thrown.

His horse galloped on a few yards, trotted, walked, then stopped, and put down its head, heaving for breath.

Red hit the ground running, just as if he had thrown a steer at some roundup doin's and was after first prize. The Devil sat back on his haunches, holding the rope taut.

Red poked Knox with a toe, not gently. Knox

was unconscious, perhaps with a broken neck. The fall had been enough to burst him wide open. Red had taken him out of the saddle with a rope instead of shooting him out of it because he wanted a live man, one that could talk about the dead boys and Kate Clayton. But if Knox were dead, it was no more than right and proper; and Red cared, but not very regretfully.

He reloaded the revolver he had emptied, all the while keeping a look about in the shadow-filled starlight just in the case the other fellow had escaped being badly hurt and wanted to come around and be troublesome. Then he rolled a cigarette and squatted patiently.

III

Knox began to squirm and groan as his hands struggled weakly. Red had laid the rope around him just below the shoulders, binding Knox's arms to his sides, and the Devil kept the rope tight with a steady backward pull.

Red dabbed out the cigarette on the ground. "Knox!"

Knox shook his head like a drunken man and rolled over. Instantly the horse, with backward shuffle of hoofs, took in the slack. Knox groaned, not yet fully conscious. It was bright enough for Red to have as good a look as he wanted at Knox's face. His hat was gone. His sleek black

hair was messed with dirt. There was a drip o
blood from Knox's nose.

"Where," said Red, "is Kate Clayton?"

Knox was a tough-bodied man, and frigh
helped bring him to his senses. His black eye
were snakelike in their steadiness, bright an
afraid.

"I don't know," said Knox sullenly.

Red pulled a gun. "Then I got no reason a-tal
for not killin' you!"

"An unarmed man!"

"Use up all your bullets missin' me, then cal
yourself unarmed? To hell with that kind of bein
unarmed, feller!"

Red fired. Knox's whole body jumped, mucl
as if he were bounced a little, as he cried out
frightened. The bullet had barely gone over him
Red said, "Shucks," and leveled the long-barrelec
gun again as if to take better aim.

"Don't! I'll tell you—tell—"

"Tell what?"

"About her!"

"You're such a liar you'd tell anything." Rec
was as conversational as if talking about branding
a calf, and as convincing. "Two or three times
now I ain't killed you when I orta, all of whicł
mistakes I figger need fixin' up."

Red cocked the .45 with twitch of thumb. Thɛ
muzzle was point-blank.

"Mell Barber got 'er!" Knox tried to sit up

ut the Devil pulled him down. " 'Fore God A'mighty, it's truth!" His tone was desperate.

"An' I s'pose," said Red coldly, "it was Mell Barber that killed my horse an' purt-near shot me h' other day up in the hills?"

Knox's lips worked hard; his voice was lesperate: "But it *was* Mell Barber and them that illed the kids last night and took her up to Joe Strumm's place!"

"Well, feller, you keep right on talkin' if you vant me not to question you some more about ayin' for me up in the hills."

Knox bent his head and moved a hand to wipe he blood trickle from his nose. It was a little as f he wanted time to think. Red didn't want him o have any time to think; and warned, "Talk fast, Knox! I'm in a hurry."

"I had nothin' to do with last night!"

"Liar!"

"I begged 'im not to! 'Fore God! And listen. oe Strumm an' me was being sent to town to tell hat Kilco is bad hurt over at your ranch so Dave Gridger and the sheriff could go catch him!"

"Who told you that?"

"Them kids!"

"You *are* a liar!"

"They did! That's truth! Mell guessed she'd ode over to meet Kilco and said he'd kill her if he didn't tell him where Kilco was, then Bobby ip and yelled out about Kilco!"

"Then why didn't you-all come a-rarin' over t[
our place to see if Kilco is there?"

"Mell had to hide her. He wouldn't leav
nobody else have her. He hates Kilco, and he'
all along wanted *her!* And," Knox said with
burst as if the words flew, "he hates you worse '
anybody!" The way he said it seemed expressin,
his own feelings, too.

"Don't he know that Clayton punchers'll fi[
him full of holes for touchin' a hair of her head?'

"Bill Clayton and him are in cahoots!"

"I said Clayton *punchers!*"

"They don't know nothin' about anything. Eve[
me, I didn't know till yesterday—"

Knox tried to make out that it was the noseblee[
trickling over his face and around his mouth tha[
made him shut up. He smeared his hand with a[
awkward swipe. His arms were tightly bound
held tight by the Devil's pull. He was taking tim[
to think.

"Untie me, will you? I'm bad hurt. Then I'[
tell you ever'thing I can."

"You're goin' to be worse hurt unless you tell!'

"Can we make a bargain, Red?"

"Me an' you don't bargain good."

"All I want is a chance to get out of the country
Then I'll tell you ever'thing. 'Fore God!"

"What you think you know that I don't—'cep[
how to get to Strumm's place?"

"I know," said Knox, mysterious and earnest

242

why Mell Barber and them shot old Sam Clayton hat day!"

"Sure. Bill Clayton put 'em up to it. Him an' our friend Gridger."

"How *you* know that?"

"I got eyes an' a nose, feller!" Then, savagely, Red asked, "Was it bargained for Mell Barber to ill her, too?"

"God A'mighty, no!" said Knox. Even he linched from such a thing. "But Mell wants ier—part to spite Kilco, part because she is urty, part because Bill will pay him in cows ind horses if he takes her off. Red," Knox vent on, almost as if talking to somebody vho was not unfriendly, "I will tell you, Bill Clayton his-self has helped us all steal Clayton ows so he could have spendin' money." Then, inxiously: "Are you goin' to give me a chance to eave the country? I want to quit. I've had—had nough!"

Red thought it over somberly.

"I'm a rustler," Knox admitted. "But I don't iurt women!"

Red grunted, thought some more; then: "Shut ip, tryin' to make yourself out as not bad some vays. You are ornery mean. But I will make you a bargain: You take me to where Mell Barber is vith his men—how many is with him?"

"Three fellers."

"You take me so they don't know I've come

till I get there. Then, if you ain't tried to be cute
I'll let you go. That there is a promise. But," Red
added solemnly, "this here is a promise, too: If
ever I catch you again, anywhere, I'll kill you.
Understand?"

"But you will let me go?"

"I'll do it."

Knox thought it over; then, with a trace of
sullen distrust: "How do I know you will?"

" 'Cause I said so. I do what I say. So don't you
try no cute tricks on me tonight about goin' to
Strumm's place. I'm in no mood to be monkeyed
with, as Mell Barber an' them are goin' to find
out."

"You—alone?"

Red glared, spoke solemnly: "Don't you think
old Sam Clayton an' them kids'll be ridin' right
along with me? *I do!*"

IV

Red took away Knox's revolver, went to his
saddle and unsnubbed the rope from the horn
and let Knox slip off the noose. Red got in the
saddle and trotted over to where Knox's horse
was standing. He rode up close and said, "Whoa,
boy," and laid rather than threw the loop about
the horse's neck.

He led the horse back and told Knox, "Uncinch
an' resaddle."

Knox unsaddled and turned the blankets, saddled again.

"Now give me the rope off your saddle."

Knox loosened the rope, tossed it down. Red pitched the loop back to him. "Fit this around your belly."

"I won't try to get away."

"You do like you're told."

Knox said, "All right." Then he said, "Now let's see here a minute, Red. I ain't goin' to say I like you any. But how they treated that girl and killed them kids—I liked them kids!"

Red was unimpressed. He knew how men with guns at their heads or ropes around their necks all of a sudden got themselves sentiments that they hoped fellows would admire. As far as Red was concerned, Knox was ornery-mean; and when Red's mind was made up, he wouldn't change it without a lot of big reasons. He asked, "How'd they kill 'em?"

Knox talked while they rode off together, leg to leg, as close as friends, but there was a noose about Knox's belly, and the rope was in Red's hand.

"Joe Strumm, at whose place we stayed, seen her ride over the hill yesterday, so Mell Barber and them—"

"With you along," said Red.

"—rode down to wait on the trail in the scrub oak for her to come back. Her and the kids come along in the dark and was covered before they knowed what was up. Mell Barber, he said, 'You tell me where Kilco is or I'll kill you!' She said 'I don't know.' That made Mell mad, and he hi her. Pete's gun had been took off him, but he jumped his horse right at Mell, and Mell sho 'im. Then Mell said to her, 'I'll shoot you next i you don't tell!' So Bobby, he up and yells abou Kilco bein' hurt at the Lazy Z ranch. Then Mell he made Bobby get off his horse and shot hin just to be mean."

Red growled far down in his throat. "With *yo* an' some more lookin' on!"

Knox acted as if he didn't hear. "There wa some talk about ridin' over to the ranch afte Kilco right then. Was old Backman there?"

"Why?"

"She said old Backman was there and stayin there to help take care of Kilco."

"An' though they was five of you, you drug your tails off between your legs! Didn't you know he would be on your trail?"

Knox said, "That is why we bunched some cows and drove 'em back and forth over the tracks to hide which way we went. Up at Strumm's place it was talked over today, and Strumm and me li out for town to tell Dave where Kilco is."

"Will somebody be on the watch at Strumm's place?"

"I ain't sure."

"Don't go hedgin'!"

"I *ain't* sure," Knox insisted. "All day we watched careful on account of thinkin' old Backman might've found them kids. Mell knows he can track like a 'Pachy. But how's anybody goin' to track in the dark? I would bet they ain't keepin' watch."

"You are bettin' your neck!"

"Then we'd better act like we thought they was lookin' out," Knox admitted.

"Does Bill Clayton know what has happened?"

"He don't, yet. He is most likely in town, drinkin'."

"Gettin' full an' havin' folks think it is from feelin' bad over his dad! Did he expect somethin' like it to happen?"

Knox studied a little, then sounded sour and earnest: "It was bargained for Mell to get rid of her. From what I guess, Mell was goin' to take her down to Mexico and marry her, then Bill was to pay him in horses and cows. But they hadn't dealt me in on the game him an' Dave and Mell is playin' for that ranch. All I know is how I heard Mell talkin' last night. That there is honest."

Red halfway believed, but did not think any the better of Knox because he believed; and he was very troubled by having to think. An idea had just come to him that was troublesome; it had to do with how pleased Dave Gridger and Bill Clayton were going to be if Mell Barber was killed.

When they were about halfway up the hogback from which Strumm's cabin overlooked the valley, Red said, "I think I'll leave you here."

"You are boss." Knox couldn't help sounding a little pleased.

"I'm goin' to use your saddle blanket to make some shoes for my horse. I'm goin' to tie you up an' leave you here. If it works out all right, when I come back I'll cut you loose an' let you go."

Red was not in the least ashamed to act carefully cautious in tying up a bad man, and he made Knox back up to a tree and put his arms behind him. He used the rope to wind it around Knox's feet and neck, too, fastening tight knots.

"I ain't doin' this to be mean," he explained. "I only want to make sure of knowin' where you are while I'm gone."

He unsaddled Knox's horse, spread out the heavy saddle blanket and with a sharp, long-bladed pocket-knife cut it into squares. He punched holes around the edges of the squares, took the buckskin thongs from Knox's saddle and threaded them into the holes he had punched.

Red lifted a forefoot of his horse, set it down on the square of blanket and drew the thong tight, pouchlike. "I know this is bunglesome," he explained to the Devil, "but you've got to go like on tiptoes. You click a shoe on a rock and I'd maybe be the one that got surprised."

The horse didn't like having his feet muffled

nd stamped and kicked a little; but Red was
entle and led the horse a little way so that he
vould get used to having his feet muffled. Then
Red mounted.

The trail was easy to follow, although the
scrub oak was thick. Where it began to thin,
pines stood up. The horse, unsure of its footing,
went cautiously, but Red was patient. Also very
thoughtful. He was troubled by how pleased Bill
Clayton and Dave Gridger would be if he killed
Mell Barber, yet the idea of not killing him was
contrary to all of Red's ideas and instincts.

The horse moved on with slow, nearly noiseless
plodding. Red kept his eyes focused on the
horse's head, watching for the sensitive outtilted
thrust of ears. He could not see very clearly in the
shadows, so he leaned forward. The Devil, being
a high-spirited horse, poked his ears inquiringly
every few steps; then, understanding that it
wasn't anything of interest, let them droop as if
moodily disgusted.

The Devil's ears went out, the head lifted, and
he stopped for a moment; then with slow unsure
steps went on, with ears still out.

That seemed the signal that Red had been
waiting for, so he said, "Whoa," softly. He
let himself down out of the saddle and stood
listening. There was no sound but the murmur
of a gentle night wind in the treetops. Red
unbuckled his spurs and hung them over the

horn, then quietly led the horse to one side of th
trail.

He reached for his rifle, but the hand fell away
empty. A rifle was troublesome, and this woul
be close work.

CHAPTER TEN

Red went forward along the trail, keeping on tiptoes as well as he could, peering intently and not at ease. Somebody might be near, silently waiting. He judged that it was near midnight, not much after if at all.

He saw a light dimly; and, edging around a turn in the trail, saw that the light came through a doorway. It was a strong light as if from a big lamp in a small room. There was the black outline of a man in the doorway. He stood looking out, shoulder against the door jamb. Every detail of shadow outline was clear, even the dog-ear flaps of his boots, the tousled tufts of his bare head. He was a tall, slim fellow, and the curved butt of his gun stuck out, low on his thigh. A dull glow brightened at his mouth as he inhaled on a cigarette.

Red, a hundred feet or more away, crouched low and was aware of an indistinct mumble inside the house. He would have to wait until the man went inside the room before he could move safely to where there was a view through the door. Three men, Knox had said. Red slowly began to suspect that Knox was a liar. It seemed that there were many voices inside the cabin. The fellow in the doorway finished his cigarette and gave it a careless flip, showering tiny spark as it struck against a rock. He turned, restin the other shoulder against the door and facin inside.

Red hesitated to stir. High-heeled boots wer awkward for stealthy movements; and if he trie to get around to the front of the door he might b seen. Pine needles were brittle, and twigs cracke under even light steps. He sat down cautiously crossed a leg, began to pull at a boot. If h couldn't risk making his way so as to see throug] the doorway, he could slip through the shadow to the other side of the cabin.

Another man came near the door. He wa shorter, broader, and without his face being seen gave the impression of being older. Red hear his voice, not his words. It was a rough, gratin; voice; and the tall man laughed with a sharp crackling sound.

Red thought, "Things ain't goin' to be so funn soon, maybe."

The shorter man moved restlessly, passin; from sight. The tall man stood with his back t the door. A mumble-grumble murmuring wa going on in the room. The few clear words wer oaths. Voices sounded discontented rather tha angered.

Red moved sideways, with slow groping o hands on the ground and stealthy shifting of feet keeping his face toward the doorway. There wa some faint rustle in every movement, and the rustle sounded very loud to his ears. The man turned in the doorway, looking out. Red drew a gun and lay low. The man evidently was thinking rather than listening. He spoke, and what he said was clearly heard, because he talked without facing those within the room:

"I think you're plumb loco, Mell. I never yet heard of a feller makin' a woman like 'im by hog-tyin' 'er!"

Laughter answered. There was more laughter than from two mouths—meaning there were more than three men in the cabin. The next voice must have been near the door. Red could not see the man's shadow, but he heard the voice:

"She shore left her mark on Mell!"

Again laughter, and a sharp voice said confidently, "Never yet seen the woman I couldn't tame! She'll be eatin' outa my hand purty soon."

Then the tones fell again to the mumble-grumble, inaudible.

Red moved on, feeling that he must know where Kate was before he broke in on these men. When he was halfway around the house he saw a ghost-dim glow through another doorway, knew that it was lighted by a candle. He came up close to the windowless wall of the cabin and felt his way around the corner.

Here was a rickety lean-to room that had been added to the cabin, probably to give more bunk space to fellows that rode in for rest and news probably had been added after the owner of the cabin became the friend of outlaws.

Red reached the lean-to doorway and crouched. A thick candle stood upright on a smear of tallow on a ledge made of a split log that had been braced against the wall of the cabin on which the lean-to rested. The candle flame was smoky and bad-smelling. The room had a sour odor, as if slept in by sweaty men who never washed. The dirt floor was not even beaten earth, but dirty with loose trash and dust. There was a wide bunk on each side. In a corner were empty whisky bottles. There was no window and only one door. To enter the lean-to from the cabin, it was necessary to come around outdoors.

Red rose slowly and stood in the doorway with finger to lips.

Kate lay huddled on the dirty-looking blankets of a bunk and gave a start at seeing him. She twisted about, half sitting up, and looked as if she could not believe what she saw. The smelly candle did not give much light to see by. She was sick with worry and fear and had been through terrible experiences, so now she felt unsure of what was fancy and what was real.

Red came in barefooted on tiptoes, opening his pocketknife. Her ankles were tied, and her hands were bound behind her. He thought that her face was dirty, but when he bent close to reach behind her to cut the rope on her wrists, he saw that her cheek was bruised. Kate gasped as if to cry out joyfully, but closed her mouth. Her eyes were feverishly bright, and it hurt him to see how pathetic she looked in smiling. She didn't feel like smiling, yet she bravely wanted to smile at him.

He cut the rope about her wrists. They had been tied so hard that the rope marks were in the flesh, and she held her hands stiff and lifelessly, as if they were frozen. Kate sat with her loosened feet hanging over the bunk and looked up at him, her face haggardly drawn, and the bruise was like a smear of dirt on her cheek.

Red touched the bruise with tip of forefinger, jerked his head toward the cabin wall. Kate nodded.

He helped her to stand, but her legs were cramped, and the muscles responded so clumsily that she tottered. He put his arm about her, lifted her, and went out slowly for fear of stumbling in the darkness outside the room. Over near the corral that was directly behind the lean-to, he put her down. The horses stirred.

When he set her feet on the ground she took hold of his shoulders with fingers that would not grip. They were still too stiff. "Red, did you come alone?" she asked.

"Um."

"What are you going to do?"

255

"What I orta do." He sounded almost sullen.

"Don't! Please, Red! There are too many, and i anything happens to you—"

"You shut up. They killed the kids. They hi you. Only I want that Mell Barber alive so, by God, he'll talk!"

"Red!"

"Yes'm?"

"T-then you know? Know about him and—and *Bill?*"

"Yes'm. How many is they?"

"Four. One rode in this evening. And Red, they have sent Joe Strumm and Frank Knox into town to tell people that Jim Kilco is wounded over a your ranch!"

"I know. I've got Knox tied up down on the trail, an' that Strumm feller is afoot som'ers down on the flat—if he ain't dead. Does tha Barber feller come in once in a while to see you there?"

"Yes, the beast!"

"Then you set right over here, an' stay set. I'l lay for him. I'll wait till he comes if it's mornin' When I want something bad as I want him, I ge it!"

"Red, please! Can't we get away?"

"No'm. I come to get you loose. You are loose So other things have got to be done next."

"But, Red!"

"Yes'm?"

"D-don't be foolish!"

"I ain't bein'."

"But four terrible men, Red!"

He spoke simply, with conviction: "Somehow I feel that old Sam an' them kids are lookin' on—waitin'!"

Kate put her arms about his neck and murmured, "I understand, Red. I'm sorry I am—am a coward!"

"You ain't got nothin' coward-shaped in you. You are just all wore out an' hurt. You just set till an' don't you peep!"

II

Red went back into the lean-to and stood beside the door. He looked toward the bunk where Kate had been. The candlelight was very dim, but Barber might guess right away that she had gone. He quickly bunched up the blankets in a way that faintly resembled the outline of someone lying down, then went back to the side of the door, standing off a little, so that Barber would have to look well to one side to see him.

Red simply waited, waited doggedly. His mind was made up. This seemed the thing to do, and do it he would. Time dragged. He knew that fifteen minutes must seem an hour long or more, but he kept waiting. Only the vaguest of voice sounds reached him at times, until he heard a voice call,

"But if you loosen her hands, you'll come back more scratched 'n you are!"

Red stooped a little, with a drawn gun in his hand. Footsteps, dragging rowels came near. The man stopped outside the lean-to door, looking in. Red was afraid that he was going to back up suspiciously. Mell Barber said, "Asleep, heh?" as if finding her asleep was unexpected.

He came in, stooping slightly at the doorway because of his high-crowned hat that was pushed back on his head. The white scar on his hatchet thin face was conspicuous. He needed a shave and the beard would not grow on the scar surface. Also there were fresh red scratches on one side of his nose. The smell of whisky was as strong as if he had been pouring it down his neck, but he wasn't drunk. Heel-and-rowel drag scuffed the dust.

Some stir of Red's movement, or some warning sense of his near presence, made Mell Barber look around with bright, squinty peering. It was dim, but he saw the lean, lithe shape not more than an arm's length away swing at him just about as the lashing heel of a mule would have swung. He gulped a vague "Ow!" and tried to jerk himself back, a hand going gunward as he bent sideways to dodge.

Red struck, not overhand, because the roof was too low, but with a rising, sidelong swing. The long-barreled .45 had started on about a level vith Red's knee. It curved up at arm's length, apped Barber's shoulder, smacked alongside his ead. Red gave the gun barrel all of his weight, utting fury into the blow. He wanted Mell 3arber alive, but struck as if to kill him.

Barber threw back his head—just about as if icked by the mule. He teetered on loose knees nd went down as limply as a wet sack, pressing is face in the dust. There had been no sound xcept his muffled, astounded grunt and the snap f gun steel alongside Barber's head.

Red slapped the gun into its holster and crambled along the rumpled blankets where Kate had been for the pieces of rope that he had ut from her wrists and feet. He was not afraid hat Barber might come to, but just wanted to e sure. He yanked Barber's wrists up behind im. The wrists and hands were small and slim or a man. Red clenched his teeth as he drew the nots, remembering the marks on Kate's wrists. He bound Barber's legs, then took off the dust-meared handkerchief from Barber's neck, gave t a shake, spreading it. When it was folded ornerwise he pushed it between Barber's loose aws and knotted it behind his head.

Red stood up, brushed his hands together, idding them of dust, hitched at his belts, gave is hat a yank to tighten it on his head. As he tepped out of the lean-to his heart jumped and a and flashed at his hip, but it was only Kate.

"I just had to see!" she murmured, touching him. There was praise in her low voice.

He gave her a shove that was not gentle. "You get back over yonder an' stay. I ain't half done!" He went on around the house, hurrying noiselessly on bootless feet.

III

There was a large, rusty tin lamp on the table near the center of the room. The lamp had round wick and a new, clean chimney. The blaze of the lamp smeared the ground outside the cabin door.

Red stepped into the lighted doorway, appearing as noiselessly as a shadow. His right leg, advanced a little, was bent at the knee, quite as if he were about to jump into the room. One gun was leveled breast high; the other had its muzzle up at the edge of the holster. The three men saw him at the same time and were completely motionless with surprise. The thought in each man's head was that Red was not alone. They imagined that armed men stood in the darkness behind him.

"All right, you fellers!" he snapped. "Do something!"

The tall man who had loitered in the doorway was sitting with hands on his knees and a tin cup in one hand. His hand opened, the tin cup

260

ell. Whisky splattered on the floor, making a dark wet spot by his feet. The shorter man had a week's beard on his jaws. His small, black eyes popped wide, looking like two burnt holes in a blanket, and his bristly lips opened, as if it were hard for him to breathe. Very slowly, with little hesitant jerks, he raised his hands, getting them higher and higher.

The third man sat at the rough table. He held a cigarette half lifted to his mouth. His hat was off. He had a bushy head and straggling tangles of hair down along the back of his neck. He was a bull-like sort of man, bulgingly muscular, with hard, bright eyes, a thick nose, thick lips. He wore a spotted fawn-skin vest from which much of the hair had been rubbed away, as if moth-eaten. He stared at Red, stared past Red as if trying to see other men, stared again at Red. His voice was low and harsh: "Who the hell?"

Red did not answer. He clicked back the hammer of the leveled gun, took his thumb from the spur.

The bristle-faced man, who already had his hands up, blurted: "W-where's Mell?"

"Hog-tied!" said Red.

The tall man who had dropped the cup looked furtively aside. He saw that Bristle Face already had his hands well up, saw that the bull-like man was lifting the hand that held the cigarette, then he, too, put his hands shoulder high and sa[t] rigidly as if with a stiff neck.

"Who are you?" the bull-necked man asked in [a] kind of calm, cautious tone.

"Red Clark!" And having spoken, Red's weak ness for talking loosened his tongue a little. Measly lot of bad men, you! You like to kill You killed them two kids! Why don't you try i[t] now? Turnin' up your bellies like a lot of dyin[g] snakes!"

Then, from the darkness beside the doorway Kate Clayton cried:

"Oh, here is Mr Backman, Red!"

Kate's voice and its nearness gave Red [a] start; and he half turned to greet the tall ol[d] frontiersman whose presence was welcome.

Within the cabin a muffled blow brought [a] swirl of vanishing light as the bull-necked ma[n] with upward sweep of muscular arm struck th[e] lamp from the table, and the lamp flew into th[e] air. The blow had jarred off the chimney, an[d] it shattered on the table. The rough wick wa[s] smothered as if blown out by a breath. The ti[n] lamp crashed against the wall, thudded to th[e] floor. Before it struck the floor there was lurc[h] and scramble, a wordless yipping as the thre[e] fellows jumped, changing position so Re[d] wouldn't know where to shoot at them. Flame laced the darkness with crisscross flashes. The smoky jar of rapid gunfire in the small room wa[s] leafening. Kate gave a shrill, agonized scream.

Red had fired twice between the time the hurled lamp hit the log wall and dropped to the dirt floor; then he moved with quick, barefooted jump to one side of the door. The darkness was smokily dense in the cabin. Dagger-pointed flames stabbed at one another rapidly. Voices, unaware of speaking, yelled. Then there was the floundering beat of badly hurt bodies on the floor, oaths, groans.

Ten seconds—scarcely more—passed, and silence, except for one hoarse voice rattling in labored breath. Ten seconds more of silence, and Kate's low voice begged:

"Red? Oh, Red?"

Red moved to the doorway, stepped outside. "I'll be damned," he said in a low, awed voice.

"Red! Are you hurt?"

"Me? No. But I'll be a—Where is Mr Backman?"

Kate took hold of him. It was almost as dead black outdoors here under the thick tops of the pines as in the cabin. Her fingers groped quickly for Red's collar, and her face was very close. She murmured humbly, "I thought—you—alone—I thought if they believed that Mr Backman—Oh, Red, you aren't hurt?"

"So you just said that? All right. It's all right. Funny, though." He sounded a little bewildered. "I just shot twict, then jumped quick off to one

side. Then—then they killed 'emselves. They
was bad scairt. They shot at who was shootin'."
Pause. Then, soft and solemn, he said, "Make
me feel funny—like maybe old Sam an' the kid
was in there!"

IV

Red went into the lean-to for the candle. He
stooped with it and saw that Mell Barber's eyes
were open in a kind of unfocused stare, not yet
quite conscious. Red pinched the candle wick,
breaking off the crust and, holding a palm before
the flame, went back to the cabin. The hoarse
breathing had stopped.

"Oh, be careful!" Kate urged. Red carried the
candle from one dead man to the other, then put
it on the table.

He figured that at least one of his two rapid
shots had hit the bull-like man in the breast and
knocked him over. Being a tough fellow, he had
begun to shoot, but was too dazed to know where
he was shooting, and had fired at flame-flashes.
So the shooting was all mixed up. Anyhow, Red
had fired but two times, and three men were
dead, and some had been hit more than once.

"I'm goin' to leave 'em lay," he said, holding
the candle in one hand as he pulled the rickety
cabin door to. "I've got to get Mell Barber down
to our house, then into town. I've got to get the

ids took care of proper. I've got to get you home to your ranch—"

"No, Red. No. I can't go home. I won't. I can't meet Bill again, ever. I have always tried to like Bill. I felt sorry for him because I thought Daddy was hard on him. But now I hate him! I more than hate him! The very name and memory of him is loathsome!"

"How it come you know?"

"Mell Barber, the beast! He was to take me to Mexico as his wife and Bill would pay him, but —I can't talk of it."

" 'Course not. Here." He gave her the candle and rolled a cigarette, put the tip of it to candle flame. He blew smoke at the candle, watched the smoke. "Mell Barber's goin' to talk. I want the judge an' Marshal Vickers to hear 'im. But I been thinkin'. Nobody is liable to believe 'im. Bill an' Dave Gridger'll lie like hell. Things'll work out somehow, 'cause they got to."

Red searched for his boots, took off his socks, shook out the dust as well as he could. He felt better as he stamped his feet down into the snug leather.

He saddled two horses, put ropes on two more and turned the others loose from the corral. Then he went for Mell Barber.

Barber had squirmed about in the dust until he was covered and almost choked. The dust clung to the moisture of the handkerchief between his

jaws and was like—*was*—mud. He had a welt o
the side of his head that was as big as a long egg
and one whole side of his face was swollen. Hi
small, mean eyes were full of hate, but also c
fear.

As soon as Red removed the handkerchie
Barber gasped, "Water!"

Red brought in a rusty tin dipper full of wate
held it to Barber's mouth. Barber swished wate
about, washing out his mouth, then drank a few
swallows. Red pitched the dipper aside.

Barber said, "For God's sake, loosen up th
ropes on my wrists. It's killin' me!" He writhe
to show how much he was in pain.

"Get on your feet, Barber. We're ridin'!"

"You're proud, ain't you, to be takin' me i
alive!"

"Nope. But if I took you in dead, Dave Gridge
an' Bill Clayton would be too happy. They coul
go on bein' thought nice, honest fellers—lik
they will be if you let yourself be hung withou
tellin' the truth. Come along!"

Barber gave Red a squinty stare. He said, "
won't never be hung!" and seemed to believe it.

Red met the squinty stare steadily, shook hi
head. "*They* won't help you get away, feller. *The*
want you dead. If you keep your mouth shut an
stay alive, they'd have to whack with you. S
they'd rather you died. An' you sure will. Yo
murdered them kids, an' Kate Clayton saw you

266

So even if you try to say Bill an' Dave put you up to killin' old Sam, they'll just call you a liar an' help hang you quick. I'm only takin' you in alive just to spite them!"

V

Red, on foot, led his little cavalcade down the trail. Kate was in a saddle. Barber, with hands bound, his feet hobbled, and two unsaddled horses on ropes, followed.

When they reached the Devil, Red cut the pieces of saddle blanket from the horse's feet, then half furtively rubbed the Devil's nose with his cheek. He fastened on his spurs and got into the saddle.

A mile or so farther down the trail he stopped again to see about Knox; but Knox was gone, Knox's horse was gone. Red said to himself, "This is funny." He groped about the tree where he had tied Knox and picked up pieces of rope. A match flare showed that the rope had been cut. Somebody had come along the trail; Knox had called out and found a friend. Red guessed that most likely it had been Joe Strumm. If so, Knox had evidently advised him not to go on.

"I promised 'im he could go," Red reflected. "And he's gone. So all is square—till we meet again."

When they came down off the hill, the moon

was up and the country had a look as if covere
lightly with snow. Kate rode beside Red, an
she did not say anything at all as they cantere
along until they came to the trail, much used b
rustlers, that wound up to the scrub oak; ther
softly: "That is why you brought the spare horses
Red?"

"Yes'm."

Kate began to cry a little, and she didn't try no
to cry. She was a pretty delicate-seeming girl, an
had been through hell. Her nerves were all tor
to pieces. When the horses slowed to a climbin
walk, she said, "They were so brave, Red."

"Yes'm."

"He killed them in cold blood!"

"Yes'm."

"He won't—won't escape hanging, will he?"

"If he does, I'll shoot 'im."

When they came to where Red had found th
bodies, he got down. Kate dismounted, too. Th
moonlight came down to the scrub oaks, foun
openings, and laid bright splotches on the groun
among the deep shadows. Red stooped low
moved slowly, frowned as if something wer
wrong with his eyes.

"Bobby was right here in the dust."

Bobby was not there now. Red sheltered
match flame and scrutinized the dust. Ther
was the plain impress of where Bobby's bod
had been. Red got down on his knees and struc

nother match, hovered close to the ground, then
hook out the match and got up.

"It's all right, Miss Kate," he said. "We'll be
idin'."

He had seen the imprint of long, moccasined
eet.

VI

t was sunup when the little cavalcade wound
lowly up from the valley and, keeping to a walk,
ame before the ranch house and stopped.

Mr Backman was standing there with his rifle
n his arm, his long beard flowing down his
reast; and he was so still that the buckskin fringe
f his shirt did not move. He scarcely looked at
Red, scarcely looked at Kate, but looked steadily
t the dust-covered, badly battered Mell Barber.

Jane's face was all tearstained, and her eyes
vere swollen. Kate jumped from the saddle, and
hey put their arms about each other and began
o cry. Together, still holding to each other, they
vent into the house.

The frowzy cook stood slope-shouldered,
vith his hands in his pockets and the corners of
is mouth dragged down. He looked sick. His
leary eyes peered inquiringly at Red, who sat
notionlessly in the saddle, hands on the horn,
vaiting for old Mr Backman to speak.

Mr Backman spoke: "That him, Red?"

"Him, dad."

"Why you brung him *alive?*"

"So we could hang Dave Gridger an' anothe feller, too!"

Mr Backman nodded gravely, not quite under standing, but willing to accept Red's judgment.

Red left Barber under the old frontiersman' eyes and took the horses to the stable, method ically watered them, pitched hay into the manger and grain into the feedbox for the Devil. H returned to the house the back way, took off hi hat and shirt, pumped a panful of water, used th strong lye soap and scrubbed head, arms, breas and face. The water was pleasantly cool.

Cook brought out a clean towel and sat or the end of the wash bench until Red was read for it. Cook said, jerking his head, "They ain' spoke, but Kilco looks like he will bite him to death!"

Red wiped himself as if scrubbing, spok through folds of the towel as he wiped his face "Bring me a clean shirt an' some socks, wil you?"

Cook looked at Red and did not move for long minute or two. "Miss Kate has told what all you done." He got up, awkwardly shuffle to Red, stuck out his hand. Without a word the shook hands, then the cook went in to find th clean shirt and socks in Red's war bag.

When he came out, Red was sitting on a

verturned bucket, washing his feet. "Fact is," he
aid, "I'm hungry."

"You'll be fed, son." The cook paused; then, in
mumble, as if a little ashamed of deep feelings:
I'd steal from a blind widder lady to make you
apjacks, any time!"

Red slipped on his boots, combed his hair
efore the broken mirror with the snaggle-toothed
ld horn comb. "Have Mr Backman bring Barber
ut here to wash up. Get him one of my shirts."

Cook scowled with tight pucker of brow. "*Yore*
hirts! But all right, if you say so."

Barber came out ahead of Mr Backman, who
ooked questioningly at Red.

"Dad, it's thisaway: I'm fixin' to take him right
long into town. In town he is goin' to talk or he
in't. He thinks he ain't. He thinks Dave Gridger
n' Bill Clayton an' maybe that rabbit-faced
heriff is goin' to get him away. But they ain't!
hey are goin' to want him hung. Well, a man
as a right to wash up an' change his shirt before
e is hung."

Red could not untie the knots on Barber's
vrists, so he cut the rope. Barber's wrists and
ands were numb. He rubbed them up and down
or a long time on his pants legs to bring back the
lood.

Mr Backman stroked his beard. "I come over
or a little visit last night, and when I heard about
he boys not comin' back, and you bein' gone, I

set out on horseback to foller. I found their bodie and saw you'd been there and gone on. I'd'v had to wait till mornin' anyhow to trail you, so come back."

Barber washed himself slowly, listening. Th cook was stirring up a breakfast. Red squatte on a piece of unsplit stovewood and gouge at his fingernails with a pocketknife blade Mr Backman was close to the wall, but he di not lean against it. His shoulders did not nee support.

"Son," he suggested, "don't you think you' better lay down and take a little nap?"

Red snapped the blade into the handle, put into his pocket, rubbed back his wet hair wit sweep of palm. "I don't sleep good when there i something orta be done." He stuck out a leg an absently jabbed the ground by lifting his foot an bringing down the rowel. Mr Backman didn't sa anything more. Red didn't say anything. The patiently waited for Barber to wash himself a well as he wanted to.

It wasn't easy for Barber to wash. He wa covered with dust. His head was sore. His fac was sore, and the blue-black bruise clear dow one side of his face showed more clearly whe he washed—the fresh red scratches on his nos too. He went to the pump three times for wate and soused his head down into the last panful Soapy water was in his eyes, and he groped fo

ie towel. Red got up and handed it to him, then
at down.

Barber wiped his head a long time. He wadded
ie towel and threw it at the wash bench, and
vithout looking at anybody he said in a mean
oice, "I sure am not goin' to take all the blame
n myself!"

Red said, "I reckon you'll purt-near have to.
They'll just call you a liar, an' you can't prove
ou ain't."

Barber was rubbing his hair with his fingers
nd paused to stare squintily at Red from the eye
hat wasn't swollen.

"Can you?" Red asked.

Barber mumbled, "Maybe I can't, but, by God,
hey was in it!"

"Feller, if I didn't believe you, you wouldn't be
ere *alive!*"

"And I never meant to hurt that girl a-tall!" said
Barber, almost righteously.

"No," Red cracked back, "no more maybe than
o make her wish she was dead!"

They all went into the house. Barber sat down,
vithout being told to, on a stool by the table and
ooked about.

There was a blanket spread smoothly, as if over
leeping bodies, on one of the bunks. Barber
ooked toward that bunk with no trace of feeling.
He stared straight toward where Kate was sitting
eside Kilco. Jane sat with her face in her hands.

She hadn't realized how much she loved thos
kids. Her black hair was all frowzy and tangled
but she did not care. The old cook made muc
noise in slamming pots about on the stove, a
if it made him mad to have to fix food for Me
Barber.

Kilco put up a hand to Red and pressed it hard
Kilco looked pretty sick and haggard, not like th
big, handsome, half-roistering fellow Red ha
first met. "Why didn't you kill him?" It was hal
snarl and wholly reproachful.

" 'Cause I wanted him alive."

"He'll get away from you!"

Red jerked his head toward Mr Backman. "Me
maybe. But not from dad there."

From clear over by the table Barber spoke up
"I'll tell you why *he* wants me killed. So I won'
tell nobody about him havin' a wife and two kid
over in—"

Kilco's face took on a spasm-look of fury, an
his whole body moved jerkily, as if trying t
jump from the bunk. Kate had an expression a
if somebody had slapped her in the face, and sh
stared at Kilco as if afraid that he wouldn't den
it.

He denied it at the top of his voice: "That's
lie!"

Barber laughed dryly. He wasn't really laughing
but was making mocking sounds. He raised hi
voice: "You've fooled her good." With a finge

aised gingerly to his scratched nose: "She done
his to me last night when I told her. But you've
ot that wife and them kids and—"

"Oh, Jim!" Kate pleaded.

Kilco roared, "It's a lie!" and swore.

Barber laughed. "I hear old Vickers is up in this
ountry. You just ask him, Kate. He knows all
bout Jim and Jim's wife, too."

"I don't believe it!" Kate cried, but she sounded
omehow as if she didn't entirely disbelieve; or
t least was afraid that it might be true. But she
vanted to be firm and loyal. Then she looked up
hankfully at Red because he said:

"You, Barber, can shut your mouth an' keep it
hut till some food is on the table!"

Red went to the bench where Jane sat with
ace downcast, and when she looked up, her
lance would go to the bunk where Bobby and
'ete lay under the blanket just as if they were too
leepy to be awakened by the stir and talk. Red
at down by Jane and took her hand. He didn't
ay anything. Jane wiped at her eyes, pushed
ndifferently at her loose hair, smiled sadly at
im. "You—you are all *my* boys!"

VII

he cook sourly called, "Here it is!" and planked
lown a big plate stacked with flapjacks.

Barber turned around and began putting food

on his plate. Red went to the table and sat dow
across from Barber. Mr Backman came and sa
by Red. Jane got up and went outdoors. Coo
took a cup of coffee across to Kate.

She said, "Oh, thank you, but—but I ough
to wash!" She stayed where she was and dran
the coffee a spoonful at a time because it wa
scalding.

Barber ate without lifting his eyes from th
food. Red ate, too, and drank many cups o
coffee, thickened with sugar. He poured a heav
stream of blackstrap over the grease-soake
flapjacks, cut them into chunks, held a drippin
chunk before his mouth and asked, "Dad, do w
make a couple of graves before we go to town?"

Mr Backman wiped his mouth with the back o
his hand. "Me and cook have done that a'ready
son."

Barber stabbed a piece of steak and drew i
dripping from the platter to his plate. "I sure a
hell ain't goin' to take all the blame," he said. H
had to chew on one side because the other sid
of his face was so swollen. He chewed awhil
and gulped coffee. He put the coffee cup dow
carefully, spread his elbows, leaned forwar
without lifting his eyes. "Jim Kilco has got a wif
and two kids over in New Mexico."

Red rolled a cigarette. Barber said, "Giv
me the makin's." Red laid tobacco and paper
on the table. Barber did not say, "Thanks.

He said, "Give me a match." Red gave him a match. He stared squintily at Red. "You are the luckiest damn fool in the world!" Red nodded, indifferently, thinking of other things.

Mr Backman said, "Son, you fetch the horses. We'll bury the boys, then set out."

Red dabbed out the cigarette, pushed back his stool. "In a minute." He walked over to Kilco. "See here, you been told, ain't you, that Bobby up an' said you was here?"

Kilco nodded. "You've got him there, and the others are wiped out!"

"Not Joe Strumm an' Knox. They know. They may tell somebody."

Kilco instantly had the outlaw's worry about being caught. "I'll be like a rat in a trap!"

"All I can promise," Red went on, "is that if Knox an' Strumm did go to town an' tell that sheriff an' Gridger, an' we meet 'em, I'll turn 'em back, 'cause I want 'em. If it's the marshal, I'll coax my best to get him to go back, but I won't pull a gun on him. Not for nobody, I won't. An' they is one thing I want to know: Have you got a wife?"

Kilco all of a sudden looked mad. He glared at Red and shouted, "No!" Then he glared some more and said, "But if I had, I don't see how it is any of your business!"

"It sure is *my* business that no man makes who I work for believe lies! An' I'm runnin' the Clayton ranch—or goin' to be about this time tomorrer!"

"Oh, you are?" said Kilco. "What about thi ranch here?"

"It too. Both of 'em. An' the whole damn country besides, if needful to make people leav my range an' cows alone!"

Kilco said, "You talk purty big!"

Then he saw the look on Kate's face an wished that he had kept a quieter tongue, becaus she showed how much she was surprised b his acting that way with Red. Red's blazin; directness appealed to her; and though sh thought of Red as only a boy, a rather awkwar and not even handsome cowboy, she admired trusted and perhaps even liked him better tha anybody else in the world. Deep down in he troubled heart she was afraid that Jim Kilc did have a wife; and if he did, then he had bee hopelessly dishonest with her, saying he woul turn over a new leaf, take her off somewhere an become a fine, respected cattleman.

"I talk purty big, do I?" Red asked somberly "Well, sir, if I wanted to brag a little, I could sa I had been big enough to purt-near wipe out a ba bunch that folks call the Kilcos!"

Then Red went out to saddle the horses.

CHAPTER ELEVEN

They jogged into Manning Springs a little after noon, and old man Manning came shambling out, with the gray dog at his heels and a wide grin. He called, "Howdy, boy!" and raised a fluttery arm. He knew who Mr Backman was. The long-haired, buckskin-shirted frontiersman was pretty well known by name. When Manning saw that the third man's arms were tied, he pushed back his old hat.

"Well now, who have you got there?"

"Mell Barber," said Red.

Manning parted his mouth in a wide gulp, said he'd be gosh-ding-damned, or words to that effect, only stronger; and he took out a hard lump of tobacco and whittled himself a chew.

Red slid from the saddle, hooked thumbs in his belt and said in a kind of now-I-don't-want-to-hurt-your-feelings voice, "Pop, I've got some news. I'm runnin the Clayton ranch an'—"

"Yo're *what!*"

"That's right. And water, it is—"

"Why, Bill, he rode by this mornin' an' he didn't say—"

"Um. He don't know it yet. Now water is mighty precious, pop—specially this time of year. You'd better clean out the ditch, plug up them leaky butts in the trough, an' I see you've got a slip. If it's too hard for you grade the water hole better, I'll get out a mule skinner an'—"

Old Manning almost wanted to be mad. "Old Sam, he never made no complaint about how I—"

"Old Sam, he owned the ranch. If he wanted his water to waste, 'twas his lookout. But me, I got to see that purt-near ever' drop goes into some cow's belly an' grows into fat."

Manning chewed and spit and fidgeted, and Red stood there with thumbs in belt and looked at him and smiled a little; then, softly:

"Supposin' it was your ranch, an' you hired me to run 'er?"

Old Manning glared for a minute, then he spit, shifted the chew until it bulged out a lean cheek, opened his mouth. "If 'twas, I'll be gosh-ding damned"—or something like it—"if I wouldn' hire you to run it! You do beat all for lookin' like a fool kid an' not bein' one! But how it come Bill don't know yet?"

"You see, pop, he asked me to be boss that day after you an' me fooled some fellers here that tried to fool us; and I said, 'No.' But I changed my mind. I've took over Miss Kate's share, and I'm takin' over the other half along with it. You say Bill rode by. Which way?"

"He rode out home last night. He had been

rinkin'. He rode back this mornin', lookin' sorta eaked and in a hurry. He is all broke up over his ad's death."

"I reckon."

Mell Barber sneered.

There was some silence, then Mr Backman aid, I am thinkin' it might be a good idee, son, if ve don't get to town till after dark."

Red nodded and squatted down to think a little. I see how you mean."

"I got a big pot o' beans." Manning was inviting hem to eat. "And I don't want you sendin' nybody out here to run that slip. You git me a ouple o' mules an' I'll fix that water hole up. I eckon old Sam was so worrit about rustlers he ever much noticed maybe that water was bein' vasted a mite."

Barber spoke up, mean and sneering: "Bill was he biggest rustler of the bunch!"

Manning said, "Wha-at?"

Barber grinned and jerked his head, then cussed 3ill and brought Dave Gridger's name into the ussing. Red looked up, slantwise, interested, ;lad to see that Mell Barber was feeling that vay. When Barber quieted down, Red asked of Manning:

"You by happenchance seen Knox ride by?"

"No."

"Nor a feller named Joe Strumm?"

"No."

"An' Bill this mornin', he didn't say nothin' about Miss Kate not bein' home?"

"No. He just watered his hoss and rode on. He looked sorta like he didn't feel good. Why would he wanta steal his own cows?"

Barber said, sneering, "He wanted to be a good sport. And he hated his old man. And Gridge hated old Sam, too. I'll fix them two sons of so-and-so . . ." Barber worked himself into quite an excitement in cussing them.

Red's look slanted up toward old Mr Backman and Mr Backman peered back at Red; they didn't give a flicker of an eyelash between them, but they understood.

Since it seemed better not to get into town until after dark, when there would be less excitement over Mell Barber being brought in, Red put the horses away. They went into the dim 'dobe and ate beans, drank coffee. Barber's hands were untied so that he could eat easily and roll cigarettes, and Mr Backman, with his rifle on his knee, sat close to the door and did not take his eyes off Barber.

Red leaned his head back against the wall and shut his eyes, but he did not sleep. His lids popped wide at the least movement. He had been through a lot that was tiring and had had no sleep, but he had a way of staying on a job as long as a job needed him.

When it was nearly sundown Red brought up

he horses. He came back into the house and
rank another cup of cold black coffee into which
e stirred some spoonfuls of sugar. Mr Backman
vas tying up Barber's wrists. Red peeled an
nion, took a plate of greasy beans, sat on a
orner of the table, ate the beans with a spoon:
ne spoonful of beans, one bite of onion. He
hewed slowly, thoughtfully enjoying the flavor.
Vhen he had finished, he announced gravely, "I
ure do like to eat!"

II

t was well after suppertime when Red left Mr
Backman and Barber some hundred yards or so in
he dip of an arroyo outside of town and rode on.
   He went straight to the back of the Saginaw
Restaurant and clattered into the kitchen, where
Mr Blanton, Prop., sat disconsolately sucking
n old pipe and watching the Chinese cook slice
oiled potatoes for tomorrow morning's hash.
   "Sure," said Mr Blanton welcomingly as Red
tamped in, "we'll fix you a bite if—"
   "I got some business. Where's Jody?"
   "In bed back there with that dog," said Mr
Blanton, grinning as if not greatly displeased and
apping the pipe bowl against his heel.
   Red dipped his fingers into the pan of sliced
otatoes. "I wonder if he wants to earn himself a
ollar?"

"Jody? Shorest thing! You know, I was jus
settin' here thinkin' this country is no place for t
bring up a boy. No lakes. No cricks. No trees. N
fishin'! I tell you, I git mighty homesick for som
green! An' all little Jody does is run around in th
dust an' listen to men cuss and talk about killin's
I think I ain't doin' my honest duty to raise a bo
out in this God-forsaken country."

"They got cows in that Michigan place?"

"Sho-ore!" proudly. "Milk cows!"

Red snorted. "You give Jody to me. I'll put hin
to work where there is trees an' fishin' an' a rea
old Injun fighter to teach him things, an' a nic
woman to tuck him in his bunk."

"Jody?"

"Jody. Only tonight"—Red took some mor
sliced boiled potatoes—"I want 'im for a specia
scoutin' job. An' I'll pay him a dollar."

"You mean," said Mr Blanton, standing u
and staring hard, "you want to take Jody to you
ranch for to work?"

"For to play. He'll draw some wages a little, an
he'll work, only he'll think it is play. I'm bossin
two ranches now, an' I need me some good men.

"Two?"

"The Clayton outfit."

"Why, that's the biggest ranch in the whol
danged country!"

"That's why maybe I need me a good helper."

"You are jokin'," said Mr Blanton.

"I may be jokin', but I ain't lyin'. I got special need for a kid of about Jody's size out where they is a nice, lonesome woman who is dyin' to squeeze somebody. She won't squeeze us full-grown fellers, 'cause she thinks that would make her look silly. But Jody is about the right size. An' I got a real old Injun fighter that hankers for a nice kid to worship him. Roust him out. I'm"— another reach for the long-suffering Chinaman's potatoes—"in a hurry."

Mr Blanton went through the door to where the boy slept and came back with a sleepy kid and a black-and-white dog that sniffed Red with far reach of nose as if Red were a stranger, then looked up to see what Jody thought.

Jody said, " 'Lo, Red," and leaned against Red to yawn sleepily. Then, in suspicious alarm: "You ain't come for Bozo?"

"Yeah. You an' Bozo both. You're goin' out to be a cowboy."

"Me?"

"Um."

Jody let out a screech and began to jump up and down, and Bozo barked and jumped up and down, too, as if greatly delighted at being a cow dog. When they quieted down, Red said, "Now you listen clost. Is Dave Gridger in town?"

"He is, Red."

"An' Bill Clayton?"

"He was in the Silver Dollar all afternoon."

"Do you know if Marshal Vickers is in town?"

"Him and the two fellers are at the hotel, Red.'

"A'right. Come on."

Outside in the dark beside Red's horse, Jody got his instructions: "You go to Mr Vickers. No matter where he is, you find him."

"I'll find 'im, Red!"

"I know it. That's why I'm hirin' you. When you find him, you get him off by hisself an' you say, 'Red told me to tell you to be over to Dave Gridger's saloon by eight-thirty.' "

"Yes'ir, Red!" Jody was ready to bolt.

Red clapped a hand on the small shoulder "Wait a minute. How little work you think you have to do for a dollar? Next you go to where the Judge is. Most likely he is playin' poker at the back of the general store. You get him outside an' you say to him alone, 'Red says for you to be at Dave Gridger's saloon by eight-thirty. An' to bring anybody you want along.' Understand?"

"You betchu!"

"Then you've got to find the sheriff. If he ain' already in the saloon, you find 'im. An' you say to *him* that the Judge wants to see him over a Dave Gridger's saloon at eight-thirty."

"I shore will!"

"All right. Here is your dollar. Now you skedaddle. An' if you do a good job you can go to work for me at two-bits a day. An' you'll earn 'er, too!"

"As a cowboy, Red?"

"As a cowboy."

Jody let go with a joyful squawk and bolted. The dark shadow that followed was Bozo.

III

Red rode slowly out of town and came to where Barber sat on the ground, his hands tied behind him. Old Mr Backman stood by, as tall and motionless as if on sentry duty.

Red got off the horse. "It's been fixed," he said. He rolled a cigarette.

Barber said, "Give me one."

Red put it into Barber's mouth, gave him a light and rolled himself another. Barber didn't say "Thanks"; but after a time he did say, "I wanta ask something."

"Ask away."

"Why do you give me cigarettes?"

" 'Cause I think you wanta smoke."

"Most fellers would say 'Go to hell' to me. You now I'd cut your heart out if I got a chanct!"

"I don't give a goddamn. I figger a man has a right to water, air, food an' some tobacco as long s he is alive. That's all."

Barber shut up as if thinking it over and not quite understanding.

Soon Red said, "Well, dad, I reckon it is gettin' long to purt-near time for us to mosey.

287

When they came to the road just outside o
the town, they rode three abreast, with Barbe
in the middle. Nobody was on the street, but a
they turned to the hitching rack they could se
through the Silver Dollar's open door that a goo
many people were there. Red grinned, bettin
to himself that spider-fat Dave Gridger wa
wondering why business was so good.

As he got out of the saddle a small shado
scooted from the darkness beside the wall an
said in a gleeful, hushed voice, "I done it, Red
All like you told me!" Bozo nudged in wit
whiplike wag of tail, as if he, too, had bee
helpful and deserved the same sort of pat on th
head that Jody got.

Mr Backman and Barber stayed outside, an
Red walked into the saloon, was well inside th
door before he stopped. He had the look of
man who had come for trouble as he sized peopl
up. Everybody was watching. Those who didn'
know that he had sent word around asking som
people to be there knew that he was on edge
dangerously.

Red stood straight and had his chin in. His eye
glowed. The more cautious fellows in the crow
began to move well away from the bar and neare
to the round poker tables that were up front. Tw
lamps were burning in front of rusty reflector
high behind the bar. The coal-oil light was so
and yellowish and threw shadows from men'

odies to the floor, made them dance on the far
wall.

The bald, red-faced Judge held his black hat
in one hand and a wadded red bandanna in the
other. It was a warm night. He had on a boiled
shirt, without a collar, and his long black coat.
Shirt and coat were a part of the legal tradition of
his day. His plump round face was puzzled and
anxious, for he knew that there was an impetuous
craziness about Red—usually commendable, but
often perilously rash. Marshal Vickers, a head
taller, stood beside the Judge up near the front
of the bar and rested, back to the bar, on the tips
of his elbows. The marshal's coat was off, but he
wore a vest. There was a black single-action .45
in a belt holster on the marshal's hip. His hat was
pushed back, and his tired, weather-worn face
was sternly set. He was deeply exasperated by
what he felt was the trick Red had played on him
with Kilco; but he had to feel that Red had played
fair even if foolishly. The Wells, Fargo men, with
half-jeers and not illogical criticism, had made
the marshal uncomfortable.

The sheriff was on the other side of the Judge
and did not look happy. He nibbled on a cigar
much as a rabbit nibbles on a cabbage leaf. The
Judge had acted funny when the sheriff asked
why he had sent Jody; and when the Judge said,
noncommittally, "Just remain here. Just remain,
and you will see," the sheriff thought that maybe

289

the Judge had something up his sleeve to discredit him.

So it was a puzzled, doubtful lot of men that Red faced. They all could see that Red was pretty worn and haggard, but his eyes had a fierce glow.

The Wells, Fargo men had come along with the marshal. They had handkerchiefs stuffed inside their neckbands to keep the collars from wilting too fast and, with fresh cigars in their mouths and filled glasses of whisky, stood well down along the bar, where they could overhear men talking among themselves and maybe learn something.

Bill Clayton had been drinking, but he could drink a lot and not be unsteady on his feet. For days he had been drinking and keeping unsociably to himself, even at the bar. "Sorrowin'," men said respectfully. He looked the next thing to shabby too, as if he had been sleeping in his clothes and not washing up. His heavy, sullen face flushed with an uneasy glower as he saw Red single him out and stare. Bill put down his glass of whisky and wiped his right hand on his trousers to get off the sweat. What Red had said about ivory handled revolvers troubled him vaguely.

Red scarcely looked at the Judge or the marshal, or even at the Wells, Fargo men because they were friends, or at least not unfriendly. And so were the old poker player that the Judge had dragged to the saloon without much of explanation. He wasn't so sure about he sheriff, but felt that the sheriff didn't count or much. Red knew that Bill Clayton could be dangerous, believed that Dave Gridger, with his smooth ooziness that covered so much meanness, was even more dangerous.

It was quiet, because everybody could see that Red was set to say something. The first thing he said was across the bar:

"Gridger, you come around on this side of the bar where you can hear good an'—"

Gridger forced a kind of laugh, trying to pass off the sharpness in Red's voice. "Oh, I can hear all right, boy!"

"—an' so I can see what you've got in your hands!"

That was a hard, insulting slap. Red had as much as said, "I don't put it past you to shoot when I'm not looking!" Gridger didn't know what to say or how to act. It was the same as a slap, but he knew that Red would do more than slap. He made a little noise in his throat before he got out some words: "I have to tend to my customers." He nodded toward the men, as if staying behind the bar was what they wanted him to do. Also he put his hands flat down on the bar to show how empty they were.

"They'll be no more drinkin' till I get done!" Red told him.

Gridger's temper came out in almost a bellow: "Who is runnin' this place, anyhow!"

Red told him, "I am!" Then: "You get aroun here like you been told!"

There was a breathless silence. Gridger looke doubtful and angry. He was afraid of Red. He ha seen Red go into action. He felt a lot safer behin the bar. All of a sudden he began to suspect tha it wasn't just happenso that had brought so man people into the saloon only a little while befor Red showed up.

Gridger was scared, and he shouted at th sheriff, "Are you goin' to stand there an' let thi Clark feller bulldoze people?"

The sheriff nibbled faster on his cigar for minute, then took it out and looked at it as if h hoped he could read something suitable to say The Judge raised his pudgy body on tiptoes an whispered to the sheriff, "You keep out of this!"

The marshal dropped an elbow, half turned looked at Gridger. "You had better come o around here like you've been asked. We all wil be the judge then of whether or not there wa good reason for askin' you."

Gridger picked up his bar towel, made a wad threw it down as if trying to break something He grumbled something or other as he poure himself a drink of whisky. He pitched it dow his throat and came waddling around the bar. H went right up close in front of Red, put his hand on his hips, looked mean and said, "Well, wha d'you want?"

Many of the people there had never seen the mooth-talking, back-patting, now-have-a-drink-n-me Gridger mad before. He was mad all right, ut he was afraid, too; not merely afraid of Red, ut of how men like the marshal and Judge were cting.

"You'll hear what I want in a minute," Red told im. Then he called, "Bill, you come right along loser up here, too."

Everybody turned to look at Bill. He glowered ullenly, not moving, not speaking. He was well iquored, and he had a flush urge to make this quarrel right now; but he remembered what Red had said about sweaty hands slipping on vory handles, and his hands were again sticky vith sweat. He could tell, too, that Red was langerously ready. Also he, like Gridger, was nade uneasy by feeling that so many of these eople had been waiting in the saloon for Red o come. People watched nervously. The silence vas like pressure. Bill had to give way or make a quarrel. As yet there wasn't much of anything to quarrel about. Bill gave his thick lips a sneering wist and swaggered with a heavy lurch that vasn't whisky, just to show everybody that he vasn't afraid. He went up alongside of Gridger nd scowled at Red: "Well, what is it?"

"I got some news that I want ever'body to hear. t ain't good news."

Men edged in, with necks stuck out to get their

ears closer. Red was not speaking loud, but h
was not mumbling any words:

"Day before yestiddy, Miss Kate rode over t
visit with my lady boss. She stayed till dark. The
the two kids as ride for the Lazy Z went along t
see her home. They didn't come back. Yestiddy
rode out to find why. I found their bodies on th
trail. Shot!"

The Judge gasped and let the black hat sli
from his fingers as the pudgy hand flew up in
shocked gesture. There was a stir of muttering
as if a wind swept over men's lips and passed
Marshal Vickers moved in closer.

Gridger wet his thick lips. "Maybe Knox don
it for spite!" he suggested helpfully. Someho
he felt a lot of relief, because nobody could ver
well accuse him of any hand in that.

Bill had something of the same feeling of relief
"And Kate?" he asked.

"Stole!" said Red. Men exclaimed about tha
It was one thing to kill men, even boys; anothe
to lay hands on a woman. Red paused till th
voices got quiet, then he snapped at Bill, "Yo
was home last night an' she wasn't. Didn't yo
wonder?"

Bill put his sullen look back on. Red seeme
accusing him. He growled, "They told m
she was over to your ranch. She don't like m
meddling. She is in love with Jim Kilco an
rides out to meet him!"

Bill must have had a hazy notion that he was making himself appear all right by telling that about Kate. It didn't work out that way, because people simply did not believe that the haughty, aristocratic granddaughter of old Sam Clayton was such a fool. The Judge frowned as if disgusted with Bill.

Marshal Vickers nudged Red and asked, "Who done it?"

"The same feller that shot Sam Clayton!"

"You mean Mell Barber?"

"I mean Mell Barber!" said Red, looking hard at Gridger. Gridger started to sweat. Red seemed to know things and to be about to say them.

The marshal asked, "How are you sure?"

" 'Cause I caught him!"

Bill Clayton's sullenness broke in the quick question, "You mean killed him?"

Red watched, noting how eager Bill sounded and was right ready to act as if he and Red were fine friends. Red waggled his head a little. "No. He ain't dead. An' he talked!"

Red paused, and people squirmed nearer. Then Red said, looking right at Bill, "He says *you* an' Gridger here put him up to shoot Sam Clayton. An' me, I believe him!"

"Red!" That was the Judge's incredulous protest. It sounded loud, because nobody else said a word. Everybody was at least a little shocked, though. They, like the Judge who thought Red was making an awful mistake, were shocked that Red would say a thing like that when Bill had been drinking so sorrowfully for days.

The sheriff had a fluttery look, as if he thought that he ought to do something but couldn't think what.

Dave Gridger took in a big gulp of air. He said "Ow!" just about as if he had been stabbed. Red had accused him of that very thing on the day Sam Clayton was shot, and Gridger had wiggled around it with smooth talk and a hurt air. He got his breath, and in trying to look like an honest man who has been terribly misjudged, he shook his head woefully and drew up a big sigh. But there was a scared look in his eyes.

Bill looked the worst hit. It was for a minute just as if he were dazed. Then his face blazed with anger. He yelled, "That's a lie!" He stood tense and glaring, ready to make a grab for his gun.

But Gridger said, "Don't, Bill!" and took hold of his arm. "He is just waitin' to kill you!"

"That is right!" said Red. "I am!"

Some men that were close edged off in a hurry. This was fight talk. Their moving shadows darted and jiggled on the far wall.

Marshal Vickers spoke up sharply: "Careful, boy!"

Red kept his eyes on Bill, pointed straight at him. "He had been in with rustlers to steal his ad's own cows! He has also rode with outlaws. He fretted his dad into bein' took to the ranch—against the doctor's advisin'!—just so the joltin' would make him worse. An' havin' killed his dad to get half the ranch, he wanted to get rid of Kate so he could get all of it! Well, he won't!"

So, having told why he meant to kill Bill, Red waited; and everybody, even Marshal Vickers, moved back. Gridger waddled backwards to the bar. Red and Bill stood out on the floor, face to face and alone.

Red looked as if he were a tightly coiled steel spring. It seemed to take some moments for Bill to get it into his head that people were waiting for him to do something. There was a confused haziness in his eyes, not fear so much as a look of being shattered inside. It sickened him to have Red tell all the things he had been up to—even the secret crafty cunning of getting his father jolted to death by the wagon ride to the ranch. That was having a secret he had never told anybody jerked right out of the darkest place in his heart and thrown to men.

Bill was bad hearted, but he wasn't wholly coward, except as fellows who think they are smarter than honest people don't like having to stand up eye to eye with somebody that is fiercely purposeful. And it was somehow as if he had never before realized just how rotten low he was until Red spread it out in plain words.

Bill made a sound almost like a sob, as when a man confusedly comes out of a bad dream. H jerked at his ivory-handled gun. His hand wa sweaty, and his fingers were nearly numb-stiff He was so nervous that they simply wouldn take hold, and he made frantic snatches. His fingers closed on the gun butt. Then Red's han flashed back, shadow-swift. His body bent wit a backward jerk, and the cocked .45 had it muzzle up over the slick holster. But he did no shoot.

Bill Clayton's gun, half out of its holste seemed to stick. His eyes wavered past Red, int a startled, widening stare. Red was onto prett near every gun trick; and the one of looking pas a man to throw him off guard did not in the leas bother him. He watched Clayton's hand and sav the hand slide laxly from the gun butt, just abou as if the wrist were suddenly broken. Then Bi lifted his hand in a swipe across his eyes, as i trying to wipe away something.

Mell Barber was coming in, with Mr Backma behind him. Mr Backman stopped in the door way, tall and straight, with flowing beard, lon hair, buckskin shirt, and stood with the rifle i the crook of his arm. He had decided that it was good time for Barber to come in.

Barber's hands were tied behind him, and hi face was black-bruised on one side, but he wa not coming with his tail between his legs. H new that he was a goner. On top of all else, here was the murder of the two kids, with Kate Clayton to say that she had seen him do it; so, being damned anyhow, he was willing to tell all about everything and make it as bad as he could, just to make it that much worse for Gridger and Bill. Red and Mr Backman had figured out that his was about the way it would happen.

Gridger and Bill looked just about as if Mell Barber were the devil walking in to grab them. Gridger's fat face all of a sudden looked flabby, and his hog-shaped belly caved in.

Bill's thick lips moved without a sound. He scraped his feet a little, as if trying to back away, but his feet seemed too heavy to move. Barber went right up close to him; and from all around men pushed in close again to see and hear.

The sheriff seemed to think that it was his place to get up alongside of Barber, as if the outlaw were his prisoner; and he put back his shoulders a little, as if some share in the capture belonged to him.

The marshal took Red by the arm, pulled him aside. "Are you *sure* Bill killed old Sam?"

"I believe for certain that him an' Gridger—an' don't you go forgettin' Gridger!—put Barber an' them up to shootin' Sam. I *know* Bill made his father get wagon jolted so he would die!"

The marshal barely said, "Poor Sam." Then he turned around to listen.

Mell Barber was talking. His voice was mean and his eyes glittered. One eye was badly swollen, but it glittered, too. He started in on Gridger first: "You begun lendin' Bill money to blow on women an' gamblin'. When he couldn' pay, you made him throw in with them rustlers you are in with!"

Gridger yelled denials, but there was some thing in his flustered loudness that was very confessional.

"Then Bill began to ride a little with the bunch An' about three months ago he first begun to tall to me about how well off he'd be if the old man died. So then—"

Bill had the look of a man who has been beaten with a club. His voice was low and strained as if he were being strangled, as he tried to shout, "No! 'Tain't so! Don't believe 'im!" But somehow there was no earnestness in his voice only the weak desperation of a man who has no real hope.

"It was planned by Dave Gridger here for us to ride in an' kill Sam, then ride out and nobody would know us and—"

Gridger was bellowing: "That's a lie!"

Barber squirmed a little and looked fierce. He yelled, "I know damn well you want to see me hung, an' I'll be hung, but you two bastards are not goin' to—"

Right then and there, there was a flurry, and

before anybody quite knew what was happening Barber had jerked the marshal's gun out of its holster. The sheriff jumped back, with hands half lifted, and yelled, "Don't!" Barber was not paying any attention to him. He fired twice right up against Bill's belly.

Bill clapped both hands to his belly and bent over, falling. He fell sideways and turned over. Barber swung the muzzle at Gridger, and Gridger just opened his mouth and yelled, with both hands out in front of him as if to push bullets away. When the gun went off, Marshal Vickers had hold of the back of Barber's neck with one hand and was grabbing at the gun with the other. There were too many people all bunched up for anybody but a madman like Barber to risk shooting. He was so jostled and hurried that when the gun went off the bullet missed Gridger and hit a man beside him in the shoulder.

Men squawked, and feet clattered, and some got down low. The marshal wrenched Barber's arm high up over his head. The pudgy Judge, who didn't know what fear was, had jumped in in a bustling, puffy way to help the marshal, and in doing so he blocked Red, who had swung up a gun to bring it down on Barber's head. But Barber dropped the gun from his uplifted hand and quit struggling.

The Wells, Fargo men had jumped in like a couple of angry bulls even while Barber was

301

shooting, but they had more or less to knock people who were trying to dodge off out of their way. Red changed his feelings a little toward the Wells, Fargo men because they certainly were no timid under gunfire.

They took hold of Barber and hustled him across the room, slammed him up against the wall, jerked him around, and before anybody could have said "Jack Robinson," one of them snapped handcuffs on Barber's slim wrists. They were smart, watchful fellows, too, because right off they saw that Barber had curiously small hands, almost as if jointless, and one of them took a piece of stout twine from his pocket and tied Barber's thumbs together. They didn't stop there. They were like bulldogs with a rag doll and took Barber at a jostling run to the back of the saloon, stood him up in a corner by the dim light and started in to work on him.

Dave Gridger was shaking. He looked down where the men were in a stooping cluster about Bill, crowding in morbidly close. Gridger gave his head a furtive twist this way and that, then sidled to the bar, sidled along it. He untied his apron and started for the back way.

There was a clatter of peg heels, jangle of spurs, a call: "Come back here, you!"

Gridger knew that voice. He turned around and explained to Red, "I was just goin' out back. I feel a little sick at my stomick!"

Red said, "I bet you do! Get back up here and et down. Maybe we can find a rope that will :ure that belly sickness."

IV

The Wells, Fargo man that had the hoarse voice :ame up front and passed close to Red, who vas beside the chair where Gridger sat looking olemn and studying his hands. The Wells, Fargo nan gave Red a queer look, grinned a little, then 1e went over to where Marshal Vickers was .tooping over Bill Clayton.

He pulled at the marshal's arm. The marshal ooked around and stood up. They walked off ome steps to be alone. The marshal listened and ugged at an ear, smiled a bit and glanced toward Red. He took off his hat, scratched his head, ind the Wells, Fargo man laughed. The marshal 1odded, and the Wells, Fargo man looked at Red igain, then went in a hurry out the front door.

Mr Backman was still there, but looked as if all his excitement did not affect him. Jody was right 1p close, and Mr Backman had an arm about the 1oy's shoulder. Jody didn't know whether he was nore interested in the crowd in the saloon or in he buckskin shirt. Bozo was crouched nervously 1ehind his legs, raising his ears, letting them fall loubtfully. Now and then, by way of reassuring 1imself, he licked Jody's hand.

Bill Clayton was flat on the floor, dying. His eyes had a hazy, all-gone look, and he groaned a little, with speckles of foam at his mouth. Judge Trowbridge was down on his knees and bent his head low as he took Bill's hand and spoke solemnly in a deep, impressive voice:

"Bill, you are dying, so now tell us the truth. Has it been as Mell Barber says?"

Bill squeezed the lids over his glazed eyes. His thick lips barely moved. The Judge put his head closer, turning an ear. Bill whispered weakly. He tried to say something more, but words would not take sound. The Judge put a hand gently on Bill's forehead and sighed. It was hard for the Judge to believe that men could be downright evil. A little later the Judge closed Bill's eyes, then got up, brushed at his dusty knees.

CHAPTER TWELVE

here was a good deal of excited talk among
ae people in the saloon; and other people,
roused by the news, came, too. Gridger and
arber would have been lynched in ten minutes
xcept for the Judge, who made a speech and had
committee formed to take care of the prisoners.
Jobody would listen to the sheriff, who almost
arfully tried to explain that he didn't know
thing about how his brother-in-law had been
arrying on.

A rasping voice told him, "Then that shows just
ow a poor a sher'ff you are!"

Marshal Vickers took hold of Red's arm and
owned. "Red, you are under arrest."

"Me?"

"You."

"What I done?"

"When I arrest a man I always take off his
uns, Red."

"You really mean—me?"

"You. I don't want to embarrass you before
eople, so will you give me your word that you
vill do as I say?"

"I reckon I will. Only what you goin' to say?"

"I am going to say that you are to keep right by
ae from now on."

"Is it on account of Kilco?"

"Yes."

"Mell Barber, he told, h'm?"

"You certainly worked it slick, hiding him behind the blankets we thought were for Miss Alvord's privacy!" The marshal almost, but not quite, smiled.

"Barber didn't know that, so how could—"

"He told where Kilco was. In what bunk. The Wells, Fargo men can add, quick!"

He made a submissive gesture. "I lose. So all right. Only you tell me, has he got a wife and some children?"

"Yes."

Red scowled, spoke moodily: "He has got a mean streak, I reckon. But he is all right, too, lots of ways. He has got grit—real grit. An' I reckon if a purty girl likes a feller, he don't much care how many wives he has got. Not if he is that kind of a feller."

The citizens' committee made up a posse to take the prisoners down to Poicoma. The Judge talked them into deciding to do that, because as soon as word got around among the cowboys, especially the Clayton boys, they would come storming into town and string up Gridger and Mell Barber.

II

he Wells, Fargo man, who had grinned queerly
t Red in passing, had left the saloon to go to
ıe livery stable for horses so that they could
ll ride out at once to the Lazy Z ranch with
ed.

It was around midnight when they set out. Mr
Backman held Jody in his arms in front of him,
nd Bozo trotted along through the dust at the
orses' heels.

The marshal and Wells, Fargo men were in a
urry; and Mr Backman didn't want to jolt
ody by trotting, so he said he would stop at
ıe Springs for the night and fell behind. Jody's
mall head was pillowed against the long beard.
ody tried to make out that he wasn't sleepy, but
is eyes just couldn't stay open, not even to hear
bout Injuns; so he slept in the arms of the last
f the old frontiersmen, at least in that part of the
ountry, who had been a fur trapper, scout and
ndian fighter all of his life.

The marshal pushed on fast. The Wells, Fargo
ıen were now friendly toward Red; too friendly.
Ie wished they would shut up. But their exas-
eration was over. Mell Barber was a prisoner,
nd they knew where to find Kilco. They laughed
bout how Red had fooled them in concealing
Kilco.

"If you ever turn bad," said the hoarse one, "there will be plenty of hell!"

Red wasn't under arrest at all. The marshal had just said that to make him promise not to go riding off in a hurry and hide Kilco again. And Red was troubled. He was, in a way, bringing the marshal to arrest Kilco. He couldn't help himself, and he knew that it wasn't any betrayal on his part; nevertheless he wished it weren't happening just this way. He felt that it was mighty mean of Kilco to have let Kate be in love with him when he already had a wife—"a half-dozen besides," said a Wells, Fargo man. But someways, Kilco was good leather. He had a mean streak all right, but he had grit. So Red didn't feel talkative, and he was not in a hurry to get to the ranch. The way they were pushing the horses would get them there about sunup or a little before.

They paused at the Springs. Old Manning put his head out of the door and hailed them. Red called, "You've got comp'ny comin' to stay the night. Mr Backman will give you the news. And they's plenty!"

III

It was dark when they came out of the timber above the Lazy Z ranch house. All of a sudden Red said, "Whoa-up!" as sharply as if he were in charge, and pulled up his horse short.

They could see that a light was burning in the house.

"No tricks now, Red!" said the hoarse man with some suspicion, but with some good nature, too. He admired Red tremendously, but was afraid his rash daredevil might be up to something.

The marshal edged his horse shoulder to shoulder to Red's black, bent his head, peered at Red's face. "You've give your word, son!"

"I smell me something wrong!" Red told him and leaned low, staring through the dimness. The moon had slid down behind a pine-crested mountain ridge, and the darkness of before dawn lay like a blanket. I can't see good, but I *think* I see a horse standin' there up close to the house. Do you?"

The marshal cupped both hands to the sides of his head, leaned forward. "I don't, no."

"You fellers?" Red asked.

The Wells, Fargo men denied that they could see anything. The hoarse one said, "Well, let's go on. If there's anything wrong, we'll damn soon fix it!"

Red swung out of the saddle. You-all need specs! They is *two* horses there! They're right up close to the house!"

"You wouldn't try to fool us, Red!" said a Wells, Fargo man, jeering a little.

"When I smell me something wrong, I go slow!"

"I've noticed just how timid you are," said the marshal, dryly.

"I am till I know what's what!"

"Just what do you think can be so wrong that riding up won't make it all right?" the marshal asked, critically.

"I ain't goin' to argy. But I'm goin' up on foot quiet. You-all can come along—on foot!" Red tossed the reins aside.

"He's up to something!" said the hoarse man, now unfriendly and suspicious.

"Look out, marshal!" said the other.

The marshal spoke calmly: "He has given his word."

"Now lissen!" Red sounded impatient. "They's horses there. I ain't put in my life readin' brands a half-mile, or nearly that, away without havin' eyes. Either friends or strangers come on them horses. If they are friends, all right. If they are strangers, it's all wrong to be there this time o' mornin' where two women are—"

"And an outlaw you are hiding!" said the hoarse man.

"Outlaw be damned! You've won the pot. Kilco is yourn, but them are *my* women and—"

The hoarse man pointed. "I'll be damned!" His companion said, "There *is* a horse!" Marshal Vickers came out of his saddle. "I apologize, Red. I thought I had as good eyes as any man."

A horse, with the slow movement of dragging

ts reins as it edged along, not walking off but
losing for wisps of dried grass to nibble, had
moved directly in front of the doorway. They
could even see the outline of the saddle.

"But we can ride up," a Wells, Fargo man
suggested.

"We are goin' to walk," Red told him.

"Walk," Red had said, but he started off at a
trot, teetering and stumbling. The marshal kept
alongside. The other men, more fattish, puffed
and nearly tripped at every few steps.

A long stone's throw away Red stopped
short, poised in listening. In the stillness he
heard a sound like that of a woman trying to
muffle sobs; just that, and not another voice.
Red stooped, unbuckled his spurs, kicked them
off. The marshal said, "Wait," and took off his
spurs. Together they went on a run for the house.
The horses, not frightened but uncertain, walked
aside, trailing their reins.

Red barely paused at the door, looked toward
where he could hear the sobs, not even glancing
toward the other end of the room. Then he
jumped through the door, and the half-drunken
Knox, who was pawing Jane Alvord, rose up,
facing about. His hat was off, and his straight
black hair, slick as if freshly greased, gave him
an Injun look.

Jane was sitting on a bench, her shoulders
hunched down sideways, and the hem of her

dress was pressed to her face. Knox rose up from beside her, stood almost against her, instinctively drawing his gun as he jumped up. A fierce squawky yell from the other end of the room carried a warning to Red, but he didn't look around, not even when a shot came from behind him. There was the mingled outcry of the cook's squawky warning and a woman's shriek, then the nearer roar of a .45 as the marshal from the doorway killed Joe Strumm over at the table near the stove.

Red had felt a flicker of hesitation about shooting, because Knox was so close to Jane, but Knox's black, whisky-lit eyes blazed, and he fired, and he was answered by Red's .45, held hip high. Once, twice and again, Red shot with a rapidity that gave the sound of more than one gun's roar. Knox was dead on his feet when the first slug smashed through his heart. Jane, as if paralyzed, did not move except to lift her face. A bullet that missed Knox six inches to the right would have killed her. But Red did not pause. He killed Knox on his feet, shot him again before he started to fall, shot him as he was spilling forward with the sagging slump of a broken legged dummy, shot him again as he flopped to the floor.

Then Red spun about, facing toward the other end of the room. The old cook, tied up like a pig for the market, was yelling a most blasphemous hant of praise. Kate Clayton was near the wall, tense and pale, with body drawn over, as if still shrinking. Joe Strumm had been making her sit by him at the table, but when Red appeared like a devil out of the darkness she had screamed and jumped up.

Marshal Vickers slowly put his gun into its holster as he walked across to the bunk where Kilco, gray and cold, lay with blood on his mouth.

The Wells, Fargo men, who never wasted time in idle gaping, pounced at the cook, lifted him up, set him on a stool, cut the rope that was wound from his ankles to his shoulders. The frowzy old cook was in a state of almost furious delight. He screeched, I kep' tellin' 'em he'd come!" He sounded like a dishonored prophet who had been vindicated.

IV

As nearly as the marshal and Wells, Fargo men could put two and two together, it appeared that Strumm, on the night Red had chased them, caught Knox and tied him up, had started back for his cabin to tell Mell Barber what had happened, and had found Knox tied to the tree. He had cut Knox loose, and they had gone off together, neither of them wanting anything more to do with Red, at least that night.

The cook had overheard enough to be sure tha they had gone to Knox's ranch to talk things ove and plan to move what cows Knox owned out c the country. They rode through the day, bunchin the cows; and when evening came they starte to drink, and with a little whisky much courag returned.

It occurred to them that Red would have gon into town to face Gridger and Bill Claytor which would mean that the crippled Kilco woul be alone with the cook and the woman. And if h hadn't gone to town, maybe they would have good chance to even things by shooting from th dark.

They rode over, found a light burning, had sneaking look and found two women, but tha didn't matter. Red was gone, so they marched in The cook was asleep and sat up helplessly. The told Kilco to throw up his hands. They had thei guns leveled, but Kilco reached under his pillov for his own revolver that he had persuaded th cook to give him. Kilco hadn't the slightes chance.

Strumm and Knox felt pleased with themselves Being a little drunk and excited, they figured tha they not only had the reward in their fingers but that they had made themselves respectabl citizens.

Strumm had made Kate sit by him and listen t him talk of all he wanted to do and the big thing e had done in the past. Knox, overliquored, got he maudlin idea that he wanted to settle down nd grow into a big rancher. His idea was to join iis little ranch with the Lazy Z, all easily done by aving Jane marry him. Then Red had walked in.

Knox lay flat, face down, legs curved up and rms out. Marshal Vickers stood above him, ooked up at Red. "That wasn't like you," he said.

"It sure was!" Red said defiantly. "I owed him hree or four killin's from time past, an' I made ure he got 'em. That's all."

V

Three months later Kate Clayton and Red, on vhom she had forced the mouth-filling title of General Superintendent," rode over from the Clayton ranch to attend the wedding of Miss Jane Alvord and Dr Price Mills.

The doctor had given up his practice at Poicoma o come to the measly little town of Nelplaid. Then he had nearly worn out the livery-stable norses to visit the Lazy Z, which was still under he management of Red Clark—assisted by Jody Blanton, Bozo, Mr Backman and the cook.

Jane had a new big house on the hill where ody and Bozo and an Indian woman lived; and it vas there that the wedding was held, with Bozo uspiciously sniffing the preacher's legs, and ody sniffling with his face tucked up against

Mr Backman's buckskin shirt as if his heart wer
broken. Jody had meant to marry Jane Alvor
himself when he grew up.

VI

Six months later, in the office of Judge Trow
bridge, the handsome agent of an Englis
syndicate laid down a certified check fo
$137,000 before Kate Clayton, and an Englis
cattle company became the owner of the Clayto
ranch.

Kate pressed her pretty lips together and foun
it hard to breathe.

The agent said, "That is a very large sum, Mis
Clayton," as if he wanted to cheer her up.

Red quit turning the brim of his hat through hi
fingers and stared at the smooth-cheeked, riding
booted agent who wore funny, tight-fitting pants
Kate reached out and took Red's hand. "I ough
to be glad," she said. "But I'm not."

The Judge clucked and beamed. The agen
thought Kate was one of the prettiest girls he ha
ever seen, and he looked as if he wanted to sa
that she would be welcome to stay on and on a
long as she wanted; but he merely cleared hi
throat and took a sidelong look at Red. He ha
heard a lot about this Red Clark, but he couldn'
see anything in this lanky, lithe, undignifie
and almost shabby cowboy that seemed to con

irm what he had heard. So the agent couldn't
understand why Kate held to Red's hand as if
he liked holding to it. The agent knew that
he had a much nicer hand, and that he never
mispronounced a word; and that he was really
a graceful rider, and that pretty girls usually
encouraged him to be nice to them.

The Judge looked at his watch and said that it
was pretty near to the time. He took up his black
soft hat and opened the door. They filed out, with
Kate keeping hold of Red's arm. They went along
the rickety board sidewalk and across over to the
hotel where Kate's trunk and bags lay waiting for
the stage.

"Red."

"Yes'm?"

Kate looked at him earnestly. "Red, please
won't you use some of this money to buy yourself
a little ranch?"

"I been tellin' you 'No'm' for a week. I don't
want no little ranch. Nor," he added quickly, "a
big un."

"Just why not?"

"Mostly, I reckon, 'cause if you get mad you
can't tell the boss to go to hell an' quit. I like
ramblin'. I *like* it. Me, I'm goin' off som'ers I
ain't known an' go to work where I can tease the
cook, put sandburs in fellers' saddle blankets,
sing night herdin', an' crawl into my bedroll
without givin' a damn what some fellers off in

317

Kan's City or Chicago say is the price of beef!

"But if ever you do want money for anything—anything at all, Red—you will, won't you, let m know?"

"Sure. You bet. Only as long as I got two leg an' a horse has got four, I can earn wages."

The six-horse stage swung up with lumberin roll in a cloud of dust. The Judge took one o Kate's arms, the handsome agent took the othe and they escorted her to the open door of th stage. She put her foot on the step, took it dowr pulled away from them and turned to Red. Kat put her two gloved hands gently against hi cheeks and kissed Red on the mouth. And sh was not smiling.

The stage rolled away, with dust boiling u under its wheels like a smoky curtain that ros from the ground. Red saw a gloved hand twinkl at him from the window, and he flourished hi hat in a last good-by.

Center Point Large Print
600 Brooks Road / PO Box 1
Thorndike, ME 04986-0001 USA

(207) 568-3717

US & Canada:
1 800 929-9108
www.centerpointlargeprint.com